THE WESTERNERS

Texas Ranger Vaughn Medill is tired of the ranger game, worn down by a life spent eternally on his guard, and grappling with his impossible love for the roguish coquette Roseta Uvalde. When she disappears one morning, it's Medill's task to track her down ... Lightning, a rogue wild horse, is causing havoc for Utah ranchers: invading their grazing spots, he fights and kills their stallions, and leads off the other horses to freedom. With a $500 price on his head, brothers Lee and Cuth Stewart are determined to corral him ... The Selwyn Ranch bunkhouse has been ransacked by the local camp robber: a thief who steals foolish trinkets, yet leaves valuables untouched. When over two thousand dollars of the cowboys' pay vanishes, the new rider Wingfield is accused — but he has his own suspicions, and sets out on the trail of the camp robber ...

THE WESTERNERS

ZANE GREY

SAGEBRUSH
Large Print Westerns

First published in the United States by Five Star

First Isis Edition
published 2015
by arrangement with
Golden West Literary Agency

The moral right of the author has been asserted

A catalogue record for this book is available
from the British Library.

ISBN 978–1–78541–006–2 (pb)

Published by
F. A. Thorpe (Publishing)
Anstey, Leicestershire

Set by Words & Graphics Ltd.
Anstey, Leicestershire
Printed and bound in Great Britain by
T. J. International Ltd., Padstow, Cornwall

This book is printed on acid-free paper

Contents

Foreword

In addition to the more than sixty novels, ten full-length fishing books, three collections of baseball stories, and several juveniles, Zane Grey still found time to write more than a hundred shorter works, mostly non-fiction outdoor stories, but also some classic fiction, as well. Most of these stories were eventually combined into book form, but those presented here are among those which never found their way into the hardcover trade book market.

These stories range in scope from classic Western tales to relatively modern works. Their locales vary vastly from the badlands of Texas' Big Bend country to the great Outback and tumultuous seas of faraway Australia. They are told in a style that is vintage Zane Grey.

This volume opens with "The Ranger," a stirring saga of a Texas Ranger whose task is to rescue the daughter of a wealthy Mexican rancher from a vengeful outlaw who has kidnapped her. In its original form the story had been published serially in *Ladies' Home Journal* (10/29 - 12/29) and contained considerably different material than did its appearance in the anthology published many years later by Harper's. The magazine version appears here for the first time.

Among other stories in this book is "Lightning," a rousing tale about the capture of a great stallion who had earned a dead-or-alive bounty on his hide; "The Camp Robber," a poignant and classic Western story; "The Westerners," a modern story about a young heiress who tries to shame her mother away from divorce by sharing her bed with a young Westerner she has picked up in a Reno casino; and "Monty Price's Nightingale," a story of a cowboy who nurtures a dark secret in his frequent disappearances from the ranch where he works. A non-fiction piece, "Death Valley," which first appeared in Harper's Weekly Magazine in the April 22, 1920 issue, displays Grey's talent for description.

The final Zane Grey selection in this collection, another non-fiction piece but, in this case, not concerned with the West, is one of the greatest true sea tales in history. It takes place near a little town called Eden, on the east coast of Australia, about three hundred miles south of Sydney, and relates how a band — now called a pod — of killer whales teamed up with a family of primitive whalers to hunt the great whales in their small boats. The orca would round up the large whales like cattle and drive them into Two-Fold Bay where the whalers were waiting with their tiny boats and harpoons. No one knows for sure when this remarkable alliance began, but it lasted at least from the 1870s to the 1930s, when petroleum was discovered and the demand for whale oil diminished along with its profitability for whalers. This was such an astonishing account that I made a special journey to Eden on my second visit to Australia, just to see if Dad's thrilling version was even remotely close to truth. What I found out was even more incredible than his stunning tale, and it is presented here in my own tale, "Of Whales and Men."

Loren Grey
Woodland Hills, California

The Ranger

CHAPTER
ONE

Periodically of late, especially after some bloody affray or other, Vaughn Medill, Ranger of Texas, suffered from spells of depression and longing for a ranch and a wife and children. The fact that few rangers ever attained these did not detract from their growing charm. At such times the long service to his great state, which owed so much to the rangers, was apt to pall.

Vaughn sat in the shade of the adobe house, on the bank of the slow-eddying, muddy Río Grande, outside the town of Brownsville. He was alone at this ranger headquarters, for the very good reason that his chief, Captain Allerton, and two comrades were laid up in the hospital. Vaughn, with his usual notorious luck, had come out of the Cutter rustling fight without a scratch.

He had needed a few days off, to go alone into the mountains, and there get rid of the sickness killing always engendered in him. No wonder he got red in the face and swore when some admiring tourist asked him how many men he had killed. Vaughn had been long in the service. Like other Texas youths, he had enlisted in this famous and unique state constabulary before he was twenty, and he refused to count the years he had served. He had the stature of the born Texan. And the lined, weathered face, the resolute lips — grim except when he smiled — and the narrowed eyes of gray fire, and the tinge of white over his temples, did not tell the truth about his age.

Vaughn watched the yellow river that separated his state from Mexico. He had reason to hate that strip of dirty water and the hot mesquite-and-cactus land beyond. Like as not, this very day or tomorrow he would have to go across and arrest some Mexican or fetch back a stolen calf or shoot it out with Quinela and his band, who were known to be on American soil. Vaughn shared, in common with all Texans, a supreme contempt for Mexicans. His father had been a soldier in both Texas wars, and Vaughn had inherited his conviction that all Mexicans were greasers. He knew that this was not really true. Villa was an old acquaintance, and he had listed among men to whom he owed his life, Martiniano, one of the greatest of Texas *vaqueros*.

Brooding never got Vaughn anywhere, except in deeper. This drowsy summer day he got in very deep, indeed, so deep that he began to mourn over the several girls he might — at least he believed he might — have married. That seemed long ago, when he was on fire with the ranger spirit, and would not have sacrificed any girl to the agony of waiting for her ranger to come home — knowing that someday he would not come. Since then, sentimental affairs had been few and far between; and the last, dating to this very hour, concerned Roseta, daughter of Uvalde, foreman for the big Glover ranch just down the river.

Uvalde was a Mexican of quality, claiming descent from the Spanish soldier of that name. He had an American wife, owned many head of stock, and, in fact, was partner with Glover in several cattle deals. The black-eyed Roseta, his daughter, had been born on the American side of the river, and had shared advantages of school and contact seldom the lot of *señoritas*.

Vaughn ruminated over these few facts as excuse for his infatuation. For a Texas ranger to fall in love with an ordinary greaser girl was unthinkable. Certainly it had happened, but it was something not to think about. Roseta, however, was extraordinary.

She was pretty, and slight of stature — so slight that Vaughn felt ludicrous, despite his bliss, while dancing with her. If he had stretched out his long arm and she had walked under it, he would have had to lower his hand to touch her glossy black head. She was roguish and coquettish, yet had the pride of her Spanish forebears. Lastly, she was young, rich, the belle of Las Animas, and the despair of cowboy and *vaquero* alike.

When Vaughn had descended to the depths and end of his brooding, he discovered, as he had before, that there were but slight grounds for hopes which had grown serious. The sweetness of a haunting dream was all that could be his. Only this time it hurt more. He should not have let himself in for such a catastrophe. But as he groaned in spirit and bewailed his state, he could not help recalling Roseta's smiles, her favors of dances when scores of admirers were thronging after her, the way she would single him out on occasions. *"Un señor grande,"* she had called him, and likewise "handsome *gringo*," and once, with mystery and havoc in her sloe-black eyes . . . "You Texas Ranger . . . you bloody gunman . . . killer of Mexicans!"

Flirt Roseta was, of course, and doubly dangerous by reason of her mixed blood, her Spanish lineage and her American development. Uvalde had been quoted as saying that he would never let his daughter marry across the Río Grande. Some rich rancher's son would have her hand bestowed upon him; maybe young Glover would be the lucky one. It was madness of Vaughn even to dream of winning her. Yet there still abided that much boy in him.

Sound of wheels and hoofs interrupted the ranger's reverie. He listened. A buggy had stopped out in front. Vaughn got up and looked round the corner of the house. Significant was it that he instinctively stepped out sideways, his right hand low where the heavy gun-sheath hung. A ranger never presented his full front to bullets; it was a trick of old hands in the service.

Someone was helping a man out of the buggy. Presently Vaughn recognized Colville, a ranger comrade, who came in assisted, limping, and with his arm in a sling.

"How are you, Bill?" asked Vaughn solicitously, as he helped the driver lead Colville into the large whitewashed room.

"All right . . . fine, in fact . . . only a . . . little light-headed," panted the other. "Lost a sight of blood."

"You look it. Reckon you'd have done better to stay at the hospital."

"Medill, there ain't half enough rangers to go . . . 'round," replied Colville. "Cap Allerton is hurt bad . . . but he'll recover. An' he thought so long as I could wag I'd better come back to headquarters."

"Uhn-huh. What's up, Bill?" rejoined the ranger quietly. He really did not need to ask.

"Shore I don't know. Somethin' to do with Quinela," replied Colville. "Help me out of my coat. It's hot and dusty . . . Fetch me a cold drink."

"Bill, you should have stayed in town if it's ice you want," said Vaughn, as he filled a dipper from the water bucket that stood in a corner of the room. "Haven't I run this shebang many a time?"

"Medill, you're slated for a run across the Río . . . if I don't miss my guess. Something's on foot, shore as shootin'."

"You say . . . alone?"

"How else, unless the rest of our outfit rides in from the Brazos . . . Anyway, don't they call you the 'lone-star ranger'? Haw! Haw!"

"Shore you don't have a hunch what's up?" inquired Vaughn.

"Honest, I don't. Allerton had to wait for more information. Then he'll send instructions. But we know Quinela was hangin' 'round, with some deviltry afoot."

"Bill, that outfit is plumb bold these days," said Vaughn reflectively. "I wonder, now."

"We're all guessin'. But Allerton swears Quinela is daid set on revenge. Lopez was some relation, we heah from Mexicans on this side. An' when we busted up the

11

Lopez gang, we riled Quinela. I reckon he's laid that to you, Vaughn."

"Nonsense," blurted out Vaughn. "Quinela has another raid on hand, or some other bandit job."

"But didn't you kill Lopez?" queried Colville.

"I shore didn't," declared Vaughn testily. "Reckon I was there when it happened, but I wasn't the only ranger."

"Wal, you've got the name of it, an' that's as bad. Not that it makes much difference. You're used to bein' laid for. But I reckon Cap wanted to tip you off."

"Uhn-huh . . . Say, Bill," replied Vaughn, dropping his head, "I'm shore tired of this ranger game."

"Good Lord, who ain't? But, Vaughn, you couldn't lay down on Captain Allerton right now."

"No. But I've a notion to resign when he gets well an' the boys come back from the Brazos."

"An' that'd be all right, Vaughn, although we'd hate to lose you," returned Colville earnestly. "We all know . . . in fact, everybody who has followed the ranger service knows . . . you should have been a captain long ago. But them pigheaded officials at Houston! Vaughn, your gun record, the very name an' skill that makes you a great ranger, have operated against you there."

"Reckon so. But I never wanted particularly to be a captain . . . leastways of late years," replied Vaughn moodily. "I'm just tired of bein' eternally on my guard. Lookin' to be shot at from every corner or bush! Why, I near killed one of my good friends, all because he came sudden-like out of a door, pullin' at his handkerchief!"

"It's the price we pay. Texas could never have been settled at all but for the buffalo hunters first, an' then us rangers. We don't get much credit, Vaughn. But we know someday our service will be appreciated . . . In your case, everythin' is magnified. Suppose you did quit the service? Wouldn't you still stand 'most the same risk? Wouldn't you need to be on your guard, sleepin' an' wakin'?"

"Wal, I suppose so, for a time. But somehow I'd be relieved."

"Vaughn, the men who are lookin' for you now will always be lookin', until they're daid."

"Shore. But, Bill, that class of men don't live long on the Texas border."

"Hell! Look at Wes Hardin', Kingfisher, Poggin . . . gunmen that took a long time to kill. An' look at Cortina, at Quinela . . . an' Villa . . . Nope, I reckon it's the obscure relations an' friends of men you've shot that you have most to fear. An' you never know who an' where they are. It's my belief you'd be shore of longer life by stickin' to the rangers."

"Couldn't I get married an' go 'way off somewhere?" queried Vaughn belligerently.

Colville whistled in surprise, and then laughed. "Uhn-huh? So that's the lay of the land? A gal! Wal, if the Texas Ranger service is to suffer, let it be for that one cause."

Toward evening a messenger brought a letter from Captain Allerton, with the information that a drove of horses had been driven across the river west of

Brownsville, at Rock Ford. They were in charge of Mexicans and presumably had been stolen from some ranch inland. The raid could be laid to Quinela, although there was no proof of it. It bore his brand. Medill's instructions were to take the rangers and recover the horses.

"Reckon Cap thinks the boys have got back from the Brazos or he's had word they're comin'," commented Colville. "Wish I was able to ride. We wouldn't wait."

Vaughn scanned the short letter again and then filed it away among a stack of others.

"Strange business, this ranger service," he said ponderingly. "Horses stolen . . . fetch them back! Cattle raid . . . recover stock! Drunken cowboy shootin' up the town . . . arrest him! Bandits looted the San 'Tone stage . . . fetch them in! Little Tom, Dick, or Harry lost . . . find him! Farmer murdered . . . string up the murderer!"

"Wal, come to think about it, you're right," replied Colville. "But the rangers have been doin' it for thirty or forty years. You cain't help havin' pride in the service, Medill. Half the job's done when these *hombres* find a ranger's on the trail. That's reputation. But I'm bound to admit the thing is strange an' shore couldn't happen nowhere else but in Texas."

"Reckon I'd better ride up to Rock Ford an' have a look at that trail."

"Wal, I'd wait till mawnin'. Mebbe the boys will come in. An' there's no sense in ridin' it twice."

The following morning, after breakfast, Vaughn went out to the alfalfa pasture to fetch in his horse. Next to

14

his gun, a ranger's horse was his most valuable asset. Indeed, a horse often saved a ranger's life when a gun could not. Star was a big-boned chestnut, not handsome except as to his size, but for speed and endurance Vaughn had never owned his like. They had been on some hard jaunts together. Vaughn fetched Star into the shed and saddled him.

Presently Vaughn heard Colville shout, and, upon hurrying out, he saw a horseman ride furiously away from the house. Colville stood in the door, waving.

Vaughn soon reached him: "Who was that fellow?"

"Glover's man, Uvalde. You know him."

"Uvalde!" exclaimed Vaughn, startled. "He shore was in a hurry. What'd he want?"

"Captain Allerton, an' in fact all the rangers in Texas. I told Uvalde I'd send you down *pronto*. He wouldn't wait. Shore was excited."

"What's wrong with him?"

"His gal is gone."

"Gone!"

"Shore. He cain't say whether she'd eloped or was kidnapped. But it's a job for you, old man. Haw! Haw!"

"Yes, it would be . . . if she eloped," replied Vaughn constrainedly. "An' I reckon not a bit funny, Bill."

Vaughn hurriedly mounted his horse and spurred him into the road.

CHAPTER
TWO

Vaughn's personal opinion, before he arrived at Glover's ranch, was that Roseta Uvalde had eloped, and probably with a cowboy or *vaquero* with whom her father had forbidden her to associate. In some aspects Roseta resembled the vain daughter of a proud don. In the main, she was American bred and educated, but she had that strain of blood which might well have burned secretly to break the bonds of conventionality. Uvalde himself had been a *vaquero* in his youth. Any Texan could have guessed this, seeing Uvalde ride a horse.

There was excitement in the Uvalde household. Vaughn could not get any clue out of the weeping folks, except that Roseta had slept in her bed, had arisen early to take her morning horseback ride. All Mexicans were of a highly excitable temperament, and Uvalde was an example. Vaughn could not get much out of him. Roseta had not been permitted to ride off the ranch, which was something that surprised Vaughn. She was not allowed to go anywhere unaccompanied. This certainly was a departure from the freedom accorded Texan girls; nevertheless, any girl of good sense would give the river a wide berth.

"Did she ride out alone?" queried Vaughn in his slow Spanish, thinking he could get at Uvalde better in his own tongue.

"Yes, *señor*. Pedro saddled her horse. No one else saw her."

"What time this morning?"

"Before sunrise."

Vaughn questioned the lean, dark *vaquero* about what clothes the girl had worn and how she had looked and acted. The answer was that Roseta had dressed in *vaquero* garb, looked very pretty, and full of the devil. Vaughn reflected that this was easy to believe. Next he questioned the stable boys and other *vaqueros*. Then he rode out to the Glover ranch house and got hold of some of the cowboys, and lastly young Glover. Nothing further was to be elicited from them, except that this thing had happened before. Vaughn hurried back to Uvalde's house.

Uvalde himself was the only one here who roused a doubt in Vaughn's mind. This Americanized Mexican had a terrible fear that he did not divine he was betraying. Vaughn conceived the impression that Uvalde had an enemy, and he had only to ask him if he knew Quinela to get on the track of something. Uvalde was probably lying when he professed to fear Roseta had eloped.

"You think she ran off with a cowboy or some young fellow from town?" inquired Vaughn.

"No, *señor*. With a *vaquero* or a *peon*," came the amazing reply.

Vaughn gave up here, seeing he was losing time.

"Pedro, show me Roseta's horse tracks," he requested.

"*Señor*, I will give you ten thousand dollars if you bring my daughter back . . . alive," said Uvalde.

"Rangers don't accept money for services," replied Vaughn briefly, further mystified by the Mexican's intimation that Roseta might be in danger of foul play. "I'll fetch her back . . . one way or another . . . unless she has eloped. If she's gotten married, I can do nothing."

Pedro showed the ranger small hoof tracks made by Roseta's horse. He studied them a few moments, and then, motioning those following him to stay back, he led his own horse and walked out of the courtyard, down the lane, through the open gate into the field.

He rode across Glover's broad acres, through the pecans, to where the ranch bordered on the desert. Roseta had not been bent on an aimless morning ride.

Under a clump of trees someone had waited for her. Here Vaughn dismounted to study tracks. A mettlesome horse had been tethered to one tree. In the dust were imprints of a riding boot, not the kind left by cowboy or *vaquero*. Heel and toe were broad. He found the butt of a cigarette, smoked that morning. Roseta's clandestine friend was not a Mexican, much less a *peon* or *vaquero*. There were signs he had waited on other mornings.

Vaughn got back on his horse, strengthened in the elopement theory, although not wholly convinced. Maybe Roseta was just having a lark. Maybe she had a lover Uvalde would have none of. This idea grew as

Vaughn saw where the horses had walked close together, so their riders could hold hands. Perhaps more! Vaughn's silly hope oozed out and died. And he swore at his ridiculous vain importunities. It was all right for him to be young enough to have an infatuation for Roseta Uvalde, but to have entertained a dream of winning her was laughable. He laughed, although mirthlessly. And jealous pangs consumed him.

"Reckon I'd better get back to rangerin' instead of moonin'," he soliloquized grimly.

The tracks led in a roundabout way through the mesquite to the river trail. This was two miles or more from the line of the Glover Ranch. The trail was broad and lined by trees. It was a lonely and unfrequented place for lovers to ride. Roseta and her companion still walked their horses. On this beautiful trail, which invited a gallop or at least a canter, only love-making could account for the gait. Also the risk! Whoever Roseta's lover might be, he was either a fool or crooked. Vaughn swore lustily as the tracks led on and on, deeper into the timber that bordered the Río Grande.

Suddenly Vaughn drew up sharply with an exclamation. Then he slid out of his saddle, to bend over a marked change in the tracks he was trailing. Both horses had reared, to come down hard on forehoofs, and then jump sideways.

"A hold-up!" ejaculated Vaughn in sudden dark passion.

Sandal tracks in the dust. A bandit had hid behind a thicket in ambush. Vaughn swiftly tracked the horses off the trail, to an open glade on the bank, where hoof tracks of other horses joined them and likewise boot tracks. Vaughn did not need to see that these new marks had been made by Mexican boots.

Roseta had either been led into a trap by the man she had met or they had both been ambushed by three bandits. It was a common thing along the border for Mexican marauders to make away with Mexican girls. The instances of abduction of American girls had been few and far between, although Vaughn remembered several whom he had helped to rescue. Roseta being the daughter of rich Uvalde would be held for ransom and through that might escape the usual terrible treatment. Vaughn's sincere and honest love for Roseta occasioned an agony of grief at the fate that had overtaken her heedless steps. This was short-lived, for the flashing of the ruthless ranger spirit burned it out.

"Three hours' start on me," he muttered, consulting his watch. "Reckon I can come up on them before dark."

Whereupon he followed the broad fresh trail that wound down through timber and brush to the river bottom. A border of arrowweed stretched out across a sandbar. All at once he halted stockstill, then moved as if to dismount. But it was not necessary. He read another story in the sand, and one spot of reddish color — blood — on the slender white stalk of arrowweed, a heavy furrow, and then a line of demarcation through the green to the river — these added a sinister nature to the abduction of Roseta Uvalde. It cleared Roseta's comrade of all complicity, except heedless risk. And it began to savor somewhat of Quinela's work. Vaughn wondered if Quinela could be, by any chance, the menace Uvalde had betrayed a fear of. If so, God help Roseta!

Vaughn took time enough to dismount and trail the line where the murderers had dragged the body. They had been bold and careless. Vaughn picked up a cigarette case, a glove, a watch, and he made sure by the latter he could identify Roseta's companion on this fatal ride. A point of gravel led out to a deep current, to which the body had been consigned. It would be days and far below where the Río Grande would give up its dead.

The exigencies of the case prevented Vaughn from going back after food and canteen. Many a time had he been caught thus. He had only his horse, a gun, and a belt full of cartridges.

Hurrying back to Star, he led him along the trail to the point where the bandits had gone into the river. The Río was treacherous with quicksand, but it was always safe to follow Mexicans, provided one could imitate them. Vaughn spurred Star, plunged across the oozy sand, and made deep water just in the nick of time. The current, however, was nothing for the powerful horse to breast. Vaughn emerged where the bandits had climbed out.

Again Vaughn loped Star on the well-defined tracks of five horses. At this gait he knew he gained two miles on them while they were going one. He calculated they should be about fifteen miles ahead, unless rough country had slowed them, and by early afternoon he ought to be close on their heels. If their trail had worked down the river toward Rock Ford he might have connected these three with the marauders mentioned in Captain Allerton's letter. But it led straight south of the Río Grande and showed a definite object.

Vaughn rode for two hours before he began to climb out of level river valley. Then he struck rocky hills covered with cactus and separated by dry gorges. There was no difficulty in following the trail, but he had to go slower. He did not intend that Roseta Uvalde should spend a night in the clutches of these Mexicans. Toward noon the sun grew hot, and Vaughn began to suffer from thirst. Star sweat copiously, but showed no sign of distress.

He came presently to a shady spot where the abductors had halted, probably to eat and rest. The remains of a small fire showed in a circle of stones. Vaughn got off to put his hand on the mesquite ashes. They were hot. Two hours behind, perhaps a little more or less!

He resumed the pursuit, making good time everywhere and a swift lope on all possible stretches.

There was a sameness of brushy growth and barren hill and rocky dry ravine, although the country grew rougher. He had not been through this section before. He crossed no trails. And he noted that the tracks of the riders gradually headed from south to west. Sooner or later they would join the well-known Rock Ford trail. Vaughn was concerned about this. And he pondered. Should he push Star to the limit until he knew he was close behind them? It would not do to let them see or hear him. If he could surprise them, the thing would be easy. While he revolved these details of the problem, he kept traveling deeper into Mexico.

He passed an Indian cornfield, and then a hut of adobe and brush. The tracks he was hounding kept straight on, and led off the desert onto a road — not, however, the Rock Ford road. Vaughn here urged Star to action, and in half an hour he headed into a well-defined trail. He did not need to get off to see that no horses but the five he was tracking had passed this point since morning. Moreover, they were not many miles ahead.

Vaughn rode on a while at a gallop, then, turning off the trail, he kept Star to that gait in a long detour. Once he crossed a streambed up which there would be water somewhere. Then he met the trail again, finding to his disappointment and chagrin that the tracks had passed. He had hoped to head them and lie in wait for them.

Mid-afternoon was on him. He decided not to force the issue at once. There was no ranch or village within half a night's ride of this spot. About sunset, the bandits would halt to rest and eat. They would build a fire.

Vaughn rode down into a rocky defile where he found a much needed drink for himself and Star. He did not relish the winding trail ahead. It kept to the gorge. It was shady and cool, but afforded too many places where he might be waylaid. Still he had to go on. He had no concern that the three bandits would ambush him. But if they fell in with others!

Vaughn approached a rocky wall. He was inured to danger. And his ranger luck was proverbial. It was only the thought of Roseta that occasioned misgivings. And he turned the corner of the wall to face a line of leveled rifles.

"Hands up, *gringo* ranger!"

CHAPTER
THREE

Vaughn was as much surprised by the command in English as at the totally unexpected encounter with a dozen or more *peones*. He knew the type. These were Quinela's bandits.

Vaughn elevated his hands. Why this gang leader held him up, instead of shooting on sight, was beyond Vaughn's ken. The Mexicans began to jabber angrily. If ever Vaughn expected death, it was then. He had about decided to pull his gun and shoot it out with them, and finish as many a ranger had before him. But a shrill authoritative voice deterred him. Then a swarthy little man, lean-faced and beady-eyed, stepped out between the threatening rifles and Vaughn. He silenced the others.

"It's the *gringo* ranger, Texas Medill," he shouted in Spanish. "It's the man who killed Lopez. Don't shoot. Quinela will pay much gold for him alive. Quinela will strip off the soles of his feet and drive him with hot irons to walk on the *chaya*."

"But it's the dreaded gun-ranger, *señor*," protested a one-eyed bandit. "The only safe way is to shoot his cursed heart out here."

"We had our orders to draw this ranger across the river," returned the leader harshly. "Quinela knew his man and the hour. The Uvalde girl brought him. And here we have him . . . alive! Garcia, it'd cost your life to shoot this ranger."

"But I warn you, Juan, he is not alone," returned Garcia. "He is but a leader of rangers. Best kill him quick, and hurry on. I have told you already that *gringo vaqueros* are on the trail. We have many horses. We cannot travel fast. Night is coming. Best kill Texas Medill."

"No, Garcia. We obey orders," returned Juan harshly. "We take him to Quinela."

Vaughn surveyed the motley group with speculative eyes. He could kill six of them at least, and, with Star charging and the poor marksmanship of Mexicans, he might break through. Coldly Vaughn weighed the chances. They were a hundred to one that he would not escape. Yet he had taken such chances before. But these men had Roseta, and when there was life, there was always some hope. With tremendous effort of will he forced aside the deadly impulse and applied his wits to the situation.

The swarthy Juan turned to cover Vaughn with a cocked gun. Vaughn read doubt and fear in the beady eyes. He knew Mexicans. If they did not kill him at once, there was hope. At a significant motion, Vaughn carefully shifted a long leg and stepped face front, hands high, out of the saddle.

Juan addressed him in Spanish

"No savvy, *señor*," replied the ranger.

"You speak Spanish?" repeated the questioner in English.

"Very little. I understand some of your Mexican lingo."

"You trailed Manuel alone?"

"Who's Manuel?"

"My *vaquero*. He brought *Señorita* Uvalde across the river."

"After murdering her companion. Yes, I trailed him and two other men, I reckon. Five horses. The Uvalde girl rode one. The fifth horse belonged to her companion."

"Ha! Did Manuel kill?" exclaimed the other, and it was certain that was news to him.

"Yes. You have murder as well as kidnapping to answer for."

The bandit cursed under his breath. "Where are your rangers?" he went on.

"They got back from the Brazos last night with news of your raid," said Vaughn glibly. "And this morning they joined the cowboys who were trailing the horses you stole."

Vaughn realized then that somewhere there had been a mix-up in Quinela's plans. The one concerning the kidnapping of Roseta Uvalde and Vaughn's taking the trail had worked out well. But Juan's dark corded face, his volley of unintelligible maledictions at his men betrayed a hitch somewhere. Again Vaughn felt the urge to draw and fight it out. What passionate fiery-headed fools these fellows were! Juan had lowered his gun to heap abuse on Garcia. That individual turned green of face. Some of the others still held leveled rifles on Vaughn, but were looking at their leader and his lieutenant. Vaughn saw a fair chance to get away, and his gun hand itched. A heavy-booming revolver — Juan and Garcia dead — a couple of shots at the others — that would have stampeded them. But Vaughn caught no glimpse of Roseta. He abandoned the grim cold impulse and awaited eventualities.

The harangue went on, soon to end in Garcia being cursed down.

"I'll take them to Quinela," rasped Juan shrilly, and began shouting orders.

Vaughn's gun belt was removed. His hands were tied behind his back. He was forced upon one of the horses, and his feet were roped to the stirrups. Juan appropriated his gun belt, which he put on with the Mexican's love of vainglory, and then mounted Star. The horse did not like this exchange of riders, and, right there, followed evidence of the cruel iron hand of the bandit. Vaughn's blood leaped, and he veiled his eyes lest someone see his intent to kill. When he raised his head, two of the squat-shaped, motley-garbed and wide-sombreroed crew were riding by, and the second led a horse upon which sat Roseta Uvalde.

She was bound to the saddle, but her hands were free. She turned her face to Vaughn. With what terrible earnest dread did he gaze at it! Vaughn needed only to see it flash white toward him, to meet the passionate eloquence of gratitude in her dark eyes, to realize that Roseta was still unharmed. She held the small proud head high. Her spirit was unbroken. For the rest —

28

what to Vaughn mattered the dusky disheveled hair, the mud-spattered and dust-covered *vaquero* riding garb she wore? What mattered anything so long as she was safe? Vaughn flashed her a look that brought the blood to her pale cheeks.

Juan prodded Vaughn in the back. "Ride, *gringo*." Then he gave Garcia a last harsh command. As Vaughn's horse followed that of Roseta and her two guards into the brook, there rose a clattering, jabbering mêlée among the bandits left behind. It ended in a roar of pounding hoofs. Soon this died out on top.

The brook was shallow and ran swiftly over gravel and rocks. Vaughn saw at once that Juan meant to hide his trail. An hour after the cavalcade would have passed a given point here, no obvious trace would show. The swift water would have cleared as well as have filled with sand the hoof tracks.

"Juan, you were wise to desert your gang of horse thieves," said Vaughn coolly. "There's a hard-riding outfit on their trail. And some of them will be dead before sundown."

"*¿Quién sabe?* But it's sure, Texas Medill will be walking *choya* on bare-skinned feet *mañana*," replied the Mexican.

Vaughn pondered. Quinela's rendezvous, then, was not many hours distant. Travel such as this, up a rocky gorge, was necessarily slow. Probably this brook would not afford more than a few miles of going. Then Juan would head out on the desert and essay in other ways to hide his tracks. So far as Vaughn was concerned, whether he hid them or not made no difference. The

29

cowboys and rangers in pursuit were but fabrications of Vaughn's to deceive his captors. He knew how to work on their primitive feelings. But Vaughn realized the peril of the situation and the brevity of time left him.

"Juan, you've got my gun," said Vaughn, his keen mind striving. "You say I'll be dead in less than twenty-four hours. What's it worth to untie my hands so I can ride in comfort?"

"*Señor*, if you have money on you, it will be mine anyway," replied Quinela's lieutenant.

"I haven't any money with me. But I've got my checkbook that shows a balance of some thousand dollars in an El Paso bank," replied Vaughn, and he turned around.

Juan showed gleaming white teeth in derision. "What's that to me?"

"Some thousands in gold, Juan. You can get it easily. News of my death will not get across the border very soon. I'll give you a check and a letter, which you can take to El Paso, or send by messenger."

"How much gold, *señor*?" Juan asked.

"Over three thousand."

"*Señor*, you would bribe me into a trap. No. Juan loves the glitter and clink of your American gold, but he is no fool."

"Nothing of the sort. I'm trying to buy a little comfort in my last hours. And possibly a little kindness to the *señorita*, there. It's worth a chance. You can send a messenger. What do you care if he shouldn't come back? You don't lose anything."

"No *gringo* can be trusted, much less Texas Medill of the rangers," rejoined the Mexican.

"Sure. But take a look at my checkbook. You know figures when you see them."

Juan rode abreast of Vaughn, dominated by curiosity. How his beady eyes glittered!

"Inside vest pocket," directed Vaughn. "Don't drop the pencil."

Juan procured the checkbook and opened it. "*Señor*, I know your bank," he said, vain of his ability to read, which to judge by his laborious task was very limited.

"Uhn-huh. Well, how much balance have I left?" queried Vaughn.

"Three thousand, four hundred."

"Good. Now, Juan, you may as well get that money. I've nobody to leave it to. I'll buy a little comfort for myself . . . and kindness to the *señorita*."

"How much kindness, *señor*?" asked the bandit craftily.

"That you keep your men from handling her rough . . . and soon as the ransom is paid send her back safe."

"*Señor*, the first I have seen to. The second is not mine to grant. Quinela will demand ransom . . . yes . . . but never will he send the *señorita* back."

"But I . . . thought . . . ?"

"Quinela was wronged by Uvalde."

Vaughn whistled his reception of that astounding revelation. He had divined correctly the fear Uvalde had revealed. The situation then for Roseta was vastly more critical. Death would be merciful compared to what the half-breed *peon* Quinela would deal her.

Vaughn cudgeled his brains in desperation. Why had he not shot it out with these malefactors? But passion could not further Roseta's cause.

Meanwhile, the horses splashed and cracked the rocks in single file up the narrowing gorge. The shady walls gave place to brushy slopes that let the hot sun down. Roseta looked back at Vaughn with appeal and trust — and something more in her black eyes, that tortured him.

Vaughn did not have the courage to meet her gaze, except for that fleeting instant. It was natural that he sank in spirit. Never in his long ranger service had he encountered such a diabolically baffling situation. More than once he had faced what seemed inevitable death, where there had been presented not the slightest chance to escape. Vaughn was not of a temper to resign. He would watch till the very last second. For Roseta, however, he endured agonies. He had looked at the mutilated, outraged body of more than one girl victim of bandits. As a last resource he could only pray for a recurrence of such unheard-of and incredible luck as had made ranger history.

When at length the gully narrowed to a mere crack in the hill, and the water failed, Juan put his men to the ascent of a steep brush slope. And before long they broke out into a trail.

Presently a *peon* came in sight astride a mustang, and leading a burro. He got by the two guards, although they crowded him into the brush. But Juan halted him, and got off Star to see what was in the pack on the burro. With an exclamation of great satisfaction he pulled out what appeared to Vaughn to be a jug or demijohn covered with wickerwork. Juan pulled out the stopper and smelled the contents.

"¡Canyu!" he said, and his white teeth gleamed. He took a drink, then smacked his lips. When the guards, who had stopped to watch, made a move to dismount, he cursed them vociferously. Sullenly they slid back in their saddles. Juan stuffed the demijohn into the right saddlebag of Vaughn's saddle. Here the *peon* protested, in a mixed dialect that Vaughn could not translate. But the content was obvious. Juan kicked the ragged fellow's sandaled foot, and ordered him on with a significant touch of Vaughn's big gun, which he wore so pompously. The *peon* lost no time riding off. Juan remounted and drove the cavalcade on.

Vaughn turned as his horse started, and again he encountered Roseta's dark, intent eyes. They seemed telepathic this time, as well as soulful with unutterable promise. She had read Vaughn's thought. If there were anything that had dominance of the *peon's* nature, it was the cactus liquor, *canyu*. Ordinarily he was volatile, unstable as water, flint one moment and wax the next. But with the burn of *canyu* in his throat he had the substance of mist.

Vaughn felt the lift and pound of his leaden heart. He had prayed for the luck of the ranger, and lo! a *peon* had ridden up, packing *canyu*.

CHAPTER
FOUR

Canyu was a distillation from the maguey cactus, a plant similar to the century plant. The *peon* brewed it. But in lieu of the brew, natives often cut into the heart of a plant and sucked the juice. Vaughn had once seen a native sprawled in the middle of a huge maguey, his head buried deep in the heart of it, and his legs hanging limp. Upon examination he appeared to be drunk, but it developed that he was dead.

This liquor was potential fire. The lack of it made *peones* surly; the possession of it made them gay. One drink changed the mental and physical world. Juan whistled after the first drink; after the second he began to sing "La Paloma."

Almost at once the pace of travel that had been maintained slowed perceptibly. Vaughn felt like a giant. He believed he could break the thongs that bound his wrists. As he had prayed for his ranger luck, so he prayed for anything to delay this bandit on the trail.

The leader Juan either wanted the *canyu* for himself or was too crafty to share with his two men, probably both. With all three of them, the center of attention had ceased to be in Uvalde's girl and the hated *gringo* ranger. It lay in that demijohn. If a devil lurked in this white liquor for them, there was likewise for the prisoners a watching angel.

The way led into a shady rocky glen. As of one accord the horses halted, without, so far as Vaughn could see, any move or word from their riders. This was proof that the two guards in the lead had ceased to ride with the sole idea in mind of keeping to a steady gait. Vaughn drew a deep breath, as if to control suspense. No man could foretell the variety of *canyu* effects, but certain it must be that something would happen.

Juan had mellowed. A subtle change had occurred in his disposition, although he was still the watchful leader. Vaughn felt that he was now in more peril from this bandit than before the advent of the *canyu*. This, however, would not last long. He could only bide his time, watch, and think. His luck had begun. He divined it, trusted it with mounting passion.

The two guards turned their horses across the trail, and that maneuver blocked Roseta's mount while Vaughn's came up alongside. If he could have stretched out his hand, he could have touched Roseta. Many a time he had been thrilled and softened and bewildered in her presence, not to say frightened, but he had never felt as now. Roseta contrived to touch his bound foot with her stirrup, and the deliberate move made Vaughn tremble. Still he did not yet look directly down at her.

The actions of the three guards were as clear to Vaughn as an inch of crystal water. If he had seen one fight among *peones* over *canyu*, he had seen a hundred. First, the older of the two guards leisurely got off his horse. His wide, straw sombrero hid all his face, except a peaked, yellow chin, scantily covered with black whiskers. His garb hung in rags, and a cartridge belt was slung loosely over his left shoulder. He had left his rifle in its saddle sheath, and his only weapon was a bone-handled machete stuck in a dilapidated scabbard on his belt.

"Juan, we are thirsty and have no water," he said.

"Gonzalez, one drink and no more," returned Juan, and lifted out the demijohn.

With eager cry the *peon* tipped it to his lips. And he gulped until Juan jerked it away. Then the other *peon* tumbled off his horse and gaily besought Juan for a drink, if only one precious drop. Juan complied, but this time he did not let go of the demijohn.

Vaughn felt a touch — a gentle pressure on his knee. Roseta had laid her gloved hand there. Then he had to avert his gaze from the Mexicans.

"Oh, Vaughn, I *knew* you would come to save me," she whispered. "But they have caught you ... For God's sake, do something."

"Roseta, I reckon I can't do much at this sitting," replied Vaughn, smiling down at her. "Are you ... all right?"

"Yes, except I'm tired and my legs ache. I was frightened badly enough before you happened along. But now ... it's terrible ... Vaughn, they are taking us to Quinela. He is a monster. My father told me so ... If you can't save me, you must kill me."

"I shall save you, Roseta," he whispered low, committing himself on the altar of the luck that had never failed him.

Her eyes held his, and there was no doubt about the warm pressure of her hand on his knee. But even through this sweet stolen moment, Vaughn had tried to attend to the argument of the bandits. He heard their mingled voices, all high-pitched and angry. In another moment they would jump at each other like dogs.

A wrestling sound, trample of hoofs, a shrill — *"¡Santa Maria!"* — and a sodden blow preceded the startling crash of a gun.

As Vaughn's horse plunged, he saw Roseta's rear into the brush, with her screaming, and Star lunge out of a cloud of blue smoke. Next moment Vaughn found himself tearing down the trail. He was helpless, but he squeezed the scared horse with his knees and kept calling: "Whoa, there . . . whoa, boy!"

Not for a hundred yards or more did the animal slow up. It relieved Vaughn to hear a clatter of hoofs behind him, and he turned to see Juan tearing in pursuit. Presently he crashed into the brush and, getting ahead of Vaughn, turned into the trail again to stop the horse.

Juan jerked the heaving horse out of the brush into the trail, then led him back toward the scene of the shooting. But before they reached it, Vaughn espied one of the guards coming with Roseta and a riderless horse. Juan grunted his satisfaction, and let them pass without a word.

Roseta seemed less terrorized and shaken than Vaughn had feared she would be. Her dilated eyes, as she passed, said as plainly as any words could have done, that they had one less captor to contend with.

The journey was resumed. Vaughn drew a deep breath and endeavored to contain himself. The sun was still only halfway down toward the western horizon. Hours of daylight yet! And he had an ally more deadly than bullets, more subtle than any man's wit, sharper than the tooth of a serpent.

Perhaps in a quarter of an hour, Vaughn, turning his head ever so slightly, out of the tail of his eye saw Juan take another drink of *canyu*. And it was a good stiff drink. Vaughn thrilled as he possessed his soul in patience. Presently Juan's latest deed would be as if it had never been. *Canyu* was an annihilation of the past.

"Juan, I'll fall off this horse *pronto*," began Vaughn.

"Very good, *señor*. Fall off," replied Juan amiably.

"I am most damned uncomfortable with my hands tied back this way. I can't sit straight. I'm cramped. Be a good fellow, Juan, and untie my hands."

"*Señor* Texas Medill, if you are uncomfortable now, what will you be when you tread the fiery cactus on your peeled feet?"

"But that will be short. No man lives through such torture long, does he, Juan?"

"The *chaya* kills quickly, *señor*."

"Juan, have you reflected upon the gold lying in the El Paso bank? Gold that can be yours for the ride. It will be long before my death is reported across the river. You have ample time to get to El Paso with my check and a letter. I can write it on a sheet of paper out of my notebook. Surely you have a friend or acquaintance in El Paso who can identify you at the bank as Juan . . . whatever your name is."

"Yes, *señor*, I have. And my name is Juan Mendoz."

"Have you thought about what you could do with three thousand dollars? Not Mexican *pesos*, but real *gringo* gold!"

"I have not thought, *señor*, because I hate to give in to dreams."

"Juan, listen. You are a fool. I know I am as good as dead. What have I been a ranger all these years for? It's worth this gold to me to be free of this miserable cramp . . . and to feel that I have tried to buy some little kindness for the *señorita* there. She is part Mexican, Juan. She has Mexican blood in her, don't forget that . . . Well, you are not betraying Quinela. And you will be rich. You will have my horse and saddle, if you are wise enough to keep Quinela from seeing them. You will buy silver spurs . . . with the long Spanish rowels. You will have jingling gold in your pocket. You will buy a *vaquero's* sombrero. And then think of your *chata* . . . your sweetheart, Juan . . . Ah, I knew it. You have a *chata*. Think of what you can buy her. A Spanish *mantilla*, and a golden cross, and silver-buckled shoes for her little feet. Think how she will love you for that! Then, Juan, best of all, you can go far south of the border . . . buy a *hacienda*, horses, and cattle, and live there happily with your *chata*. You will only get killed in Quinela's service . . . for a few dirty *pesos* . . . . You will raise mescal on your *hacienda*, and draw your own *canyu* . . . . And all for so little, Juan!"

"*Señor* not only has gold in a bank but gold on his tongue . . . It is, indeed, little you ask and little I risk."

39

Juan rode abreast of Vaughn and felt in his pockets for the checkbook and pencil, which he had neglected to return. Vaughn made of his face a grateful mask. This *peon* had become approachable, as Vaughn had known *canyu* would make him, but he was not yet under its influence to an extent which justified undue risk. Still Vaughn decided, if the bandit freed his hands and gave him the slightest chance he would jerk Juan out of that saddle. Vaughn did not lose sight of the fact that his feet would still be tied. He calculated exactly what he would do in case Juan's craftiness no longer operated. As the other stopped his horse and reined in Vaughn's, the girl happened to turn around, as she often did, and she saw them. Vaughn caught a flash of big eyes and a white little face as Roseta vanished around a turn in the trail. Vaughn was glad for two things, that she had seen him stop and that she and her guard would be unable to see what took place.

All through these tingling, cold-nerved moments Juan appeared to be studying the checkbook. If he could read English, it surely was only familiar words. The thought leaped to Vaughn's mind to write a note to the banker quite different from what he had intended. Most assuredly, if the El Paso banker ever saw that note, Vaughn would be dead, and it was clearly possible that it might fall under his hands.

"*Señor*, you may sign me the gold in your El Paso bank," at length said Juan.

"Fine. You're a good fellow, Juan. But I can't hold a pencil with my teeth."

40

Juan kicked the horse Vaughn bestrode and moved him across the trail so that Vaughn's back was turned.

"There, *señor*," said the bandit, and his lean dark hand slipped book and pencil into Vaughn's vest pocket.

The cunning, thought Vaughn, in sickening disappointment! He had hoped Juan would free his bonds and then hand over the book. But Vaughn's ranger luck did not yet ride so high.

He felt Juan tugging at the thongs around his wrists. They were tight — a fact Vaughn surely could attest to. He heard the bandit mutter a little and then curse.

"Juan, do you blame me for wanting those rawhides off my wrists?" asked Vaughn.

"*Señor* Medill is strong. It is nothing," returned the Mexican.

Suddenly the painful tension on Vaughn's wrists relaxed. He felt the thongs fall.

"*¡Muchas gracias, señor!*" he exclaimed. "Aghh! That feels good."

Vaughn brought his hands around in front to rub each swollen and discolored wrist. But all the time he was gathering his forces, like a tiger about to leap. Had the critical moment arrived?

"Juan, that was a little job to make a man rich . . . now wasn't it?" went on Vaughn pleasantly. And leisurely, but with every muscle taut, he turned to face his guard.

CHAPTER
FIVE

The bandit was out of reach of Vaughn's tense hands. He sat back in the saddle with an expression of interest upon his swarthy face. The ranger could not be sure, but he would have gambled that Juan did not suspect his deadly intentions. Star was a mettlesome horse; Vaughn did not like the other's horse, upon which he sat bound; there were at least several feet between them. If Vaughn had been free to leap he might have, probably would have, done so.

He swallowed his eagerness and began to rub his wrists again. Presently he removed pencil and book from his vest pocket. It was not pretense that occasioned a few labored moments in writing out a check for Juan Mendoz, for the three thousand and odd dollars in his balance at the bank.

"There, Juan. There it is . . . all made out and signed. May some *gringo* treat your *chata* as you treat *Señorita* Uvalde," said Vaughn, handing the check over to the Mexican.

"*Gracias, señor,*" replied Juan, his black eyes burning upon the bit of colored paper. "Uvalde's daughter then is your *chata?*"

"Yes. And I'll leave a curse upon you, if she is mistreated."

"Ranger, I had my orders from Quinela. You would not have asked more."

"What has Quinela got against Uvalde?" queried Vaughn.

"They were *vaqueros* together years ago. But I don't know the reason for Quinela's hate. It is great and just . . . Now, *señor*, the letter to your banker."

Vaughn tore a leaf out of his notebook. On second thought he decided to write the letter in the notebook, which would serve in itself to identify him. In case this letter ever was presented at the bank in El Paso he wanted it to mean something. Then it occurred to Vaughn to try out his captor. So he wrote a few lines.

"Read this, Juan," he said, handing over the book.

The bandit scanned the lines, which might as well have been Greek.

"Texas Medill does not write as well as he shoots," said Juan.

"Let me have the book. I can do better. I forgot something."

Receiving it back, Vaughn tore out the page and wrote another as follows:

Dear Mr. Jarvis:

If you ever see these lines you will know that I have been murdered by Quinela. Have the bearer arrested and wire to Captain Allerton, of the Rangers, at Brownsville. At this moment I am a prisoner of Juan Mendoz, lieutenant of Quinela. Miss Roseta Uvalde is also a prisoner. She will be held for ransom and revenge. The

place is in the hills somewhere east and south of Rock Ford trail.

Medil

Vaughn, reading aloud to Mendoz, improvised a letter which identified him, and cunningly made mention of the gold.

"Juan, isn't that better?" he said as he handed the book back. "You'll do well not to show this to Quinela or anyone else. Go yourself at once to El Paso."

As Vaughn had expected, the other did not scan this letter. Placing the check in the book, he deposited it in an inside pocket. Then without a word he drove Vaughn's horse forward on the trail and, following close behind, soon came up with Roseta and her guard.

The girl looked back. Vaughn contrived, without making it obvious, to show her that his hands were free. A radiance crossed her wan face. The exertion and suspense had begun to tell markedly. She sagged in the saddle.

Juan appeared bent on making up for lost time, as he drove the horses at a trot. But this did not last long. Vaughn, looking at the ground, saw the black shadow of the bandit as he raised the demijohn to drink. What a sinister shadow! It forced Vaughn to think of what now should be his method of procedure. Sooner or later he was going to get his hand on his gun, which stuck out in back of Juan's hip and hung down. That moment would see the end of the fellow. But Vaughn remembered how this horse he bestrode had bolted at the other gunshot. He would risk more, shooting from the back of this horse than by the hands of the other Mexican. Vaughn's feet were tied in the stirrups, with the rope passing underneath the horse. If he were thrown sideways out of the saddle, it would be a perilous and very probably a fatal accident. He decided that at the critical time he would grip the horse with his legs so tightly that he could not be dislodged, and let the moment decide what to do about the other man.

After Juan had a second drink, Vaughn slowly retarded the gait of his horse until that of Juan came up to his flank. Vaughn was careful to keep to the right of the trail. One glance at his captor's eyes sent a gush of hot blood over Vaughn. The canyu had been slow on this tough fellow, but at last it was working.

"Juan, I'm powerful thirsty," said Vaughn.

"We come to water hole bime-by," replied Juan thickly.

"But won't you spare me a nip of canyu?"

"Our mescal drink is bad for gringos."

"I'll risk it, Juan. Just a nip. You're a good fellow, and I like you. I'll tell Quinela how you had to fight your men back there, when they wanted to kill me. I'll tell him Garcia provoked you . . . Juan, you can see I may do you a turn."

Juan came up alongside Vaughn and halted. Vaughn reined his horse just head and head with Juan's. The Mexican was sweating; his under lip hung a little; he sat loosely in his saddle. His eyes had lost the beady light and appeared to have filmed over.

Juan waited till the man ahead had turned a curve in the trail with Roseta. Then he lifted the demijohn from the saddlebag and extended it to Vaughn.

"A drop . . . *señor*," he said.

Vaughn pretended to drink. The hot stuff was like vitriol on his lips. He returned the vessel, making a great show of the effect of the *canyu*, when as a cold fact he was calculating distance. Almost he yielded to the temptation to lean and sweep a long arm. But a ranger did not make mistakes. If Juan's horse had been a little closer . . .

"Ah-h-h! Great stuff, Juan!" Vaughn exclaimed, and relaxed again; the moment for action would reveal itself.

They rode on, and Juan either forgot to drop behind or did not think it needful. The trail was wide enough for two horses. Soon Roseta's bright red scarf burned against the gray-green again. She was looking back. So was her escort. And their horses were walking. Juan did not appear to make note of slower progress. He had passed the faculty of minute observation. Presently he would take another swallow of *canyu*.

Vaughn began to talk, to express more gratitude to Juan, to dwell with flowery language on the effect of good drink — of which *canyu* was the sweetest and fieriest in the world — of its power to make fatigue as if it were not, to alleviate pain and grief, to render the dreary desert of mesquite and stone a region of color and beauty and melody — even to resign a doomed ranger to his fate.

"Ai, *señor* . . . *canyu* is the Blessed Virgin's gift to the *peones*," said Juan, and emphasized this tribute by taking another drink.

They rode on. Vaughn asked only for another mile or two of lonely trail, of uninterruption.

"How far, Juan?" queried Vaughn. "I cannot ride much farther with my feet tied under this horse."

"Till sunset, *señor* . . . which will be your last," replied the other.

Juan could still speak intelligibly, but he was no longer alert.

They rode on, and Vaughn made a motion to Roseta that she must not turn to look back. Perhaps she interpreted it to mean more, for she immediately began to engage her guard in conversation — something Vaughn had observed she had not done before. Soon the guard dropped back until his horse walked beside Roseta's. He was a *peon*, and a heavy drink of *canyu* had addled the craft in his wits. Vaughn saw him bend over and loosen the rope that bound Roseta's left foot to the stirrup. Juan did not see this significant action. His gaze was fixed to the trail. He was singing: *"Ai, querida chata mía."*

Roseta's guard took a long look back. Evidently Juan's posture struck him apprehensively, yet did not wholly overcome the interest that Roseta had suddenly taken in him. When he gave her a playful pat, she returned it. He caught her hand. Roseta did not pull very hard to release it, and she gave him a saucy little slap. He was reaching for her when they passed out of Vaughn's sight around a corner of the green-bordered trail.

Vaughn gradually and almost imperceptibly guided his horse closer to Juan.

47

"Juan, the curse of *canyu* is that once you taste it you must have more . . . or die," said Vaughn.

"It is . . . so . . . *señor*," replied Juan.

"You have plenty left. Will you let me have one more little drink . . . My last drink of *canyu*, Juan! I didn't tell you, but it has been my ruin. My father was a rich rancher. He disowned me because of evil habits. That's how I became a ranger."

"Take it, *señor*. Your last drink."

Vaughn braced every nerve and fiber of his being. He leaned a little. His left hand went out — leisurely. But his eyes flashed like cold steel over the unsuspecting Mexican. Then, as a striking snake, his hand snatched the bone-handled gun from its sheath. Vaughn pulled the trigger. The hammer fell upon an empty chamber.

Juan turned. The gun crashed. "*¡Dios!*" he screamed in a strangled death cry.

The leap of the horses was not quicker than Vaughn. He lunged to catch the bandit — to keep him upright in the saddle. "Hold, Star!" he called sternly. "Hold!"

Star came down. But the other horse plunged and dragged him up the trail. Vaughn had his gun hand fast on the cantle and his other holding Juan upright. But for this grasp the frantic horse would have unseated him.

It was the ranger's job to manage both horses and look out for the other guard. He appeared on the trail riding fast, his carbine held high.

Vaughn let go of Juan and got the gun in his right hand. With the other, then, he grasped the Mexican's coat and held him straight to the saddle. He drooped himself over his pommel, to make it appear he had been the one shot. Every second also he increased the iron leg grip on the horse he straddled. Star had halted and was being dragged.

The other bandit came at a gallop, yelling. When he got within twenty paces, Vaughn straightened up and shot him through the heart. He threw the carbine and, pitching out of his saddle, went thudding to the ground. His horse bumped hard into the one Vaughn rode, and that was fortunate, for it checked his first mad leap.

In the mêlée that ensued Juan fell off Star, to be trampled under hoofs. Vaughn hauled with all his might on the bridle. But he could not hold the horse, and he feared that he would break the bridle. Bursting through the brush the horse ran wildly. But presently he got the horse under control and back onto the trail.

Some rods down he espied Roseta, safe in her saddle, her head bowed with her hands covering her face. Then Vaughn called eagerly, as he reached her.

"Oh, Vaughn!" she cried, lifting a convulsed and blanched face. "I knew you'd . . . kill them . . . But, my God . . . how awful!"

"Brace up," he said sharply.

Then he got out his clasp knife and in a few slashes freed his feet from the stirrups. He leaped off the horse. His feet felt numb.

He cut the ropes that bound Roseta's feet to her stirrups. She swayed out of the saddle into his arms. Her eyes closed.

49

"It's no time to faint," he said sternly, and carried her out off the trail to set her on her feet.

"I . . . I won't," she whispered, her eyes opening, strained and dilated. "But hold me . . . just a moment."

Vaughn enfolded her in his arms, and the moment she asked was so sweet and precious that it almost overcame the will of a ranger in a desperate plight.

"Roseta . . . we're free, but not yet safe," he replied. "We're close to a *hacienda* . . . maybe where Quinela is waiting . . . Come now. We must get out of here."

Half carrying her, Vaughn hurried through the brush along the trail. The moment she could stand alone he whispered: "Wait here." He ran onto the trail. He still held his gun. Star stood waiting, his head up. Both horses had disappeared. Vaughn looked up and down the trail. Star whinnied. Vaughn hurried to bend over Juan. The Mexican lay on his face. Vaughn unbuckled the gun belt Juan had appropriated from him, and put it on. Next he secured his notebook. Then he sheathed his gun. With that he grasped the bridle of Star and led him off the trail into the mesquite, back to where Roseta stood. She seemed all right now, only pale. But Vaughn avoided her eyes. He mounted Star.

"Come, Roseta," he said. "Up behind me."

He swung her up and settled her on the saddle skirt.

"There. Put your arms around me. Hold tight, for we're going to ride."

When she had complied, he grasped her left hand with his where it fastened in his coat. On the moment he heard voices up the trail and the *clip-clop* of hoofs. Roseta heard them, too. Vaughn felt her shake.

"Don't fear, Roseta. Just hang on. Here's where Star shines," whispered Vaughn, and, guiding the nervous horse onto the trail, he let him have a loose rein. Star needed not the shrill cries of *peones* to spur him into action.

CHAPTER
SIX

As the fleeing ranger sighted the *peones*, a babel of shrill voices arose. But no shots. In half a dozen jumps, Star was going swift as the wind, and in a moment a bend of the trail hid him from any possible marksman. Vaughn's poignant concern for Roseta broke and gradually lessened.

At the end of a long straight stretch he looked back again. To his intense relief there was no one in sight.

"False alarm, Roseta," he said, craning his neck so he could see her face, pressed cheek against his shoulder.

"Let 'em come," she said, smiling up at him. Her face was pale, but it was not fear he read in her eyes. It was fight.

Vaughn laughed in sheer surprise. He had not expected that, and it gave him such a thrill as he had never felt in his life. He let go of Roseta's arm and took her hand, which was fastened in his coat. And he squeezed it with far more than reassurance. The answering pressure was unmistakable. A singular elation mounted in Vaughn's heart.

It did not quite render him heedless. As Star turned a corner, Vaughn's keen glance took in a widening of the trail blocked by the motley crew of big-sombreroed

Mexicans and horses he had been separated from not long before that day.

"Hold tight!" he cried warningly to Roseta as he swerved Star to the left. He threw his gun and fired two quick shots. He needed not to see that they took effect, for a wild cry pealed up, followed by angry yells.

Star beat the answering rifle shots into the brush. Vaughn heard the sing and *twang* of bullets. Crashings through the mesquites behind, added to the gunshots, lent wings to Star. This was a familiar situation to the great horse. Then for Vaughn it became a strenuous job to ride him, and doubly fearful owing to Roseta. But Star appeared gradually to be distancing his pursuers. The desert grew more open with level gravel floor. Here Vaughn urged Star to his limit.

Roseta stuck like a leech, and the ranger had to add admiration to his other feelings toward her. Vaughn put his hand back to grasp and steady her. And it did not take much time for the giant strides of the horse to cover miles. Finally Vaughn pulled him to a gallop and then a lope.

"*Chata*, are you all right?" he asked, afraid to look back, after using that compelling epithet.

"Yes. But can't . . . hold on . . . much longer," she panted. "If they catch us . . . shoot me first."

"Roseta, they will never catch us," he protested.

"But . . . promise," she entreated.

"I promise they'll never take us alive. But, child, keep up your nerve. It's sunset soon . . . and then dark. We'll get away sure."

Again they raced across the desert, this time in less of a straight line, although still to the north. The dry wind made tears dim Vaughn's eyes. He kept to open lanes and patches to avoid being struck by branches. And he spared Star only when he heard the heaves of distress, but at length Vaughn got him down to a walk.

"We're . . . far . . . far . . . ahead," he panted. "They'll trail us till dark." He peered back across the yellow and green desert, slowly darkening in the sunset. "But we're safe . . . thank God."

"Oh, what a glorious ride," cried Roseta between breaths. "I felt that . . . even with death close . . . Vaughn, I'm such a little . . . fool. I longed . . . for excitement . . . But for you . . ."

"Save your breath. We may need to run again."

She said no more. Vaughn walked Star until the horse had regained his wind, and then urged him into a lope.

The sun sank red in the west; twilight stole under the mesquite and the *palo verde;* dusk came upon its heels; the heat tempered to a slight breeze. When the stars came out, Vaughn took his direction from them, and pushed on for miles.

The moon brightened the open patches and the swales. Vaughn halted the tireless horse in a spot where grass caught the moonlight.

"We'll rest a bit," he said, sliding off, but still holding to the girl. "Come."

She fell into his arms; when he let her feet down, she leaned against him.

"Can you stand? You'd better wait a little," he said.

"My legs are dead."

"I want to go a few steps and listen. The night is still. I could hear horses at a long distance."

"Please, don't go far," she entreated.

Vaughn went back out of earshot of the heaving, creaking horse, and turned his keen ear to the gentle breeze. It blew from the south. Only a very faint rustle of leaves disturbed the desert silence. He held his breath and listened intensely. No sound! He returned to Roseta.

"No sound. It is as I expected. Night has saved us," he said.

"Night and *canyu*. Oh, I watched you, ranger man."

"You helped, Roseta. That bandit who led your horse was suspicious. But when you looked at him . . . he forgot. Small wonder . . . Have you stretched your legs?"

"I tried. I walked some, then flopped here . . . Oh, I want to rest and sleep."

"I don't know about your sleeping, but you can rest riding," he replied and, removing his coat, folded it around the pommel of his saddle, making a flat seat there. "Give me your hand . . . Put your foot in the stirrup. Now." He caught her and lifted her in front of him, and, settling her comfortably upon the improvised seat, he put his left arm around her. Many a wounded comrade had he packed this way. "How is . . . that?" he asked unsteadily.

"It's very nice," she replied, her dark eyes inscrutable in the moonlight. And she relaxed against his arm and shoulder.

Vaughn headed Star north at a brisk walk. He could not be more than six hours from the river in a straight line. Cañons and rough going might deter him. But even so he could make the Río Grande before dawn. Then and then only did he surrender to the astonishing presence of Roseta Uvalde, to the indubitable fact that he had saved her, and then to thoughts wild and whirling.

"Vaughn, was it that guard or you . . . who called me *chata?*" she asked dreamily.

"It was I . . . who dared," he replied huskily.

"Dared! Then you were not just carried away . . . for the moment?"

"No, Roseta . . . I confess I was as . . . as bold as that poor devil."

"Vaughn, do you know what *chata* means?" she asked gravely.

"It is the name a *vaquero* has for his sweetheart."

"You meant it, *señor?*" she queried imperiously.

"Lord help me, Roseta, I did, and I do . . . I've loved you long."

"But you never told me!" she exclaimed with wonder and reproach. "Why?"

"What hope had I? A poor ranger. Texas Medill! Didn't you call me 'killer of Mexicans'?"

"I reckon I did. And because you *are* that, I'm alive to thank God for it. Vaughn, I always liked you, respected you as one of Texas' great rangers . . . feared you, too. I never know my real feelings . . . But I . . . I love you *now.*"

★   ★   ★

56

In the gray of dawn, Vaughn lifted Roseta down from the weary horse upon the bank of the Río Grande.

"We are here, Roseta," he said gladly. "It will soon be light enough to ford the river. Star came out just below Brownsville. There's a horse, Roseta! He shall never be risked again. In an hour you will be home."

"Home? Oh, how good! But what shall I say, Vaughn?" she replied, evidently awakening to facts.

"Dear, who was the fellow you ran . . . rode off with yesterday morning?"

"Didn't I tell you?" And she laughed. "It happened to be Elmer Wase . . . that morning . . . Oh, he was the unlucky one. The bandits beat him with quirts, dragged him off his horse. Then they led me away toward the river, and I didn't see him again."

Vaughn had no desire to acquaint her with the tragic end that had overtaken that young man.

"You were not . . . eloping?"

"*Vaughn!* It was only fun."

"Uvalde thinks you eloped. He was wild. He raved."

"The devil he did!" ejaculated Roseta rebelliously. "Vaughn, what did you think?"

"Dearest, I . . . I was only concerned with tracking you," he returned, and even in the gray gloom of the dawn those big dark eyes gave him a start.

"Vaughn, I have *peon* blood in me," she said, and she might have been a princess for the pride with which she confessed it. "My father always feared I'd run true to the Indian. Are you afraid of your *chata*?"

"No, darling."

"Then I shall punish Uvalde . . . I shall elope."

"Roseta!" expostulated Vaughn.

"Listen." She put her arms around his neck, and that was a long reach for her. "Will you give up the ranger service? I . . . couldn't bear it, Vaughn. You have earned release from the service all Texans are proud of."

"Yes, Roseta. I'll resign," he replied with boyish, eager shyness. "I've some money . . . enough to buy a ranch."

"Far from the border?" she entreated, as if thrilled.

"Yes, far. I know just the valley . . . 'way north, under the *Llano Estacado* . . . But, Roseta, I shall have to pack a gun . . . till I'm forgotten."

"Very well, I'll not be afraid . . . 'way north," she replied. Then her sweet gravity changed. "We will punish Father, Vaughn, we'll elope right now! We'll cross the river . . . get married . . . and drive out home to breakfast . . . How Dad will rave! But he would have me elope, though he'd never guess I'd choose a ranger."

Vaughn swung her up on Star, and leaned close to peer up at her, to find one last assurance of the joy that had befallen him. He was not conscious of asking what she bent her head to bestow upon his lips.

Lightning

REWARD
$500 WILL BE PAID FOR
THE DEATH OF LIGHTNING,
LEADER OF THE SEVIER RANGE
OF WILD HORSES.
UTAH CATTLE COMPANY

This notice, with a letter coming by stage and messenger to the Stewarts, brightened what had been a dull prospect. Seldom did a whole year's work, capturing and corralling mustangs in the cañons and on the plateaus, pay them half as much as the reward offered for this one stallion. The last season had been a failure altogether. A string of pintos and mustangs, representing months of hazardous toil, had climbed out of a cañon corral and escaped to their old haunts. So on the strength of this opportunity the brothers packed and rode out of Fredonia across the Arizona line into Utah.

Two days took them beyond and above the Pink Cliffs to the White Sage plateau, and there the country became new to them. From time to time a solitary sheepherder, encountered with his flocks on a sage slope, set them in the right direction, and on the seventh day they reached Bain, the most southerly of

61

the outposts of the big Utah ranches. It consisted of a water hole, a corral, a log cabin, and some range riders.

Lee and Cuth Stewart were tall, lean Mormons, as bronzed as the desert Navajos, cool, silent, gray-eyed, still-faced. Both wore crude homespun garments much the worse for wear; boots that long before had given the best in them; laced leather wristbands thin and shiny from contact with lassoes; and old gray slouch hats that would have disgraced cowboys.

But this threadbare effect did not apply to the rest of the outfit, which showed a care that must have been in proportion to its hard use. And the five beautiful mustangs, Bess in particular, proved that the Stewarts were Indians at the end of every day, for they certainly had camped where there was grass and water. The pack of hounds shared interest with the mustangs, and the leader, a great yellow, somber-eyed hound, Dash by name, could have made friends with everybody had he felt inclined.

"We calculated, boys," held forth the foreman, "that if anybody could round up Lightnin' and his bunch it'd be you. Every ranger between here an' Marysvale has tried an' failed. Lightnin' is a rare cute stallion. He has more than hoss sense. For two years now no one has been in rifle shot of him, for the word has long since gone out to kill him.

"It's funny to think how many rangers have tried to corral him, trap him, or run him down. He's been a heap of trouble to all the ranchers. He goes right into a bunch of hosses, fights an' kills the stallions, an' leads off what he wants of the rest. His band is scattered all over, an' no man can count 'em, but he's got at least five hundred hosses off the ranges. An' he's got to be killed or there won't be a safe grazin' spot left in Sevier County."

"How're we to know this hoss's trail when we do cross it?" asked Lee Stewart.

"You can't miss it. His right foretrack has a notch that bites in clean every step he takes. One of my rangers came in yesterday an' reported fresh sign of Lightnin' at Cedar Springs, sixteen miles north along the red ridge up there. An' he's goin' straight for his hidin' place. Whenever he's been hard chased, he hits it back up there an' lays low for a while. It's rough country, though I reckon it won't be to you cañon fellers."

"How about water?"

"Good chances for water beyond Cedar, I reckon, though I don't know any springs. It's rare an' seldom any of us ever work up as far as Cedar. A scaly country up that way . . . black sage, an' that's all."

The Stewarts reached Cedar Springs that afternoon. It was a hot place; a few cedars, struggling for existence, lifted dead twisted branches to the sun; a scant growth of grass greened the few shady spots; and a thin stream of water ran between glistening borders of alkali. A drove of mustangs had visited the spring since dawn and had obliterated all tracks made before.

While Cuth made camp, Lee rode up the ridge to get a look at the country. "We're just on the edge of wild-hoss country," he said to Cuth when he returned.

"That stallion probably had a picked bunch an' was drivin' them higher up. It's gettin' hot these days, and the browse is witherin'. I see old deer sign on the ridge, an' cougar, an' coyote sign trailin' after. They're all makin' fer higher up. I reckon we'll find 'em all on Sevier plateau."

"Did you see the plateau?" asked Cuth.

"Plain. Near a hundred miles away yet. Just a long flat ridge black with timber. Then there's the two snow peaks, Terrill an' Hilgard, pokin' up their cold noses. I reckon the plateau rises off these ridges, an' the Sevier River an' the mountains are on the other side. So we'll push on for the plateau. We might come up with Lightnin' and his bunch."

Sunset found them halting at a little water hole among a patch of cedars and boulders.

Cuth slipped the packs, and Lee measured out the oats for the mustangs. Then the brothers set about getting supper for themselves.

Cuth had the flour and water mixed to a nicety, and Lee had the Dutch oven on some red-hot coals when, moved by a common instinct, they stopped work and looked up.

The five mustangs were not munching their oats; their heads were up. Bess, the keenest of the quintet, moved restlessly and then took a few steps toward the opening in the cedars.

"Bess!" called Lee sternly. The mare stopped.

"She's got a scent," whispered Cuth, reaching for his rifle. "Mebbe it's a cougar."

64

"Mebbe, but I never knowed Bess to go lookin' up one . . . *Hist!* Look at Dash."

The yellow hound had risen from among his pack and stood warily, shifting his nose. He sniffed the wind, turned around and around, and slowly stiffened with his head pointing up the ridge. The other hounds caught something — at least the manner of their leader — and became restless.

"Down, Dash, down," said Lee, and then with a smile to Cuth: "Did you hear it?"

"Hear what?"

"Listen!"

The warm breeze came down in puffs from the ridge; it rustled the cedars and blew fragrant whiffs of smoke into the hunters' faces, and, presently, it bore a call, a low, prolonged call.

Cuth rose noiselessly to his feet and stood still. So horses, hounds, and men waited, listening. The sound broke the silence again, much clearer, a keen, sharp whistle. The third time it rang down from the summit of the ridge, splitting the air, strong, trenchant, the shrill, fiery call of a challenging stallion.

Bess reared an instant straight up and came down quivering.

"Look!" whispered Lee tensely.

On the summit of the bare ridge stood a noble horse clearly silhouetted against the purple and gold of sunset sky. He was an iron-gray, and he stood wild and proud, with long silver-white mane waving in the wind.

"Lightnin'!" exclaimed Cuth.

He stood there one moment, long enough to make a picture for the wild horse hunters that would never be forgotten; then he moved back along the ridge and disappeared. Other horses, blacks and bays, showed above the sage for a moment, and they, too, passed out of sight.

Before daylight the brothers were up, and at dawn filed out of the cedar grove. The trained horses scarcely rattled a stone, and the hounds trotted ahead mindful of foxes and rabbits brushed out of the sage as they held back their chase.

The morning passed, and the afternoon waned. Green willows began to skirt the banks of a sandy wash, and the mustangs sniffed as if they smelled water. Presently the Stewarts entered a rocky corner refreshingly bright and green with grass, trees, and flowers, and pleasant with the murmur of bees and fall of water.

A heavily flowing spring gushed from under a cliff, dashed down over stones to form a pool, and ran out to seep away and lose itself in the sandy wash. Flocks of blackbirds chattered around the pool, and rabbits darted everywhere.

"It'd take a hull lot of chasin' to drive a mustang from comin' regular to that spring," commented Cuth.

"Sure, it's a likely place, an' we can make a corral here in short order."

In a day's hard work, they completed the corral. The pool was enclosed, except on the upper side where the water tumbled over a jumble of rocks, a place no horse could climb out, and on the lower side where they left the opening for the ponderous pine-log gate which would trap the mustangs once they had entered the corral.

At nightfall they were ready and waiting for their quarry. At midnight the breeze failed, and a dead stillness set in. It was not broken until the afterpart of the night and then, suddenly, by the shrill, piercing neigh of a mustang. The Stewarts raised themselves sharply and looked at each other thoughtfully in the dark.

"Did you hear that?" asked Lee.

"I just did. Sounded like Bess."

"It was Bess . . . darn her black hide. She never did that before."

"Mebbe she's winded Lightnin'."

"Mebbe. But she ain't hobbled, an', if she'd whistle like thet for him, she's liable to make off after him. Now, what to do?"

"It's too late. I warned you before. We can't spoil what may be a chance to get the stallion. Let Bess alone. Many's the time she's had a chance to make off an' didn't do it. Let's wait."

"Reckon it's all we can do now. If she called thet stallion, it proves one thing . . . we can't never break a wild mare perfectly. The wild spirit may sleep in her blood, mebbe for years, but sometime it'll answer to . . ."

"Shut up . . . listen!" interrupted Cuth.

From far up on the ridge came down the faint rattling of stones.

"Mustangs . . . an' they're comin' down," said Lee.

"I see 'em," whispered Cuth.

It was an anxious moment, for the mustangs had to pass hunters and hounds before entering the gate. A black bobbing line wound out of the cedars. Then the starlight showed the line to be the mustangs marching in single file. They passed with drooping heads, hurrying a little toward the last, and unsuspiciously entered the corral gate.

"Twenty-odd," whispered Lee, "but all blacks an' bays. The leader wasn't in that bunch. Mebbe it wasn't his . . ."

Among the cedars rose the peculiar halting thump of hobbled horses trying to cover ground, and following that snorts and crashings of brush and the pound of plunging hoofs. Then out of the cedars moved two shadows, the first a great gray horse with snowy mane, the second a small, graceful, shiny black mustang.

Lightning and Bess!

The stallion, in the fulfillment of a conquest such as had made him famous on the wild ranges, was magnificent in action and mien. Wheeling about her, whinnying, cavorting, he arched his splendid neck and pushed his head against her. His importunity was that of a master.

Suddenly Bess snorted and whirled down the trail. Lightning whistled one short blast of anger or terror and thundered after the black. Bess was true to her desert blood at the last. They vanished in the gray

68

shadow of the cedars, as a stream of frightened mustangs poured out of the corral in a clattering roar.

Gradually the dust settled. Cuth looked at Lee, and Lee looked at Cuth. For a while neither spoke. Cuth generously forbore saying: "I told you so." The failure of their plan was only an incident of horse wrangling and in no wise discomfited them. But Lee was angry at his favorite.

"You was right, Cuth," he said. "That mare played us at the finish. Ketched when she was a yearling, broke the best of any mustang we ever had, trained with us for five years, an' helped down many a stallion . . . an' she runs off wild with that big, white-maned brute!"

"Well, they make a team, an' they'll stick," replied Cuth. "An' so'll we stick, if we have to chase them to the Great Salt Basin."

Next morning, when the sun tipped the ridge rosy red, Lee put the big yellow hound on the notched track of the stallion, and the long trail began. At noon the hunters saw him heading his blacks across a rising plain, the first step of the mighty plateau stretching to the northward.

As they climbed, grass and water became more frequent along the trail. For the most part Lee kept on the tracks of the mustang leader without the aid of the hound; Dash was used in the grass and on the scaly ridges where the trail was hard to find.

The succeeding morning Cuth spied Lightning watching them from a high point. Another day found them on top of the plateau, among the huge brown pine trees and patches of snow and clumps of aspen. It took two days to cross the plateau — sixty miles. Lightning did not go down, but doubled on his trail. Rimming a plateau was familiar work for the hunters, and twice they came within sight of the leader and his band.

Sometimes for hours the hunters had him in sight, and always beside him was the little black they knew to be Bess. There was no mistaking her.

There came a day when Lightning cut out all of his band except Bess, and they went on alone. They made a spurt and lost the trailers from sight for two days. Then Bess dropped a shoe, and the pursuers came up.

As she grew lamer and lamer, the stallion showed his mettle. He did not quit her, but seemed to grow more cunning as pursuit closed in on them, choosing the open places where he could see far and, browsing along, covering rods where formerly he had covered miles.

One day the trail disappeared on stony ground, and there Dash came in for his share. Behind them the Stewarts climbed a very high round-topped mesa, buttressed and rimmed by cracked cliffs.

It was almost insurmountable. They reached the summit by a narrow watercourse to find a wild and lonesome level rimmed by crags and gray walls. There were cedars and fine thin grass growing on the plateau.

"Corralled!" said Lee laconically, as his keen eye swept the surroundings. "He's never been here before, an' there's no way off this mesa except by the back trail, which we'll close."

70

After fencing the split in the wall, the brothers separated and rode around the rim of the mesa. Lightning had reached the end of his trail; he was caught in a trap.

Lee saw him flying like a gleam through the cedars and suddenly came upon Bess, limping painfully along. He galloped up, roped her, and led her, a tired and crippled mustang, back to the place selected for camp.

"Played out, eh?" said Cuth, as he smoothed the dusty neck. "Well, Bess, you can rest up an' help us ketch the stallion. There's good grazin' here, an' we can go down for water."

For their operations the hunters chose the highest part of the mesa, a level cedar forest. Opposite a rampart of the cliff wall they cut a curved line of cedars, dropping them close together to form a dense, impassable fence. This enclosed a good space free from trees. From the narrowest point, some twenty yards wide, they cut another line of cedars running diagonally back a mile into the center of the mesa. What with this labor and going down every day to take the mustangs to water, nearly a week elapsed.

"It'd be somethin' to find out how long thet stallion could go without waterin'," said Lee. "But we'll make his tongue hang out tomorrow! An' just for spite we'll break him with black Bess."

Daylight came cool and misty; the veils unrolled in the valleys; the purple curtains of the mountains lifted to the snow peaks and became clouds; and then the red sun burned out of the east.

"If he runs this way," said Lee, as he mounted black Bess, "drive him back. Don't let him in the corral till he's plumb tired and worn out."

The mesa sloped slightly eastward, and the cedar forest soon gave place to sage and juniper. At the extreme eastern point of the mesa Lee jumped Lightning out of a clump of bushes. A race ensued for half the length of the sage flat, then the stallion made into the cedars and disappeared.

Lee slowed down, trotting up the easy slope, and cut across somewhat to the right. Not long afterward he heard Cuth yelling, and saw Lightning tearing through the scrub. Lee went on to the point where he had left Cuth and waited.

Soon the pound of hoofs thudded through the forest, coming nearer and nearer. Lightning appeared straight ahead, running easily. At sight of Lee and the black mare he snorted viciously and, veering to the left, took to the open.

Lee watched him with sheer admiration. He had a beautiful stride and ran seemingly without effort. Then Cuth galloped up and reined in a spent and foam-flecked mustang.

"That stallion can run some," was his tribute.

"He sure can. Change hosses now an' be ready to fall in line when I chase him back."

With that Lee coursed away and soon crossed the trail of Lightning and followed it at a sharp trot, threading in and out of the aisles and glades of the forest. He passed through to the rim and circled half the mesa before he saw the stallion again. Lightning stood on a ridge, looking backward. When the hunter yelled, the stallion leaped as if he had been shot and plunged down the ridge.

Lee headed to cut him off from the cedars, but he forged to the front, gained the cedar level, and twinkled in and out of the clump of trees. Again Lee slowed down to save his mustang.

Bess was warming up, and Lee wanted to see what she could do at close range. Keeping within sight of Lightning, the hunter chased him leisurely around and around the forest, up and down the sage slopes, along the walls, at last to get him headed for the only open stretch on the mesa. Lee rode across a hollow and came out on the level only a few rods behind him.

"*Hi! Hi! Hi!*" yelled the hunter, spurring Bess forward like a black streak.

Uttering a piercing snort of terror, the gray stallion lunged out, for the first time panic-stricken, and lengthened his stride in a way that was wonderful to see. Then at the right moment Cuth darted from his hiding place, whooping at the top of his voice and whirling his lasso. Lightning won that race down the open stretch, but it cost him his best.

At the turn he showed his fear and plunged wildly first to the left, then to the right. Cuth pushed him relentlessly, while Lee went back, tied up Bess, and saddled Billy, a wiry mustang of great endurance.

Then the two hunters remorselessly hemmed Lightning between them, turned him where they wished, at last to run him around the corner of the fence of cut cedars down the line through the narrow gate into the corral prepared for him.

"Hold hard," said Lee to Cuth. "I'll go on an' drive him 'round an' 'round till he's done . . . then, when I yell, you stand to one side an' rope him as he goes out."

Lightning ran around the triangular space, plunged up the steep walls, and crashed over the dead cedars. Then as sense and courage gave way more and more to terror, he broke into desperate headlong flight. He ran blindly, and, every time he passed the guarded gateway, his eyes were wilder and his stride more labored.

"*Hi! Hi! Hi!*" yelled Lee.

Cuth pulled out of the opening and hid behind the line of cedars, his lasso swinging loosely. Lightning saw the vacated opening and sprang forward with a hint of his old speed. As he passed through, a yellow loop flashed in the sun, circling, shimmering, and he seemed to run right into it. The loop whipped close around the glossy neck, and the rope stretched taut. Cuth's mustang staggered under the violent shock, went to his knees, but struggled up, and held. Lightning reared aloft.

Then Lee, darting up in a cloud of dust, shot his lasso. The noose nipped the right foreleg of the stallion. He plunged, and for an instant there was a wild straining struggle, then he fell heaving and groaning. In a twinkling, Lee sprang off and, slipping the rope that threatened to strangle Lightning, replaced it by a stout halter and made this fast to a cedar.

Whereupon the Stewarts stood back and gazed at their prize. Lightning was badly spent, but not to a

74

dangerous extent, dabbled with foam but no fleck of blood appeared; his superb coat showed scratches, but none cut the flesh. He was up after a while, panting heavily and trembling in all his muscles. He was a beaten horse, but he showed no viciousness, only the wild fear of a trapped animal. He eyed Bess, then the hunters, and last the halter.

"Lee, will you look at him! Will you just look at thet mane!" ejaculated Cuth.

"Well," replied Lee, "I reckon that reward, an' then some, can't buy him."

The Camp Robber

"What the deuce!" exclaimed Hoff Manchester, the Selwyn Ranch foreman.

"Boys, it ain't no joke," said cowhand Slab Jacobs. "Shore as the Lord made little apples, we been robbed!"

The boys of the Selwyn Ranch had returned from the spring roundup . . . to find their bunkhouse door standing open, and their quarters ransacked.

Yet a quick search, punctuated by an infinite variety of cowboy speech, revealed only a few valueless trinkets missing; untouched were a set of silver-mounted spurs, money, and a diamond stickpin.

"Hoff, the laugh's on us. What's your idea?" Jacobs asked.

"By gum, I think we've had a visit from the camp robber."

"Who's this camp robber?" asked one of the cowboys.

The foreman answered him. "Well, I reckon the camp robber always has been a joke 'round the range. But I can conceive of that joke wearin' out. He's been crackin' them jokes for a good while now. I've heard them from all over, an' this is no slouch of a range. But for the most part, such stealin' seems to have been confined to Clear Creek, Cottonwood, an' the Verde. Whatever or whoever this thief is — he comes in the day time, when there's nobody home, an' he takes some fool thing or other, leaving articles of real value. This bird sure is a slick one, whoever he is. Last year he stole two dolls we know of."

"Dolls?"

"Yes, dolls. Stimpson over on Clear Creek has a little girl. She lost a doll. Missus Stimpson said the kid was sure she never lost it . . . that it was took. Wal, they got her another doll, an', by golly, not long after, when the family was all away, that doll disappeared, too."

"Now I tax myself, I can remember the darnedest lot of things the loss of which was laid on thet locoed thief. Comb an' brush, silver buckles, beads, handkerchiefs, socks, cough medicine, face powder, lace curtains, towels, mirror, bell, clock. Oh, Lord, there's no end to them. Yet nothin' worth much, so to speak. Everybody just laughs an' says . . . 'Wal, by gosh, the camp robber has been here.'"

Stimpson pushed back his papers on the desk and looked up at the rider with a keen interest.

"So your name's Wingfield?"

"Yes, sir," was the quiet reply.

The rancher surveyed the lithe figure, dusty and worn, the dark, lined face and its piercing eyes, with appreciation of the strong impression they gave.

"Where have you been ridin'?" Stimpson asked.

"I rode for Stillwell durin' the spring roundup. But he didn't need me longer. I got on at Brandon's. Lasted only one payday. Next got a job at Hall's. Couldn't stay there. Then Randall's. An', as I told you, I've been ridin' a grub line since."

"Wingfield, tell me just why you couldn't hold a job?" asked Stimpson.

"It was my fault, sir."

"You don't look like a drinkin' man."

"Well, I hit the bottle pretty stiff some years ago . . . just after . . . But I tapered off . . . an' lately I haven't drank at all."

"Because you were broke?"

"No. I've a little money left. I just got sick of it."

"I can understand that. Now, if you want to work for me, come clean about this trouble you've been havin'. Tell me why a man of your evident intelligence an' ability can't hang on here."

Wingfield looked out of the window, across the summer range, where the heat veils were rising. His face twitched. It was somber and sad. And when he turned again, Stimpson saw that the dark lightning of his eyes had dimmed.

"Seems, sir, that I can't stay anywhere long. I've been restless, an' I reckon I'm irritable. Can't make friends. I don't care about anythin'. But I realize now that I've got to correct that. An' I promise you, if you'll take me on, I'll try to overcome it."

"I'll take you on, Wingfield. Thanks for your confidence. I appreciate it. I'd like to know more, though. What happened to such a fine fellow as you . . . that you don't care for anythin'?"

"Some years ago I . . . I lost my wife . . . an' it knocked me out," said Wingfield.

"Uhn-huh. Too bad . . . I didn't take you for a married man. How old are you, Wingfield?"

"I'm twenty-nine."

"Well, that surprises me. You look older . . . All right, Wingfield, you're on. An', let us hope, to your advantage as well as mine. Report to Neff an' ask for quarters, by yourself, if you prefer. Later today we can talk wages an' what this particular job is."

That deal was consummated in July. Wingfield made a valiant effort to prove worthy of the opportunity Stimpson had placed in his way. And he succeeded so far as the work was concerned. He overcame much to stick to that job, but he could not correct his taciturn habit, his aloofness, and sharpness of tongue, when he did speak.

Naturally he had not made friends with Stimpson's foreman, Neff. Signs were not wanting, however, that some of the riders looked favorably upon him. He had even been asked to accompany them to town this Saturday night, which was the end of August, and payday.

Late that afternoon Wingfield rode back to the ranch, and before he dismounted in front of Neff's cabin, he sensed trouble. All the riders were in. Wingfield went in without greeting any of those who regarded him curiously.

82

"Wingfield," spoke up Stimpson, "the payroll is missin'.'"

"It is, sir? Well! How you mean . . . missin'?" asked Wingfield, flashing his eyes from Neff to the rancher.

"I don't know how," said Stimpson, slowly guarding his speech. "I just got here . . . Speak up, Neff."

"It . . . it was this way, boss," replied Neff hurriedly. "Reckon I got here about ten o'clock. Straight from the house, when you gave me the money. Wally Peters, over there, helped me count it. Didn't you, Wally?"

"Yes, I did," answered a clean-cut young cowboy, stepping forward to confront the rancher. "There was two thousand, three hundred an' sixty dollars. Neff put it in the desk here, shut the drawer . . . this one, sir, but he didn't lock it. Then we went out together."

"Had there been anyone about the place?" inquired Stimpson.

"Yes, sir. Wingfield must have been in . . . I found the paper . . . here it is . . . shows the time of his outfit. I always pay from his figures . . . This paper was here when I came back. But not when I left," said Neff.

Wingfield spoke up instantly. "That is correct, sir. I left my time paper here about noon. There was no one in."

A silence ensued that developed from embarrassment to a strained suspense.

Then Stimpson, seeing that Neff would not or could not accuse Wingfield to his face, burst out impatiently.

"Wingfield, I'm sorry I have to explain. Neff has charged you with theft of the payroll."

Wingfield gave a gasp that sounded like suppression of a cry of pain. His dark face went ashen. With one swift lunge he struck Neff a terrific blow, knocking him over a chair, to crash into a corner. Then Wingfield leaped clear, drawing his gun.

The spectators of that move waved in noisy pell-mell to one side, leaving Stimpson standing his ground. With a long stride he got in front of Wingfield.

"Hold on!" he called sharply. "There's no call for gun play."

Indeed, there did not appear to be, at least at the moment, for Neff had been completely knocked out. Wingfield slowly sheathed his gun. The fury that had actuated him seemed to shudder out.

"My God . . . you don't believe I stole that money?" he asked Stimpson.

The rancher took one long look at the man's convulsed face.

"No, Wingfield, I don't," he replied feelingly. "But Neff does, an' no doubt he's not the only one. Somethin' must be done about it."

"Thank you, Stimpson," said Wingfield huskily. "I swear to God I didn't take the money."

"You need not deny that to me," replied the rancher. "But you can see, Wingfield, if you're to stay on here, you must try to prove you didn't."

"Yes, I see. An' I've fallen pretty low . . . when any rider dares think me a thief," muttered Wingfield.

"Circumstantial evidence has hanged many a man. Don't let it beat you here. You're valuable to me. An' it's sure plain, Wingfield, either you crack an' lose out, or you prove what I think you are."

Wingfield raised his bowed head, and the harshest of the bitter darkness left his face. He made no move to reach the rancher's half-proffered hand.

"I'll take your hand when I show these men your faith in me is justified."

That night Wingfield lay dressed on his bed in the darkness and silence. All hands had gone to town for the dance. Lying there in the blackness, he waged the battle. If he had not become a sore and strange outsider all over the range, if he had hid the secret of his misery in wholesome labor and friendliness, he would never have been accused of theft. That was the last straw.

He did not choose to sink under that. He would disprove the charge, and thereafter regulate his conduct to harmonize with his environment. Stimpson had been right — he must mend his character or crack for good.

But there could never be any mending of his broken heart. In the five years since the catastrophe, there had never been a single night, when he was sober, that he had not lain awake, thinking, remembering, suffering. He had wronged his wife, and in the shame of his unworthiness he had augmented the quarrel that had ended in her leaving him. It all came back mockingly, and he lived over again his fruitless search for her, and then his despair.

He beheld for the thousandth time a vision of the bonnie head, with its curly golden locks, and the flower-like blue eyes, and the frail, graceful shape. Long ago he divined she was dead. She could never have borne grief and privation together. She had never been strong, although she had gained somewhat after he took her from schoolteaching and married her. He recalled with agony his panic, his joy, his pride, when she shyly imparted a secret, and how zealously from that moment he had guarded her health.

Then came his fall, a natural although despicable thing. Vain regret! Sleepless and eternal remorse! But these pangs were softening with the years. He knew that before she died she had forgiven him, and that, if he could have found her, they would have been reunited.

There in the dead hour of midnight he struggled for faith to believe she might hear his whisper and give him strength to live better the life that had to be lived.

Sunrise found him out behind Neff's cabin, studying, in the clear light of day, some strange tracks he had found. A faint long flat depression of grass and dust and on each side of it a small round mark, scarcely a hole. Wingfield followed the tracks at a walk into the woods. In places, where the pine needles formed a thick springy mat, devoid of grass or flowers, he passed quickly on in the direction in which the trail headed, and sooner or later, on more favorable ground, he would find it again. It led deeper and deeper into the woods.

In the afternoon on the first clear spot of soft ground that he had encountered in miles he found the well defined print of a large flat foot. Close on each side was the accompanying little round mark.

"A-huh! He's slipped off that long thing which gave me such trouble," said Wingfield, as he surveyed the trail. "Quit on me, huh? Feelin' pretty safe now! One foot track . . . By thunder! I've got it. He's a cripple. A one-legged man! An' these little round tracks were made by crutches . . . I'm a locoed son-of-a-gun!"

With renewed enthusiasm and stronger resolve and curiosity, Wingfield pressed on, and now, owing to the slackened vigilance of the man he was trailing, he made fast time. Almost at his feet showed a narrow trail leading down the precipitous wall. And the tracks he was trailing stood out like print on a page.

Five hundred feet down, the trail emerged from the shade into the open cañon, where Wingfield's advent scarcely disturbed the turkeys and deer. He proceeded slowly and cautiously. A little gray burro grazed in the one open glade. Beyond this, a jutting wall shut off extended view. He kept close to the wall, under cover, and soon peeped around the yellow stone corner. He was amazed to discover a child playing in front of an old weather-beaten cabin.

Wingfield sheathed his gun and stepped out to approach the little girl. She saw him before he spoke.

"Hello, little girl. Do you live here?"

"Who's you?" she asked, without alarm, although she ceased her play.

"I'm a cowboy. Where's your mother . . . an' your daddy?"

"My muvver's dead . . . I never had no daddy," she said.

She could not have been more than five years old. She was very pretty with eyes as blue as cornflowers. It needed not a second glance at her crude strange garments for even Wingfield to see that no woman had made them. Her little dress had been fashioned from a cowboy's shirt.

Upon her feet were moccasins made from sheepskin, with the wool outside, and Wingfield believed that material had come from a range rider's vest. Then the thought that had been dammed by his consciousness burst through — he had stumbled upon the retreat of the camp robber.

"My grandad's sick," said the little girl seriously.

"Where is he?" asked Wingfield thickly.

She pointed toward the cabin. The door was open, and the sunlight poured in.

An old man, with face as gray as his hair and beard, lay upon a bed. His bright eyes fixed in terrible earnestness upon the visitor.

"Well, old-timer, who are you?" burst out Wingfield, taking in the gaunt form and the wooden leg strapped to a short thigh.

"Did you ever . . . hear . . . of Pegleg Smith?" came the husky response.

"Sure I have. Old prospector . . . traveled 'round with a burro. I've heard the cowboys talk . . . Uhn-huh! Are you that *hombre?*"

"Yes . . . Did you trail me?"

"I did . . . old-timer. I'm sorry. The little girl said you were sick."

"Aye, I am, indeed . . . sick unto death."

"Aw, no. Don't say that. Maybe I can do somethin'. What ails you?"

"Old age. Love an' . . . fear," he returned.

"I don't just savvy the last," said Wingfield, approaching the bed in quandary. But pity was paramount.

"Did you trail me?"

"Yes, but you needn't fear me. Only tell me, old-timer."

"You trailed me to get back the money I stole from Stimpson's ranch?"

"I did, Smith. You see, they accused me of stealin' it."

"It is here . . . every dollar," hurriedly cried the man, and, laboriously fumbling under his head, he found a packet, and held it out with shaking hand.

"Thanks, old-timer. That'll help a lot," said Wingfield huskily. "How'd you come to . . . to take it?"

"Stranger, I never stole a cent in my life, until then. All I stole was for the child. But that day . . . when was it? Yesterday? When I saw the money, I had a wild idea. I would steal that . . . and with it . . . I would take my little girl away . . . and find a home and comfort for her . . . someone to love her . . . So I stole it. And when I got back . . . I fell here . . . it's the end . . . Thank God, you came. I can die in peace."

"Is this child related to you?" asked Wingfield.

"No. Five years ago . . . over on the mountain range I happened to find a woman along the road . . . She was a crazed thing . . . ill . . . suffering. I put her on my burro. Fetched her here. She gave birth to a child . . . She lingered a few days and died. The child lived. Meant to take her . . . somewhere . . . to a home. But I loved her. I kept her. All these years I've kept her. No cowboy or hunter ever found me, until now. No one ever dreamed old Pegleg Smith became the camp robber of the range. Many's the time I have laughed over my other name . . . The camp robber!"

Wingfield fell on his knees beside the bed.

"Old-timer, tell me . . . her name?" begged Wingfield hoarsely, his lean hands clutching at the blanket.

"Her name is Fay."

"No. Not the child . . . the woman . . . her mother . . . her name?"

"I never knew. She never told. But in her delirium she would cry out . . . 'Lex . . . Lex, my husband!' . . . an' she died crying that name. I've never forgotten."

"Merciful God!" moaned Wingfield, sinking down. "Man . . . I was that husband . . . this is my baby."

"Who are you?" queried Smith, rising upon his elbow, with hope illuminating his face.

"Lex Wingfield . . . Her name was Fay Kingsley. We were married in Denver. It was here in Arizona . . . on this range . . . at Springer that I made her unhappy, and she left me."

"Kingsley . . . Denver . . . Springer, yes, she mentioned those names," replied Smith eagerly and softly. "How strange! I never wanted to leave this cañon. Something

90

chained me here . . . So, it was the camp robber who found little Fay's father."

Wingfield leaped up with a start. The child had come in.

"Is you better?" she asked with sweet solicitude.

"No, little Fay . . . You are losing your grandad . . . But you . . . are gaining . . . your daddy."

The Westerners

CHAPTER
ONE

All the way west to Reno, Katherine Hempstead had a growing realization that her desire to save her mother from disgrace might develop a far-reaching good for herself.

The journey had been a revelation. She belonged to the Eastern class who preferred to travel abroad rather than discover their own country. The Great Plains, the grand Rockies, the glorious desert had charmed and fascinated Katherine, and finally had awakened in her a strange longing. Had she really ever known what it meant to be free, alone, self-sufficient? Her mother's ridiculous affair with the fortune-hunting Leroyd had shocked Katherine out of her gay devotion to amusement, and had driven her post-haste across the continent to try to prevent the impending Hempstead divorce and scandal. Long gazing from a Pullman window through saddened and thoughtful eyes had worked upon her the alchemy of wonder and discontent.

To Katherine's surprise, Reno did not disgust her. A vague anticipation of crude people, raw life, hideous buildings did not materialize. She registered at the famous Hotel Reno, where her mother and Leroyd were staying, and sallied forth to see the town, conscious of an unfamiliar sensation of excitement. It was her first experience on foot, at night, in a strange city. Unconsciously she shrank from the meeting with her mother. She wanted to compose herself to new surroundings, to a perplexing situation, to think. And to her amazement she found that the process of constructive thinking was difficult and elusive. Now there was a new sensation, not experienced since her sixteenth year. Katherine had to laugh at this, and label it as a girlish dream of adventure that never would materialize. At twenty she seemed sophisticated, worldly, old in the modern outlook on things.

It was a Saturday night in early May. She needed the coat she had put on. The air was keen, cold, sweet, but did not appear to have enough oxygen in it for her. A few blocks of quick walking took her breath. This distance brought her apparently into the center of Reno. The street was crowded with cars and pedestrians, moving under the garish red and purple neon lights. Jazz music pealed out from somewhere. The atmosphere and brilliance were suggestive of holiday. Katherine felt it incongruous to be reminded of the Riviera, Monte Carlo, even Coney Island. Presently she grasped that the significance of this must be what she had sensed coming West, the loosening of restraint, the effect of open spaces, the spirit of play. She did not need to be told that Prohibition was on its last legs.

Between almost every store and restaurant there was a garish or elaborate edifice devoted to games of chance. The names intrigued her. Golden Fleece, The Elite, Nevada Club, Last Chance, The Show Down were among the names she passed within two blocks. The clink of silver and rattle of roulette wheels were not unenticing to Katherine. She loved to gamble. It was in her blood. But her bridge and golf gambling, like that onboard continental liners and in the gilded palaces of Europe, had been indulged in with her own class. Here, if she wanted to play, it would be among a motley crowd. Her training forbade that. But as the subtle thing stirred within, she yielded so far as to decide that, if she could find a suitable companion, she certainly would not leave Reno without taking a fling at the gambling tables.

Katherine was aware that men stared at her. Not that this was an unusual state of affairs, except that she was in a town of unknown possibilities and alone. The fact, however, that she was not accosted reassured her. Reno, she had heard, was a city where all women and especially women unaccompanied could feel safe from annoyance, and so far there seemed justification for the statement. That fact alone would be something of a novelty to Katherine. She had never been able to escape from the tributes to striking beauty.

Crossing the street, she suddenly surrendered to temptation, and entered the most pretentious of the gambling halls. A blaze of light and wave of sound assailed her. The place appeared to be an enormous hall, crowded by rings of men and women around the different games. She stood a while, watching.

Many of the numerous people around her appeared to be merely spectators, some of them quite apparently tourists. She went closer, presently, to get a view of the players around one of the roulette wheels, and discovered men and women in evening dress at elbows with pale-faced gamblers and rough-visaged miners and ranchers.

No one appeared to notice Katherine, an omission that grew upon her and at first piqued her. So accustomed had she always been to the immediate attention that her beauty attracted, that the lack of it seemed almost strange. But when she analyzed it, it was with a growing appreciation of the new sense of freedom her apparent insignificance engendered.

Presently, when Katherine had satisfied her curiosity, she left the hall. Upon emerging on the street, she found she had become turned around and was unsure of her direction. She did not want to inquire of any of the doubtful-looking loungers lined up outside, so started walking slowly along. About half a block farther on she hailed a tall young man who looked reassuring.

"Will you please direct me to the Hotel Reno?"

"Yes, ma'am," he replied, halting. "Six squares this way."

"Thank you. I was completely turned around."

"But see heah, lady. You cain't find it without turning off. Street's closed. That's a fire."

The shrieking siren of a fire-engine and a congestion down the street verified his statement.

"Oh! Can I go in a taxi?" inquired Katherine.

"Sure, if you can find one."

"I'm a stranger in Reno."

"So am I. Got in today. I'm not crazy about it. My mother is at the Reno. I am going there. If you like, you can come with me."

Katherine gave him an appraising glance. He was tall and had wide shoulders. His face, clean-cut and tanned, proclaimed him to be around twenty-five or twenty-six years old. She could not determine the color of his eyes, but they were piercing and troubled. They certainly were not taking stock of her. And that gave Katherine a chance for a keener glance. During the last half of her journey to Reno, she had seen cowboys, cattlemen, rangers, and this superb young Westerner belonged to this class.

"Thanks. I can risk it, if you can," she replied, with her low laugh. And then she was walking beside him.

Naturally she expected him to speak. But he was silent. She had to quicken her stride a little. She felt something shy or aloof about him, and she was prompted to feel him out. "Is it safe . . . and proper for a girl to be out alone at night in Reno?" she asked, to get his reaction.

"Safe heah, if anywhere in the West. But I reckon hardly proper."

"Oh! You see, I just arrived. I wanted to look around. I walked down the street. Then I went in one of the gambling places."

Her confidence did not seem to arouse his interest or curiosity. For all she could tell, this Westerner might think she was a moving-picture actress or a schoolteacher or an adventuress, or he might not have thought about it at all. This was a new type of individual to Katherine Hempstead. She kept pace with his long stride, which she saw he at least tried to accommodate to her shorter one. They walked on half a block in silence. Katherine could not recall when she had wanted to giggle as she wanted to now. She looked up at him and decided that she could no longer deny he was more than handsome. His hair appeared to be tawny or chestnut, and it had the little curl or wave women admired. She was struck again by an impression of trouble that emanated from him.

"Didn't you say you just arrived in Reno?" she asked, becoming uncomfortable at his protracted silence.

"Yes. This afternoon. My train was late."

"I'm from New York. Where did you come from? I can tell you're Western."

"California. But I'm not native. I was born in Arizona and lived there on a ranch till I was twenty. Then Dad sold his cattle, and we went to California."

"Do you like California as well?"

"It's shore fine. But not Arizona. I cain't explain."

"You miss the range?" she queried sympathetically.

"'Deed I do, lady."

"The way you say that makes me think you've been a cowboy. But I never heard a cowboy speak, save in a movie."

"I rode the range from the time I could fork a hoss until I was twenty."

"How interesting! And how soon could you fork a horse?"

"Guess I was close to being born on one and bareback at that. But I was six when I took to herding cattle."

"Goodness! Didn't you ever go to school?"

"Yes. I went through high school and had two years ... I should say terms ... at Normal College in Flagstaff."

"I was wondering how ... when you ever got the education you seem to have, if you rode a horse all your life."

"We go to school in winter out heah."

He led Katherine off the main street, to make a detour around a block. It was evident from the noise and smoke that the fire was located on the far side of this square. Katherine had another new sensation — an urge to run to a fire. She was finding unplumbed capacities in herself. The young Westerner, however, was more interesting than the fire. Katherine waited again for him to speak voluntarily. But he did not, nor look at her.

"Your mother is staying at my hotel?" she inquired.

"Yes. I haven't seen her yet. And I shore hate to ... I've come to try to ... I've come to try to stop Mom from divorcing Dad."

"Ah!" Katherine was startled almost to the point of halting in her tracks. The information frankly volunteered by her escort, given with a poignancy of emotion in sharp contrast to his former reserve, found an instant response in her. This meeting was becoming a more than casual one.

Suddenly it seemed potent. The young Westerner's trouble found an answering chord in her heart. "I'm sorry," went on Katherine slowly. "This divorce craze ... It's not so very bad though for grown-up children like you ... and me."

He did not catch the import of her last words. "It's a craze, all right. Not so wrong for young folk like us. But for old people, Mother and Father, it's daid wrong."

"I agree with you. Oh, I hope you can stop your mother . . . persuade her to patch it up!"

That expression appeared to hit the young man hard. "I'm afraid you don't know Mom. It'll take an earthquake to shake her. If it was only something else . . . anything else."

"Another woman?" interposed Katherine.

"A girl! Only a girl sixteen years old . . . and a Mexican girl at that," he burst out, as if it relieved him to unburden himself.

"A Mexican *señorita!* She'd be pretty, of course?"

"Pretty? Why Marcheta is the prettiest kid that ever bloomed in California. I was sweet on her myself before I got wise to Dad's break. Funny thing. Marcheta liked Dad more than she did me. But then Dad is a grand guy. You'd never guess he is fifty . . . I don't blame him much for falling for Marcheta. Mom cain't or won't understand. I reckon you savvy, ma'am. It's Dad's only slip, so far as I know. And we've been like brothers. When Mom found out, I tried to take the blame. I lied myself blue in the face. But Dad would have none of that. So Mom is heah to divorce Dad . . . and I reckon we're ruined."

There was a poignant misery in this outburst that entirely disregarded the fact that it was to an entire stranger that such confidences were made. Katherine was quick to understand and respond.

"Surely it is not so bad as that. Don't give up," she rejoined eloquently. "Perhaps I can help you, Mister Arizona. You and I have something in common."

"What do you mean . . . ma'am?" he queried, with a catch in his breath. And for the first time he turned to look at her. They had gone around another block. Katherine saw the hotel looming up and beyond it a dark mountain, crowned by white stars. She was in the grip of a swiftly developing and thought-arresting situation. But her impulse brooked no restraint.

"I am from New York," she said earnestly. "My mother is here with her boyfriend. He is a fortune-hunter. My father . . . well, he maintained an expensive apartment uptown and spent much time away from home. That gave my mother the chance she was looking for, I fear. She came out here to divorce him, and she brought this man with her. If I can't persuade or force her to her senses, she will go on with it and marry this person. That will raise a rotten scandal. It will ruin Mother."

"Aw! Shore it will . . . What damn' fools these old people are!" ejaculated the young man with passion. "Your case is worse than mine. It just makes me see red."

"What's your name?" asked Katherine, inspired in spite of an effort to restrain the drift of this interview.

"Phil Cameron."

"Mine is Katherine Hempstead. Let's combine our nerve and our wit. Let's stop our mothers from doing this thing." The words were out before Katherine stopped to consider.

"What? Why . . . why . . . Miss Hempstead," Cameron stammered, blushing like a girl. "You mean for you and I to put our heads together . . . to help one another . . . to . . . ?"

"Precisely. Two heads are better than one. You are Western. I am Eastern. We might make a pair to draw to . . . to use poker lingo. How about it, Arizona?"

They had halted on the corner, under the bright light. Katherine did not flinch under the most searching scrutiny to which she had ever been subjected. But her heart did skip a beat at the look that marked the keen glance of appraisal. It told her that she had more than passed muster.

"It's a great idea, Miss Heapstead," he finally burst out. "What luck for me! I felt so . . . so sick and blue I wanted to die. How did you ever drop out of the sky like this? It's just wonderful. I cain't believe my eyes and ears. But I say yes, ma'am, bless you! And if it's fighting you need, I'll never fail you."

"I believe it. I'm lucky, too. We don't need to inquire into the workings of fate . . . Shake hands, Phil."

He appeared awkward and under a spell, but his hand left hers paralyzed.

"Oh! Ah, Arizona, I'll want to use this member again," she said. "Call for me here or give me a ring at nine in the morning. Now let's go in and beard our respective lionesses in their dens."

CHAPTER
TWO

On the way to her room Katherine observed that the hotel appeared to be patronized by well-dressed people; there was music and dancing in the dining room, flowers everywhere, and all the appointments indicated a catering to a cosmopolitan elite.

Katherine telephoned the office from her room and asked for Mrs. Henry Watson Hempstead. The clerk informed her that Mrs. Hempstead was at dinner. Katherine had dined on the train. She took off her coat and hat, all at once aware that she was tired, and that excitement still abided with her. Deciding to put off seeing her mother until next day, Katherine changed her traveling clothes for comfortable pajamas, and sat down to rest and ponder.

She was here in Reno. She had met an interesting young Westerner and had impulsively made a compact with him. The three facts had given rise to a feeling which she could not analyze, except that it was not disagreeable. Katherine got no further than that in her pondering.

Presently she called Mrs. Hempstead again and received an answer. "Hello. Who is this?" How well Katherine recognized that voice.

"Mother, it's Kay."

"*Kay!* Where are you?"

"Here."

"In Reno?"

"Yes. At this hotel."

"My God! You would. But I never thought you'd follow me. Kay, why in the world did you come?"

"Do you need to ask?"

"Yes, I do. Who told you?"

"Father. He let me read your letter. I had just arrived home from Miami. I didn't even unpack . . . and here I am."

"Darling, it was adorable of you. But so foolish. That horrible train ride . . ."

"Was glorious for me, Mother. It made me ashamed that I knew so little about my own country. It did something else to me . . . I don't know what."

"Indeed? How interesting! My eyes were so full of dust I couldn't see out. You like the West, Kay?"

"I believe I will love it."

"You always had different notions from anyone else. I'm glad your trip will not be altogether wasted."

Katherine caught the rather broad inference, and she replied that she was sure her purpose in coming West would be fulfilled.

"Not if it's what I imagine it is," returned Mrs. Hempstead with asperity. "Come to my room at once."

"Not tonight, Mother. I regret to say that I must give you a very disagreeable few minutes. But I'll put it off until tomorrow. Meanwhile, you can think a little over the horrible blunder you have made."

"Kay, I'm breaking all ties," cried her mother with emotion.

"You are not doing anything of the kind."

"Kay," rejoined Mrs. Hempstead faintly, "have I ever . . . interfered with your peculiar ways of being happy?"

"Not lately. For years, though, you were an unnatural mother . . . Is your boyfriend, Jimmy, here with you?"

"Certainly he's here. Where would he be? But I detest your vulgarity."

"He ought to be somewhere else, my dearest mother. If you haven't any sense of decency, he ought to have . . . Does his apartment adjoin yours?"

"Don't insult me, Kay."

"I'll certainly insult him, if that is possible."

"My dear daughter, you seem to be taking a great deal upon yourself. Did you come out alone?"

"Yes, I came alone."

"I rather hoped you'd brought Brelsford . . . Kay, did you accept him?"

"No."

"Did you refuse him?"

"No."

"But Kay, you will marry him? You must. He's the most eligible and desirable young man you know."

"So you think, Mother dear. I like Victor, but marriage . . . You and Father furnish a perfect example of marital felicity, don't you?"

"But Kay, you absolutely must marry. You're twenty-two."

"Quite ancient, in fact. That is, I was . . . until I dropped down here into God's country. I feel very young and romantic. Yes, that's it. I was wondering what ailed me. I've gone back to sixteen, Mother. And I think one of these tall sun-browned cowboys will get me."

"Cowboy!" screamed Mrs. Hempstead. "Are you crazy, Kay? You, a Hempstead . . . with your background . . . your money! I'll wire to Brelsford to fly out here."

"Don't you dare. *I* don't need anyone to look after me, it's you. But wait, Mother darling. That might be a capital idea . . . sending for Vic. I'd like to see how he'd stack up beside one of these strapping Westerners. Go ahead. Get Victor out here. It might precipitate things."

"You devil!"

"Good night, Mother. I'll see you tomorrow. Sweet dreams."

Katherine turned off the steam heat and opened a window. The desert air blew in, cold, fresh, with a dry tang that was new to her. White stars studded the velvety blue sky. Beyond the narrow border of the town limits stretched a vast space ending in black hills. She gazed a moment, shivering, and then ran to get into bed, grateful for warm blankets.

When she reviewed the conversation with her mother, Katherine felt that she had reason to be encouraged. It had been several months since she had heard her voice. If there was anything she could be sure of, it was her mother's love for her and her sister Polly. That Katherine felt anew, and it softened her scorn and anger. It strengthened the conviction upon which she had dared to come West — that her mother was vulnerable through her one sincere affection. But what course to pursue, Katherine had not yet decided. Persuasion, argument would be futile. Ridicule and scorn were weapons Mary Hempstead could not endure. She believed in Leroyd's attachment with all a disappointed middle-aged woman's egotism. Probably that would prove ineradicable. Katherine pondered over the problem a while and dismissed it with the decision to let her opposition in this affair rise out of the exigency of future contacts.

Then she fell to pleasant reverie. She recalled the boy with whom she had made the appointment for the morrow. *I like him,* she mused to herself. *He just fell perfectly into the picture. Strange how things happen! Was it romance? Did I have a thrill? I . . . Kay Hempstead? . . . Yes, I did . . . and couldn't recognize it . . . Well, Mother darling, it's an ill wind that blows nobody good. I'm glad, at least, that your affairs brought me out West.*

Upon such thoughts Katherine drifted into sleep. When she awakened, golden sunshine shone through the window upon her bed. She saw a wide reach of rolling bronze desert ending in blue-hazed hills. When had she awakened with such exhilaration? Not in the Alps nor the Adirondacks. And when, scorning the hot water for the cold, she rubbed her cheeks, she found that they would not need any rouge.

The thought uppermost in Katherine's mind was what to wear. Usually such consideration did not dominate her. And she was distinctly amused when she guessed the reason. *That nice Western boy!* she soliloquized. *I wonder, would he be flattered if he knew Kay Hempstead desired to look well in his eyes . . . But he really isn't a boy.*

She ordered breakfast to be brought to her room and asked for a maid to unpack her bags and have her clothes pressed. Nine o'clock found her dressed in a new sport suit of violet blue that perfectly matched the color of her eyes. She guessed it must be this invigorating Western air that made her so radiant. Precisely on the dot of nine the telephone rang.

"Hello," answered Katherine.

"Hello . . . Is this you . . . Miss . . . Miss Hempstead?" came the query in a halting voice with a drawl.

" 'Mawnin', Phil. Yes, this is Miss Hempstead. Kay to her friends."

"Kay?"

"Yes. It's shorter. Not so high-hat."

"May I call you Kay?" he asked in boyish eagerness.

"I'd like it."

"Thanks. That'll be swell . . . You asked me to call you at nine. I've been up since five o'clock waiting. Dog-gone! I never knew hours could be so long."

"Are you downstairs?"

"No. At the Elk Hotel. It's a dump about four blocks away."

"Have you a car?"

"Yes. I mean . . . it was one."

"All right. Call for me at once."

Five minutes later Katherine walked through the lobby, running the gauntlet of staring guests and reporters and agents, out into the brilliant Nevada sunlight. A dilapidated car had just drawn up to the curb. Young Cameron stepped out, bare-headed, a flush on his tanned cheek.

"Howdy, Phil," drawled Katherine, and offered her hand.

"Good mawnin'," he returned.

Katherine looked up at him as he shook hands with her. In broad daylight she recalled only his height, his wide shoulders, the glint of his chestnut hair. It did have a curl in it. Gray-blue, piercing eyes shed a glad and incredulous light upon her. Katherine thought he was handsomer than she had remembered.

"Phil, does your Western sun shine this way often?"

"Yes. Every mawnin' about the whole year 'round. But I reckon it never yet shone on anything so lovely as you."

"What? The language of compliment! And I imagined you a shy tongue-tied Arizona cowboy. Thank you, Phil. You don't distort the general landscape yourself."

"Come 'round and get in the front seat. I shore have a nerve taking you out in this tin can."

"Don't apologize for your car. It might be a chariot drawn by four white horses. Phil, drive me around the town and out into the country."

"Reno isn't much to see. But the desert is worth a lot of trouble on a May mawnin'."

Cameron showed her the town, without being able to tell her what was what. Then he drove her out beyond the auto camps, speak-easies and road houses, and

111

small ranches into the desert. It did not take long to get out of sight of Reno and its environs.

The air was cold, nipping, fragrant, and so dry that Katherine felt it drawing her delicate skin. When she inhaled deeply, she felt as if she had drawn of the elixir of life. The desert at close hand seemed to claim some kinship deep within her. Yet it was all wasteland, ridge after rolling ridge, rocks endlessly everywhere, bronze mounds and buttes here, and black walls and lava fissures there, and all around, in the distance, bold mountains veiled in blue.

"Phil, I have ridden a camel on the Sahara. I've seen the Arabian desert, the lapis-lazuli desert along the Jordan. But they never affected me like this."

"Kay, this is America. This is home. And you ought to see our Arizona desert! Not like this at all. Heah you see only a two-bit, four-flush bit of outdoors. Why, north of Flagg you can see two hundred miles. Down and down over the gray cedar flats and the grassy range, the yellow bare valley of the Little Colorado, and then up and up over the Painted Desert, the dunes of clay in all colors, the slopes to the escarpments, up to the great red walls that burn into the blue. Oh, I'd love to show you Arizona."

"I'd love to have you. Color is my weakness, Phil. I adore blue. I love red and purple."

"Then you should see our purple sage in bloom."

"Purple sage. I've read of it. Perhaps I'll have you show it to me, if . . . I mean when we have been successful here with our recalcitrant mothers. Oh, I'd like to ride on and on."

"Kay, can you ride a hoss?"

"I play polo, Mister Cameron."

"My Gawd, I'd love . . . Aw, excuse me, Kay. But to see you on a hoss."

"That wouldn't be difficult, if you find the horses. I have my riding togs . . . Oh, how splendid! Stop the car here, Phil."

The road had turned on the edge of a high promontory from which Katherine had a superb view of leagues of desert, where lava cones and black beds led the eye to bleached alkali flats, and on across the land of mirage to the inevitable barriers of mountains. Katherine gazed long at this desolate scene. It approached the sublime in its overpowering starkness. She had never dreamed that the wasteland could affect her like this. It provoked thought; it faced her with herself. Was she really as honest and sincere as she believed herself? What good was she to anybody? Certainly she had not helped materially to make a home for Polly and her mother. All of which restless query and deduction went tumbling through Katherine's consciousness, until a movement on her companion's part brought her back to the present.

"Here I am dreaming, when we should be discussing our problem," she said, rousing. "Where shall we begin?"

"I shore don't know. It's got my goat, if you know what I mean," returned Cameron in perplexity.

"Did you talk to your mother last night?"

"I should smile I did. I pleaded with her. I used every argument and persuasion in the world. But Mom's as bull-headed as any old cow on the range."

"Naturally, being a wronged woman. But most women do not see clearly. All through the ages they have been wronged . . . that way. It can't be helped. Religion, morals, education, ties . . . all these things are lost in the shuffle now and again. A modern woman should recognize that and realize that the lapse may be only temporary. She should bow to what she cannot break."

"Not many girls take such views. I never heard one. I wish you could talk to Mom."

"Perhaps I can, sometime. But don't you speak of me. She'd resent it. I'll make her acquaintance before she learns that my mission out here is the same as yours. Phil, it strikes me that, if you and I are really going to present a united front in battle against these destroyers of happy homes, we should know more about each other."

"You said you'd risk that walk last night if I would, or something like that. I've gone a long way."

"But don't you want to know anything about me?" asked Katherine in surprise.

"To see you heah is enough."

"Be serious, Phil. Haven't you thought about me at all?"

"I lay awake most of the night . . . thinking. There's one thing though that . . . that . . . Shore, I know you're not married. But are you engaged?"

"No, I'm not. I should tell you, though, that I know a fine chap, Victor Brelsford, whose people have always been close to mine. They all want me to marry him.

Mother is rabid on that subject. I haven't been able to make up my mind."

"Well, I should think if you were put on the spot, you'd savvy *pronto* what was what," declared Cameron bluntly.

"I didn't know, but I do now," she rejoined thoughtfully. "I never loved Victor. I shall never marry him."

"That's that. I shore feel sorry for the *hombre*," said Phil feelingly.

"Mother threatened she'd wire for Victor to come out West to take care of me. You see, I'd confessed my interest in cowboys."

"Aw, don't kid me," implored Cameron, with the blood leaping to his face.

"Phil, I wasn't altogether in fun. To be sure, I wanted to upset Mother. But I know I'd like cowboys. I like you. I've been used to men too soft, too effete, too civilized, except perhaps in the case of a college football player or two."

"Shore you'd like cowboys. They are the salt of the earth . . . those I was brought up with. Clean, straight, hard chaps, who'd fight and shoot, too, as quick as that."

"Shoot! In this modern day? You mean in the movies, Phil?"

"Well, I've been off the range for some years, worse luck. All the same that holds good . . . I'm shore proud you like me, Kay. I'll try to deserve it."

"Boy, you're taking me for granted. Face value, you know, is risky. But I want to know more about you."

115

"OK with me. Just ask?"

"This first one is funny. Are you married?"

"Good Lord . . . no!"

"Well, perhaps you're engaged? Girls, even in California, must be like those I know."

"I'm not engaged," replied Phil soberly.

"But you must have lots of girls?"

"Why must I?"

"Never mind. But have you?"

"I'd shore like to lie and say I had. Only the fact is I haven't a single darn girl."

"What a terrific waste of good looks and sterling young manhood!" rejoined Katherine flippantly. Then more seriously: "But I'm glad, Phil. It wouldn't be so good if you were. Your lady love would come over here and upset our apple cart . . . How old are you, Phil?"

"I feel fifteen this mawnin', but I'm twenty-six. No boy any more, as Mom said."

"You adore her, don't you?"

"I reckon."

"You work, of course. I felt your hand. It was as rough as sandpaper. But what kind of work?"

"All kinds, believe me. My job is to superintend Dad's ranch. He has a thousand acres in grapes and a couple of hundred in oranges. Dad employs a good many Mexicans. Our ranch is one of the biggest in Southern California. Near Redlands. At this season you can see orange blossoms and oranges, and right above them the mountains white with snow."

"How beautiful! I've read of that, too. And to think I've never seen California."

116

"If you ever come, *I* want to show it to you."

"That's a promise. I'll come, Phil."

"Too good to ever come true. But I mustn't forget about my ranch. An aunt left me some money a couple of years ago. I blew ten thousand of it for a mile square of land down in the Coachella Valley near the Saltan Sea. It's way below sea level there. Hell in summer. Dad swore I was crazy. But I developed water . . . two dandy artesian wells. Hot water. I irrigated and put in dates and grapefruit. The fellow I have in charge made fourteen thousand dollars on five acres of grapefruit on his place adjoining last year. Well, my vineyard and orchard sprang up over night, almost. Just grew grand. You see, after all, the land didn't have any alkali. I'd picked a winner. I had a gold mine. Then the Depression hit the coast. Dad almost went under. He couldn't help me. I'm deep in debt now, and if I cain't get a loan, a mortgage on my ranch, I'm going to lose it. Aw, but that will be tough."

"Loan? How much will you need, Phil?" she asked quietly.

"Not so much, I reckon. Only a few thousand to save the ranch. But where'n he . . . heck can a fellow get a loan these days? The banks are no good. They're crooked. Aw, if I had fifteen or twenty thousand dollars to develop my ranch in five years, I'd be drawing down that much a year profit."

"Phil, would it make you sick to hear that I spend that much on my clothes alone, every year?"

"My Gawd! You don't say . . . ? Kay, you don't need so many clothes. They cain't make you any lovelier."

"More compliments! Can't we be serious? I guess I know all I want to know about you . . . And now to our problem. What to do with our mothers. Mine is the limit. She's nutty. Thinks she is in love. Thinks she's young still and adored for herself. She's furious with my father. She will be with me. She's stubborn. She's strong-willed. What can we do with women like that?"

"You said the *hombre* she brought out is a fortune-hunter?"

"I know it. I knew that before I was told. Leroyd is a gambler, too."

"He'll get cleaned proper out heah, believe me. Does she know he's a gambler?"

"Probably not. She has lent him money, though. My banker told me."

"Kay, I'll sort of trail that gent up in good old Arizona fashion. *¿Quién sabe?* I might get something on him . . . I'm getting a hunch that my case with Mom is hopeless, unless I can scare her."

"Scare her? Phil, you don't mean physically?"

"No. About me, I mean. I've got a hunch I must do something terrible."

"On her account!" exclaimed Katherine breathlessly.

"Shore."

She clasped his arm tightly and looked up into his eyes, unmindful of the effect upon him. "Phil! You're a darling. You're a genius! You've hit it . . . plumb center. I, too, must do something terrible. I must scare my mother out of her wits. I am her weakness . . . the same as you are your mother's. But what to do . . . how . . . how?"

118

"Kay, do you take . . . spells like this often?" asked Phil huskily.

"Spells! I never had one before," replied Katherine innocently enough. She had not intended to practice any charm of glance or word or person upon him. But the havoc had been wrought. Katherine could not be sorry. As she drew away, she felt an unusual warmth creep from neck to cheek. "Phil, I'll probably have more of them . . . spells, I mean," she went on joyously. "It's just marvelous . . . my coming West . . . this intrigue we're involved in . . . the outwitting of our mothers . . . the romance of it!"

"Yeah? Well, it's marvelous, all right. And I'll be game. But it's my finish, Kay."

CHAPTER
THREE

Late in the afternoon of that day Kay sought her mother. She had deliberately refrained from an earlier meeting because she had found, on previous occasions, that the longer her mother waited the more amenable she became. Mrs. Hempstead was a nervous, imperious, high-strung woman, more governed by emotion than by reason. Katherine entered the room with her usual cool poise, and for the first time in her life she omitted to kiss this parent. It was an omission that apparently stung.

"Well, Missus Henry Watson Hempstead, here I am."

"So I observe. It took you a long time. I've waited all day."

"Now that I've gotten here, I'll make my appeal short and to the point."

"Appeal? Oh, Kay! You insulted me last night . . . You freeze me today. I'm your mother. I'm not an old woman, nor a stone. Have you no feeling?"

"I am conscious of a great deal of feeling. But how much of it is sympathy with your mad project will appear presently."

"Kay, how stunning you look!" exclaimed Mrs. Hempstead, as if impelled against her will. "I never saw you look so wonderful!"

"Thanks, Mother. You can lay it to this glorious West. I've got the desert air in my lungs . . . the sun in my blood . . . Forgive me, if I fail to return the compliment in any measure. You don't look so well."

Mrs. Hempstead's pale worn face flushed. She looked all of her forty-eight years. Her make-up failed to hide a pallor of lassitude. She was still handsome, but there was a shadow, a blight of worry and strain on her face.

Katherine became prey to a suspicion that had not before beset her in her brooding. It rankled. It motivated against the love and pity she still had in goodly measure. Nevertheless, her sense of tolerance and justice, her own outlook on life, rebuked her with the thought that her mother had a right to love. On the moment, but for one single fact, Katherine would have made friends with her mother and have abandoned her resolve to prevent the divorce. If Jimmy Leroyd had not been a ruined man about town, a spendthrift, and a fortune-hunter, Katherine would have surrendered gracefully and have sanctioned the affair. But she knew Leroyd. She sensed here that the intimacy between him and her mother had gone far. Such a thing was as common in her set as conversation over the breakfast table. But coming at last to her own home, it sickened Katherine a little and steeled her nerve.

"How far have you gone with your divorce proceedings?" queried Katherine abruptly, as she sat down opposite Mrs. Hempstead's reclining chair.

"I haven't engaged my lawyer yet. They ask too much. Twenty-five hundred dollars seems excessive to pay . . . even for desirable freedom."

121

"You can get your divorce for two hundred and fifty," returned Katherine brusquely. "If you must go through with it, don't let them rob you. That's far too much to pay for Jimmy Leroyd."

"Don't be catty, Kay. Let me tell you once for all, I . . . I must go through with it."

"Nevertheless, Mother darling, I will have my say, as a dutiful daughter . . . Father is sorry. He told me he thought you knew . . . that you just wanted an excuse you didn't need. He would not have opposed your friendship with Leroyd. But to go to extremes . . . to divorce him . . . that cut Father deeply. He cannot see any sense in it. Neither can I."

"I want my freedom," protested Mrs. Hempstead. "I never loved Henry. It was my mother's match."

"Like your obsession to give me to Brelsford," murmured Katherine. "It's a fine world to live in . . . if you don't weaken. Mother, it's not true that you never cared for Father. I know better than that."

"Kay, I . . . I . . . care a great deal for Jimmy Leroyd."

"I confess there must be something," rejoined Katherine with a calculated brutality. "You're a sentimental old woman."

"I am not . . . at least not old," cried her mother, cruelly hurt.

"Listen, Mother, before I lose my temper and tell you what you don't know. Never mind Father. And leave me out of your consideration. But think of Polly. She loves you . . . far more than you deserve. She loves Father, too. It'll be rotten of you to turn her over to the

122

ranks of children without mothers. Polly is fine, sweet, deep. She has brains and soul. If you do this absurd thing, it will absolutely damn that child . . . wreck her life."

"Does she . . . know yet?" asked Mrs. Hempstead in a suffocated voice.

"No. Father didn't tell her. But if you persist, I must tell her."

"She will get over it," said the mother, breathing hard.

"You force me to be brutal," returned Katherine with cold scorn, as she arose. "I see that you have lost all sense of responsibility. You are conscienceless. Your fortune-hunting gambler has made you lose all sense of proportion and decency, has enmeshed you in a middle-aged love affair that makes you ridiculous."

"Say your worst, Kay. You always had a two-edged tongue. But you . . . can't change me," whispered Mrs. Hempstead, looking as if she were on the point of collapse.

"I've lost my desire to," returned Kay bitterly. "Go to hell in your own way. I'll go in mine."

"You'll . . . what?" cried her mother hoarsely, revived as by a lash on a raw wound.

"I'll dispense with a lot of my ideas on the subject of decency. A fine example you give me to marry. My God . . . the idea turns my stomach. Father will take Polly. That leaves me free. The Hempsteads are done. What do I care?" The scorn and bitterness that Kay managed to inject into her voice was not all acting.

"But my daughter! You have Brelsford. He adores you. He can save your name, at least. For heaven's sake, don't let my . . . my affair ruin you."

"Victor is probably all any woman might want. But I don't love him. I won't marry him."

"Oh, Kay! You've decided that?"

"Yes."

"Since you came West?"

"Yes."

"Mercy! You'll be the death of me. Have you forgotten . . . your position . . . your wealth . . . your duty to your class?"

"Almost, thank God. After all, such things don't amount to anything in this country out here."

"This country! This wilderness of dust and wind? These sordid little towns . . . these crude people? You wouldn't live here?"

"Why couldn't I? I'm sick of that idle deceitful world. I'd love some dust and wind in my face. I have begun to believe these Westerners you call crude are fine, simple, honest, true. True! They work . . . I think I'll go to the movies."

Mrs. Hempstead screamed and sank back almost fainting. Katherine's random shot seemed to her mother a terrible threat.

In the hall outside, Katherine encountered Leroyd. He appeared younger, more debonair than when she had met him last, some months ago. Well-groomed, handsome in his fair way, a man of good family, Leroyd looked more than ever the cavalier for such idle and unsatisfied women as Mrs. Hempstead. He greeted

Katherine in his smooth manner, not in the least concerned by the intent look she bestowed upon him.

"Lovelier than ever, Kay. It's great to see you," he added.

"Jimmy, I've had it out with Mother," replied Katherine peremptorily. "You will please give me a few minutes of your valuable time."

"Delighted, I'm sure. Where shall we proceed to the execution?"

"There's a sitting room on this floor."

"Will you smoke? It might soothe your ruffled nerves."

Katherine declined with thanks and led him to the far end of the corridor, where an intimate little lounge opened upon a balcony above spacious gardens. But she did not go outside. Kay sat down and motioned him to a seat beside her.

"Jimmy, I came West to try to persuade Mother not to sue for a divorce," began Katherine deliberately. "She refused."

"I fear yours are vain oblations, my dear Kay."

"Indeed, they are. But it just struck me that you might not be so difficult."

"How flattering! Go on."

"Jimmy, you have taken money from my mother. I have found out. A considerable sum, altogether."

"Certainly, I borrowed it," replied Leroyd blandly, but the red came up in his face.

"Permit me to be slangy," retorted Kay flippantly. "Baloney to that. You never intended to pay it back. You

125

never will. Jimmy, you'd not the kind of gambler who pays."

"Gambler? You are disposed to be facetious," he said not so imperturbably as before.

"I mean what I say. I had you looked up, Jimmy. And in further parlance of the age, I have your number . . . What'll you take in cold cash to ditch my mother?"

"Kay, you surprise me . . . not to say more."

"Would you take a hundred thousand dollars?"

"No," he replied.

"That's my limit. Has it occurred to you, Jimmy, that I could take you away from Mother, if I wanted to?"

"It has not. What an enchanting prospect."

"You know I could do it?"

"Kay, a denial of that would be absurd. You could take any man away from any woman."

"You're not worth what it'd cost. Nor is Mother worth it. Nor is Father. But poor Polly!"

"Kay, I swear I love that child as dearly as if she were my own," declared Leroyd with indubitable sincerity.

"Your one saving grace, Jimmy. But who could help loving that exquisite little girl? Well, there doesn't seem to be any more to say. There isn't any more . . . to you."

"I'm sorry, Kay. I bear you no resentment. Really. But I'm devoted to your mother. And that's that . . . I advise you to go back home."

"Not much. I'm going to paint this Reno the most beautiful flaming red that it ever saw."

"Kay! You're not serious!" he expostulated in consternation, his languid eyes starting and his jaw dropping.

126

"I was serious. Now I will be gay."

"But your mother could not stand your . . . such notoriety . . . here in the limelight. Good God!"

"I'll wash my hands of her. Go your dirty ways, both of you."

"Kay!"

But Katherine was sweeping down the corridor, her head high, with bells of inspiration and triumph in her ears.

Not until the following day did opportunity arise for Katherine to make the acquaintance of Phil Cameron's mother. Then, as luck decreed, it came about naturally and without the slightest apparent design on her part.

She found Mrs. Cameron a comely woman somewhat over fifty with a lined sweet face upon which was written a record of the years of hard Western life. She had been handsome once. Katherine traced some resemblance to Phil in her features. A few minutes of casual conversation were sufficient for Katherine to discern the woman's simplicity, that she was as transparent as an inch of crystal water. That was long enough, too, to divine that her heart was almost broken. Katherine experienced a warm rush of emotion at the thought that this was Phil's mother and that she might help her.

Mrs. Cameron, evidently, in this crisis of her life, was not proof against sympathy, and the evident interest Katherine did not need to pretend. The distracted mother and wronged wife wanted to unburden herself. She needed a women to confide in. Fate had it in the fact that, with a hotel full of women from all over the United States, society women, business women, motion picture stars and stage actresses, all wronged or unsatisfied or dissatisfied wives seeking freedom from their fetters, Katherine should be the one to draw lovely unhappy Mary Cameron.

"What are you here for, Miss . . . Miss Wales, I think the clerk said was your name?" asked Mrs. Cameron earnestly, on the full tide of her yearning to unburden herself, yet dubious about this brilliant girl who appeared so kindly.

"Hilda Wales. But that's not my real name. I'll tell you my story sometime. Oh, such a miserable story! I hate to think of it."

"But you're so young! You don't wear a wedding ring. So you cain't be heah to . . . for the same reason all these poor women are."

"Including you, Missus Cameron?"

"Alas, too true. I came to divorce my husband."

"Ah, I'm so sorry. What is wrong? Don't you care for him . . . forgive me. That just popped out. I can see whatever the trouble is, it's not your fault."

Then briefly the sordid little drama, as old and bitter as life, yet different because of the anguish and intimacy of the sufferer, unfolded itself to Katherine's ears. She replied as earnestly and simply as she knew how, intensely relieved and glad that she could be honestly sorry. There could be only one reason in the world why Phil Cameron's father could wound so mortally the woman who had grown up with him, fought the desert and the battle of life beside him, and then, because nature is crueler than life, had faded and lost her bloom, her youth, her response. The blame and the wrong, if there were one, could not be laid to Mary Cameron, and, viewed with the wisdom and understanding of modern thought, hardly upon Frank Cameron.

Katherine asked a number of simple questions, easy for the troubled woman to answer, the last of which brought the scarlet to her livid cheek.

"Does he want you to divorce him?"

"Oh, dear, no. All Frank wanted was to keep me from finding out. He could never manage that ranch without me."

"Missus Cameron, I . . . I wonder if you are doing right."

"That's just what Phil said," flashed the mother, showing that she still had spirit and fire. "You young folks are all alike. Naturally, of course, I'm old-fashioned, I know. But so Frank ought to be."

"Phil, your son, tell me about him," suggested Katherine. She desired to hear this boy's praises sung by his mother.

They were sung in full measure, and Katherine reflected that, if Phil were worthy of them, he was a paragon among mothers' only sons.

"Phil is heah at Reno now," went on Mrs. Cameron. "He came to stop me from getting the divorce. We quarreled last night. He didn't come to see me this mawnin' . . . Phil didn't take Frank's part, Miss Wales. Don't misjudge him. Why, he knocked his father flat for . . . You see, Frank was furious, and he swore at me . . . slapped my face. I reckon I . . . I was some sharp. But I was jealous of that black-eyed little hussy. *Jealous!* There, it's out, and it'll do me good. Marcheta is the prettiest girl in Southern California . . . Well, Phil cain't see my side. And I cain't see his."

"Tell me Phil's side, Missus Cameron."

"Oh, it's kept me awake all night," replied the mother, in distress. "I know I'm old and out of date. But I cain't help my feelings. Phil says I'm wrong. That I should never have let on I knew. That if there was anything wrong, it was Frank and me marrying when we were the same age. Because only for so long was I able to be Frank's mate. He didn't say wife or comrade. He just said mate, as if I was some kind of an animal . . . Oh, it was terrible to heah Phil say such things. I felt like the world had gone on leaving me out, which it has! Then he softened it all by saying this . . . this thing would peter out of its own accord. Marcheta would marry some young buck and everything would be all right again. But I *cain't* see that. I'll never get over it. I . . . I want to make Frank suffer."

"Being a woman, I'm on your side," returned Katherine. "But Phil is right. The bitter fact is one of evolution, not right or wrong."

"That may all be true. I don't understand it, and I don't care," replied Mrs. Cameron stubbornly.

"Have you thought that you might lose your son by this step?"

"Oh, never! My son! Phil? He would not desert me," cried the little woman, in poignant anguish.

"He might. If he's such a wonderful boy, I wouldn't risk it. I can tell he's modern. If I were you, Missus

130

Cameron, I'd settle this vexatious question on one score only. I'd let my decision depend on what it did to my son."

"Decision! I've sued my husband for a divorce. The case will come up presently. It's too late, even if . . . if . . ."

"You can withdraw your suit."

"I won't do it."

"But suppose this home-breaking course of yours threatens to ruin your son?" asked Katherine, launching her last and strangest shaft.

It struck home. Of all catastrophes, Mrs. Cameron had never imagined such a one. She was shocked. Doubt and fear added their dark shadows to her sad face. Katherine's heart ached for her. Yet it was singing, too, for she saw sure victory for Phil in his mother's love. Through that she could be won or driven.

And on the moment Phil entered the hotel reception room, hat in hand, his striking face and form instinct with vivid life. He gave a start at sight of Katherine with his mother, then he came up to them, smiling, his eyes like blue flames.

"Mom Cameron! How'd you meet my girl friend?"

"Phil, do you . . . know Miss Wales?"

"I'm happy to say I do."

"But you said a Miss Hemp . . . something or other," faltered his mother.

Katherine rose, to give Phil a significant glance of hope, of assurance.

"I have a number of names, Missus Cameron," she said with a laugh. "Missus Hempstead is my last. I'm here to divorce my third husband. Hilda Wales is my screen name. I'm a motion picture actress . . . We'll talk again about this miserable divorce business. For me, though, it's good publicity. I'm awfully happy to find you're Phil's mother. We must be great friends."

Then ignoring the utter consternation in Mrs. Cameron's countenance, she faced Phil, finding him pale, stern, yet with a fascinated understanding.

"Phil darling, don't forget our date tonight. Formal. But we're painting the town red."

CHAPTER
FOUR

That Phil Cameron would fall in love with her had
been a foregone conclusion to Katherine. Not egotism,
but experience had taught her that this was almost
inevitable. Propinquity with her seemed to have but one
result. As a girl up to eighteen she had been sorry over
many a boy's heartbreak, and had excessively grieved
herself more than once. As a woman she had learned
that men desired her kisses while they were deaf to her
thoughts. That had not made her callous. But it had
encased her in a mocking unattainable shell, through
which men, with the perversity of masculine nature,
tried only the harder to break.

But Katherine knew, not quite at first, but soon,
that she was different with Phil. It was the complex
situation, the intense resolve to circumvent her mother,
the frank manliness of this Western boy, and a revolt in
herself that seemed to be the influence of the desert —
these were the factors which were apparently placing
her restrained past further and further behind her.

The plot she had concocted to defeat her mother's
aims, which she was convinced would succeed equally
well in the case of Mrs. Cameron, she had not yet
entirely disclosed to Phil. During these few glamorous

days she grew to know him better. He would have to be terribly in love with her before he would consent to her plan. And there was something inexplicably sweet in helping this along by all the honest charms and wiles of woman. When Phil protested that they were letting the hours slide by, doing nothing, while the divorce proceedings were working toward fruition, she merely smiled and bade him wait.

Katherine had no difficulty, however, in contriving to keep Phil with her from early morning until late at night. They drove all over the desert, which she particularly loved, gambled in the casinos, went to the movies, dressed and dined at the hotels, all the time avoiding their mothers as much as possible. To Katherine's delight this procedure had begun to annoy and perplex Mrs. Hempstead, as it had distressed Mrs. Cameron. The former saw her darling flirting with a common cowboy, and the latter saw her darling in the clutches of a beautiful siren from Hollywood. If Phil had not been so worried, he, too, would have been gleeful over this mental state of the two mothers.

In Phil's case, Kay discerned that it was going to require more than propinquity. He was Western. He had been brought up in the open country. He had been taught respect for women. He was tremendously proud that Kay chose to spend all her time with him, that she never so much as met the eyes of other men. Her beauty dazzled him. He had fallen in love with her from the first. He knew it and had no regrets. But so far, he had not even permitted himself to imagine a closer relation. Kay was a gorgeous creature from another and different world than his. The boyish homage he accorded her was fit for a princess. But to possess her he did not even dream of.

He's the finest, cleanest man I ever knew, mused Kay before her mirror that night, as she proceeded with an exquisite toilet. *I'm falling in love with Phil . . . and I'm glad. It's like my few cases when I was sixteen, only worse. It'll make easier what I must do . . . But afterward . . . oh, dear!*

And at that stage of soliloquy, Kay studied her image in the mirror. It was not to satisfy her vanity or to draw pleasure from that beautiful reflection. She suddenly felt that she saw another and different Kay Hempstead. The golden hair that crowned her head, the broad low brow, the serious violet eyes, the curved red lips — these she had gazed at innumerable times, but never as now. She imagined there was a new spirit actuating her.

"I will *not* think. Sufficient unto the day!" she said, and in those deliberate words crossed her Rubicon.

That evening at dinner in the spacious dining room of the Reno, Katherine had eyes for no one but Phil. When they danced, she dropped that instinctive bar that she had always placed between her and her partner and leaned to him so close that she felt the pounding of his heart. Immediately her own became unruly.

From that time on, Katherine drifted into perilous ways with her eyes wide open. Deliberately, she exercised all the arts of coquetry. She gave royally of her smiles, her glances, her laughter and whisper, of the beauty and lure of her person. But such dangerous

135

tactics, although they awakened in Phil all she wanted, reacted with irresistible rebound upon herself. This she deserved, this she made light of, this she hoped would last long and hurt deeply, although the worldly cynicism in her raised wild scornful doubts. Nevertheless, she forgot the fleeting of the days, and almost the vital reason for her sojourn in Nevada.

One night, when the moon was full, she persuaded Phil to drive her out on the desert, to the promontory which had become her favorite place. With furs around her bare arms and shoulders she leaned silently against him, conscious that the critical hour had come. That, or the mystic and profound splendor of the desert by night, somehow saddened her into reticence. The dark gulf of the Mediterranean, the Vale of Cashmir, the Valley of Yumuri, none of the voids in the earth that she had viewed from heights, had ever had power to affect her as this naked rent in the desert, lonely, fierce, primitive as ever back in the ages that had formed it. Again she felt that this primal thing had much to do with the influence the West had upon her. Desert and elements, the men out here were far closer to the primitive than all she had known in the East and abroad. They had awakened a response in her heart. And someday there would come a reckoning and a choice.

"Have you ever seen anything more wonderful than this desert in the moonlight?" she asked presently.

"Yes, Kay," he replied with an unsteady note in his voice. "You!"

136

"But you haven't looked at the desert under the moon," she complained.

"How can I?"

"Oh . . . Then you like how I look tonight?"

"Kay, I haven't caught my breath yet . . . Aw, what luck for me to be with you . . . to dance with you . . . hold . . . to see you so many different ways, each one lovelier than the last."

"Good luck or bad luck?"

"Good, Kay. Wonderful luck! Something to sustain me . . . when you go back home."

"Then you'll not be unhappy?"

"I can't swear that, though my whole life should be a paradise of memory."

"Phil, do you love me?"

"Do you need to ask? Doesn't every person in Reno, almost, know that I'm mad about you. Didn't Mom accuse me of being the playboy of a movie queen?"

"Nevertheless, I do ask."

He uttered a short laugh. "Kay, I love you so well it's heaven to be with you . . . hell to be away from you. No man was ever so uplifted, so happy."

"Phil! So well? Yet, my boy, you have never asked me for anything. And your one wild break was to hold my hand in the dark movie theater."

He was too sincere, too terribly in earnest to see anything strange in her surprise or the import of her statements, and he let them pass unanswered.

"Time is flying, Phil. And we have done so little to block these divorce proceedings," said Kay, at last reverting to the issue at hand.

137

"Aw, I get sick when I think of that," replied Cameron feelingly. "I just hate to see Mom. She won't give in. She's more set than ever. And when I do see her, she raves so about you that I rush right away. Kay, I wish you'd let me correct that idea you gave her . . . that you were a much-divorced movie girl."

"Not yet. It was an inspiration. Phil, my mother moans about my affair with you. 'That strapping cowpuncher! Why, he might kidnap you and pack you off to the desert.' When I told her I hoped you would, she nearly had hysterics. If we could only see the humor of this situation."

"Humor? Huh, it's about as funny as being rolled on by a hoss."

"Phil, I've solved our problem," declared Kay solemnly. "I've found out how to bring my mother and your mother to their knees."

"For Pete's sake, spring it on me."

Kay felt the need of a deep full breath. It was not so easy to make a perfectly atrocious, deliberately abnormal proposition to this clear-eyed, clean-minded young Westerner who worshipped her and held her little less than an angel. But the exigency of the case justified such an appalling plot as she had conceived. Already she had devoted days and nights of thinking and feeling toward that end.

"Listen . . . Phil," she began haltingly, "and hear me through before you break over the traces . . . There is only one way to change our mothers. That is to justify the dread they already have. We must scare them to death. Ruthlessly. Mother loves me. Your mother adores

138

you. They live in us, if they only knew it. If they could be shown that you and I were going 'plumb to hell,' as you call it . . . that their disregard of children's rights and loves had ruined us, made us bitter, reckless, *bad* . . . they would be horribly upset. They would weaken. They would give up this divorce proceeding. Well, let's do it. That is, let's *pretend* to go to the bad. We'll rent a cottage. I already have one picked out! Don't look at me like that, Phil Cameron. I *have*. You'll say it's swell. We'll have the car I've hired. We'll move into this cottage, bag and baggage, unmarried, brazen as brazen can be. Then we'll cut loose to scandalize even Reno. We'll bet the roof off these gambling places. We'll mop up hard liquor, apparently, in sight of the high and low of this town. We'll make them think that we have thrown decency to the winds . . . that my mother's disgusting affair and your mother's hard and narrow creed have opened our eyes to the bald realism of life. We're sick of it all. We'll have no more of it. We'll take the fleshpots of Egypt and to hell with the rest . . . There, Phil! That's my plan. Whatever you think . . . you can't say it's not original. Come. Don't slay me . . . with your eyes!"

It had been his piercing gaze that made Kay falter at the close. She had expected anything but cool stern composure.

"My God! You're a wonder. The nerve of you! Kay, it's a swell idea. But I cain't see it your way."

"Do you think it'd work?" she queried.

"Shore it would. Absolutely. Mom just couldn't see my falling that way on her account. And that stuck-up

139

mother of yours would fall like a ton of bricks. They'd be knocked out, Kay."

"You are sure, Phil? From your man's viewpoint?"

"Yes. It'd work. Pity we cain't floor them. But we just cain't, Kay."

"Why not?" began Katherine, gathering strength with the rebellious query.

"It'd ruin you . . . disgrace you."

"Boy, we'd only pretend. We'd play a game . . . a great game. Be actors. All for a good purpose. Oh, the idea thrills me!"

"But the harm would be done, darling. No matter where you went afterward, there'd be some dirty *hombre* or some catty woman bobbing up to tell it."

"Let the future take care of itself," retorted Kay enigmatically. "We must win this game. I tell you that, even if we really went to the bad . . . it'd be worth it to save little Polly's love for her mother and save your mother from a lonely miserable old age."

"I get you, Kay," returned Phil hoarsely. "But I happen to love you . . . and your honor . . . more than the good you name."

"Won't you do it, Phil?" entreated Kay.

"I shore won't."

"Please . . . darling."

"No, by God!"

"We could correct . . . all the slander, the misunderstanding . . . somehow . . . later."

"Even if we could . . . which I shore doubt . . ."

"Phil, wouldn't it mean anything, if you really love me, to have me alone that way . . . seeing me at all

140

hours . . . and every way . . . trusting you where I would trust no other man on earth?"

"Yes. I reckon it'd mean a hell of a lot," burst out Phil, his eyes flaming. "But I'm damned if I'll give these men heah . . . that you wouldn't wipe your little shoes on . . . a chance to point the finger of shame at you."

"Why, you child, what do *I* care for the opinions of men? I'd never see them point . . . never hear them speak. I am aloof from all that."

"Kay, it hurts me to see you so daid set on this," rejoined Phil hurriedly. "I never reckoned I could refuse you anything. Aw, you're putting me in a tough spot."

"Yes. But it's for me." She threw wide the furs that enveloped her and, turning, lay back in his arms. The moonlight shone upon her golden head, upon her lovely neck and breast. "Phil, don't let me fail in this. I give you my word . . . I'll pay whatever it costs."

"Kay, you're talking wild," he said hoarsely.

"You're the dearest boy I ever knew," she rejoined dreamily.

"Boy? I reckon . . . and pretty callow at that."

She lay there gazing up at him, conscious of an emotion which she took for happiness at being in his arms, mocking herself with the thought that it was only stooping to gain her end.

"Kiss me, Phil," she whispered presently.

"Kay . . . you . . . Aw, it's only you want your way," he cried in torment.

"Suppose it is. I ask you. Here I am in your arms. I must care . . . something . . . or I wouldn't want to . . ."

141

Cameron wrenched his powerful shoulders in his effort to resist, yet they were bending closer over her all the time. He was so blind that his lips did not at first find hers. When they did, they merged a boy's soul into a man's passion. Kay felt suffocating in that embrace. But the response she gave, which her sincerity made her think was the least she could do, rewarded her with the sweetest sensation of her whole life, and then flooded her heart with sadness over a hollow victory. He was won. But then her conscience flayed her.

Next day Katherine and Phil moved into the cottage she had chosen. It was one block from the center of town, directly across, with several other cottages, from Reno's second large and fashionable hotel. It sat back among green shrubbery, quite isolated, but the gravel driveway and the path were open to idle, curious eyes. It had been newly decorated and furnished, and contained one bedroom with bath, a living room, a kitchen, and a small room for a servant. Kay had to put part of her baggage in the living room. She assured the dubious Phil that to dispense for once with maid and luxury would be a very good experience for her, and one she expected to enjoy because of its novelty.

When they had established themselves, Kay and Phil sat down deliberately to plan their campaign of deviltry. Whatever had been Phil's scruples and pangs, they were gone or hidden under a rapt reckless cowboy's exterior. Kay could not doubt that he was in a transport. She could not probe his thought as to the future, after this débacle. She feared he had burned his bridges behind him, and that the future beyond was blank. It did not take long for their quick wit to shape events.

Phil made off downstreet to purchase cowboy garb, to ingratiate himself into the good graces of the press reporters, to make friends with the chief of police whom he already knew.

Kay drove to the Hotel Reno, and the opening shot fired in the battle was to snub her mother deliberately in front of guests who knew Kay's relation to her. Leroyd she passed with an icy stare. When Mrs. Hempstead could not hide the sting of a cut, it was pretty deep. Well satisfied with this start, Kay sat down to wait for Phil and to think about him. Actually, the grave side of this drama had reverted to this Western boy. Kay had made no other acquaintances, and her part was to be absolutely oblivious to her surroundings. An expert in the art of make-up, she was to strive for as tragic and lost an appearance as possible, and to act accordingly.

At last Phil strode in, somehow different, although spurs and boots and belt with empty gun sheath, and a huge sombrero in his hand scarcely accounted for the change. He looked the true range man, splendid, lithe, hard, and the shyness, the diffidence that had marked his demeanor were gone. It struck Kay that Phil was not an actor. He was being himself.

"Howdy, honey," he called, loud enough for nearby watchers to hear. "What do you know about this?"

He laid an open letter upon Kay's lap. It was a notification from the Desert Bank of Indio, California, that there was a balance of twenty-five thousand dollars there to his account.

"Oh, that? I'd forgotten," she replied, with a smile, as she handed it back. "I notified my banker in New York to forward this amount. Just a loan, Phil . . . or an interest in your ranch, as you like."

His eyes were beautiful to see and terrible to look into. He bent over to whisper: "Kay, what good will saving my ranch do . . . if I die of love?"

"Boy, that never kills."

"¿Quién sabe? . . . Com' on, beautiful, let's go tear things."

Kay drove the big white car with such speed, and apparent recklessness, that a traffic officer caught up with them, and presented them with a ticket. Phil gave the officer such a berating that a crowd gathered. After that incident, they ran the gamut of the more pretentious gambling halls. To all appearances they had been drinking. In places frequented by all classes of people, where nothing save a big wager or a fight ever caused gamblers and spectators to turn away from the games, Phil and Kay created a sensation. He looked like a handsome motion picture cowboy, enamored of his companion. Kay knew she could play a part, and hers was that of a wealthy Easterner with a passion to gamble, to whom money was as the dust under her feet. A crowd followed them from table to table. Phil lost more than he won. But Kay could not lose, and her wagers were as large as the games permitted.

That night Kay, resplendent and patrician in white, blazing with jewels, walked with Phil into the

144

fashionable dining room of the Reno, timing her advent to her mother's dinner hour. It so happened that Mrs. Hempstead had guests that evening. The head waiter, generously bribed by Kay beforehand, had reserved a table close to her mother's. Kay might not have known her mother was alive, so oblivious did she appear to all save this stalwart cowboy, pale, fire-eyed, by far the handsomest man in a room full of handsome men.

They were the cynosure of all eyes. They must have been the despair of Kay's mother and the little drab woman who sat in a far corner, fascinated as by a snake, clasping and unclasping her hands. Like all cowboys, Phil could stand a few drinks of hard liquor. But this night they had champagne. It went to Phil's head. To Kay's delight and intense gratification he transgressed all the laws of etiquette, as well as decorum. Phil simply overplayed his part. But Kay felt sure she was perfect in hers — that of a disillusioned woman to whom the world was dross, who knew her class to be rank with hypocrisy, who had chosen a primitive cowboy to be her dissolute consort.

Before the dinner was half finished, Mrs. Hempstead, suffering from horror and shock, had to be escorted from the dining room.

"How'm I doin', Kay?" quoth Phil gaily. "Did you get a peep at your old lady as they were packing her off?"

"Yes, I saw her, and I'm divided between joy and sorrow," replied Kay. "You're doing fine. In fact, you're very natural. You're not over-acting at all. Don't drink any more champagne."

"All right. We've shot the works. Let's dance once more . . . then go back to our hogan."

"Hogan?" queried Kay, as she rose.

"Darling, a hogan is Indian for domicile, wigwam, shack, cabin, home, or what have you."

"You show your Indian tonight, Phil, more than in language. But as Polly would say . . . 'I think you're just grand!' Oh, where will this end?"

"Don't lose your nerve," returned Phil sternly. "You're the spirit of this deal. We're in it. We got it half won now. Let's cut the dance. My God, get a look at *my* mother's face."

CHAPTER
FIVE

Every morning Kay drove out into the desert with Phil, where they could be themselves for a few hours. Kay forgot her mother, then, and addressed herself to her own increasing problem, which confronted her in each thoughtful hour. If this stark and rugged Nevada affected her so powerfully, what would golden California be like, and especially purple-saged, cañon-walled Arizona? Kay could only guess at it and revel in her intention to see for herself. At the least, she meant to stay a very good while out West, and if she still maintained a home in New York, on which question she was dubious, she would come back West again and again, for long stays, always.

That much was settled. Still, it did not seem to solve her problem. And it did not, because Phil Cameron had become her problem. At this stage of pondering she always threw up her hands. To give him up was unthinkable, even if she wanted to, which was, indeed, very far from her desires. That part did not perplex Kay. She thought she was waiting for this Reno situation to end, when she was actually waiting for herself. What was the true state of her heart? As she dreaded to search it, as she put off and off the inevitable, she drifted further and further with Phil, the sweetness of their companionship when alone equaling the audacity and thrill of their appalling rôle before the Reno crowd.

In mid-May the desert was abloom with spring flowers, the fragrance and color of which enraptured Kay. She had been quick to grasp that the desert intensified everything. Nowhere else had she seen the vividness that burned in desert flowers, in desert colors.

This particular morning Phil sat in the car, with a sheaf of unanswered reports and letters from his California ranch on his lap, and, instead of attending to them, he watched Kay. She was aware of it. When she was far enough away not to see the yearning, the tragedy in his eyes, the havoc in his lean pale face — for his tan had long gone — she found pleasure in his watching her. But on occasions like this, when she came back to him, she always fell prey to a wild unconsidered impulse to tell him there might not really be any reason to dread the future. She had a secret that she had not yet divulged to herself. If she voiced it, made it tangible, then she would have to reckon with it, to try to explain it to an overwhelmed young man. And Kay was not ready for that.

Kay resisted a strong desire to steal away on the desert to a lonely spot far from the road, and there, under the white sun, look out to the wasteland for an answer to her problem. The rocks, the sage, the flowers, the cacti, the flint ridges and the dry arroyos, the wide heat-veiled stretch leading to the encompassing mountains, spear-pointed and aloof against the sky — all these called her, almost availingly. How splendid and

148

incomprehensible that such a solitude, such a lifeless area, could be pregnant with spirit. Kay felt it, and almost understood it, and feared it because it spoke to her of the uselessness and barrenness of her life. Should she flee from it as from a pestilence or embrace it with all her soul?

"Phil," she said, as she returned to him and the car with her hands full of desert wildflowers, "I've had some beautiful thoughts that no one at home would believe could dwell in Kay Hempstead's head, and that time-killing, divorce-waiting crowd back in Reno could not credit to Hilda Wales, mysterious adventuress and notorious woman."

"Yeah. I'm about fed up on that outfit, Kay," he replied gloomily. "When I know you're as good as you're lovely. I damn' near told Mom the whole story the other night when she called me a low-down bum that the toughest cowboys would scorn . . . and you a rich hussy."

"Phil, it hurts you, I know," returned Kay earnestly. "Because you're a man. But somehow it doesn't bother me in the least. I forget it the moment we get away together."

"But, how *can* you?" queried Phil desperately.

"I know that it's not true, not one word of all the rotten gossip we have created. I know that our debauchery, as Mother called it, does not exist. I know that the game has been in a good cause, which we've almost won."

"Uhn-huh . . . Well, I've had a couple of thoughts, too. Not very beautiful. If you don't care a damn whether or not this shame follows you, then you've got it beat. What people think cain't hurt you if you don't let it. And that's that . . . But how about me?"

"Phil!" she flashed, turning to him.

"Yes, Phil! You knew I wouldn't give a whoop for gossip. I could go to my ranch, or back to the Arizona range and never heah a word of it again. What misery I've had has been solely that *you* have been dishonored in the eyes of this cheap Reno crowd."

"Then why ask 'how about me?' "

"Kay, in some way you're not understandable. You're ice and flint. But, God, you've been wonderful to me. Only I've been thinking what's to become of me? Could *any* man, much less a Western fellow like me who never had serious love affairs, live with the loveliest girl in the world, be seen everywhere with her by hungry-eyed jealous *hombres*, dance and eat and gamble and play with her, and come out to the quiet desert with her, where she's her true self . . . could any man do that and get over it? You've kissed me, Lord knows, seldom enough, but you *have* . . . and you've lain in my arms like that night in the moonlight, and, most terrible of all, you haven't had any conscience or modesty or anything, about how you let me see you, all but undressed . . . you've stayed under the same roof with me day and night. After this . . . this is over, which'll be soon now, do you think I can live without all that?"

Kay put a hand on his strong brown one, as it clenched the wheel, and she looked straight ahead and across the desert, which would have answered this very question for her, if she had had the courage to ask.

150

"Phil, it didn't seem so terrible . . . the aftermath . . . when we undertook this thing," replied Kay gravely. "I was so obsessed I wouldn't face the cost. But now I begin to see the wrong I've done you."

"No, no," he interrupted. "I cain't see any wrong to me. I'm no child. My eyes were wide open. But it'll seem like being thrust out of heaven . . . Aw, Kay, don't cry. I'll take my medicine."

"But I'm the one that should have to take it," replied Kay, as she wiped the tears from her eyes. "And despite everything, we must not weaken on the main issue."

When they returned to town there was a message for Kay. Victor Brelsford had arrived from New York and desired an interview with her.

"Brelsford is here, Phil," explained Kay, and handed him the message. "Mother sent for him. It's a complication that will be a boomerang for her."

"Yeah. Mister Victor Brelsford, the swell *hombre* who's going to marry you," returned Phil in his cool drawl. But his eyes were on fire with jealousy.

"He is not. I told you, Phil. I'll tell him instantly, if he broaches that old subject. Does that satisfy you?"

"Aw, I believe you . . . trust you, Kay," he rejoined. "I'll bet my soul you're on the level . . . But I *cain't* be satisfied."

"You've been happy, for the most part. What would satisfy you?"

"Kay, I've concealed it from you," he said hoarsely. "But since that night in the moonlight I've . . . I've been mad for your kisses."

"Is that all? Why didn't you take them, then?" she retorted, with a bewildering smile. "I confess to a hankering for yours."

Phil stared with starting eyes, his face turned red, and then went pale.

"We'll have a long while to . . . to enjoy each other's kisses. Let's forget that, too, for the present. Brelsford's coming will upset Mother terribly. Because I'll refuse him finally, irrevocably. She has wanted me to marry into the Brelsford family more than she ever wanted anything. I'll change my clothes and meet him for luncheon. You call for me, say in an hour. Look and be your Western self, darling. We can't fool a Brelsford."

A little later Katherine met Brelsford in the lobby of the Reno. His faultless correctness and his fair blasé face brought back New York vividly. That first reaction of Kay's was a comparison, not greatly favorable to her own class. After the greeting, she led him to the drawing room, to a secluded corner.

"Mother sent for you?"

"Yes. A frantic appeal for help, it seemed to me. I had my doubts, but, of course, I came."

"I'm glad, Victor. After all, you are a friend of the family. Mother precipitated the mess, and I've made it worse. Have you seen her?"

"I was with her for two hours. An ordeal, by Jove! She's a wreck, Kay. She poured out a long dissertation on your primrose path to degradation. And the epitome of it was that I rescue you before you sank into the gutter."

"By the sacrifice of your good sense and position, I presume," replied Kay with sarcasm.

"Kay, I didn't believe all that trash. Besides, if it were true, I'd still repeat the proposal I've made you so often."

"Thank you, Vic. You're loyal and fine. I wish I could accept it. But since I came West I am . . . well, on the trail of my real self. Once more, and definitely, Vic, with infinite regret and appreciation of the honor, I must say no."

Flushing, he bowed silently to that decree.

"You can still be my friend without betraying Mother. I hope you will be."

"Always, Kay."

"That increases my regrets. But, Vic, tell me what do you make of this situation?"

"I'm puzzled and bewildered. Disgusted with your mother, of course, as everybody is. Amazed at you . . . and, frankly, now I've seen you, up in the air."

"Have you seen Leroyd?"

"No. And don't desire to."

"What have you heard about me?"

"Oh, gossip, here and there," he replied evasively. "There seems to be a confliction between Kay Hempstead and an actress, Hilda Wales. That you were masquerading under her name, going Hollywood, and a lot of rot. You may be sure it never affected any of your friends who know you."

"Vic, I have to confess some of that gossip has foundation. I'm going to trust you now and tell you the truth."

Whereupon Kay related in detail her plot to frighten her mother into abandoning her desertion of the family, and also what relation Phil Cameron and his mother bore to the situation.

"By Jove! It'd take Kay Hempstead to invent such a scheme and to carry it out," declared Brelsford, both intrigued and astounded. "Very clever of you. Then, as I suspected, all this . . . this rotten talk about you . . . your flagrant immorality, you know, is just what you worked for, and has no true grounds?"

"Precisely, Victor. It is a colossal bluff, and it is going to succeed."

"Kay, I don't blame you. I uphold you. What do you want me to do?" he rejoined warmly.

"Go to Mother. Be utterly shocked and heartbroken over my depravity. Assure her that you would not marry me now if I threw myself at your feet. Convince her that *she* is to blame for my revulsion against mothers, husbands, homes, and that, if she does not come to me and promise to give up these divorce proceedings, you are absolutely certain that I will be utterly lost, damned forever."

Brelsford laughed. "What a beautiful devil you are, Kay! I'll do it. I'll give her the damnedest raking over on my own score. And then do your bidding to the top of my bent."

"Vic, what a good sport you are!" exclaimed Kay radiantly. "I'll be everlastingly in your debt . . . Come now, let's hie ourselves to luncheon. I'm famished."

"Kay, wait a minute. In the dynamic whirl of your presence, I forgot the young man, Phil Cameron. What of him? What kind of a fellow?"

The keen intuition of a jealous and vanquished lover became obvious to Kay.

"He's Western. Comes from good old pioneer stock. He rode the range for years, before going to California with his father, where they have large holdings in vineyards and orchards. He's twenty-six years old, a stunning-looking boy, the finest and cleanest I ever knew."

"Well! You are enthusiastic . . . and for once you eulogize a member of my sex. I'd like to meet Cameron. If he's all you claim, Kay, then you are playing him a rotten trick."

Hot blood leaped stingingly to Katherine's very temples. The truth, spoken and not without a hint of contempt, by a gentleman, and one of her class, found the mark.

"Rotten! Why so unpleasant a word, Victor?"

"You can't tell me this boy is not in love with you," declared Brelsford. "I wouldn't believe you if you did. For I know what it means to be with you. And if you're living with Cameron . . . in a cottage . . . alone . . . *Whew!*"

"Please elucidate the *whew*, Victor," demanded Kay coldly, with a level glance at him. "I made you my confidant. I didn't lie about Phil or our intimacy."

"Forgive me," he returned hastily. "I didn't insinuate that you lied. The blood just went to my head. That explains the *whew*. But see here, Kay Hempstead, you should be told things. You have the old Helen beauty that is enough in itself. To see you is to worship. But to see you in all your outrageous shameless lack of modesty . . . that would be too much for any man. You simply should be torn to pieces."

The language of compliment was always wine to Kay's senses.

"Why, Victor, do you imagine I disrobed before Phil as Aphrodite did before Paris?" she asked gaily.

"If you felt like it . . . and the flowers in the grass enhanced the color of your skin . . . you would."

"Oh, Victor. I don't think I'd ever go to such lengths to satisfy my vanity . . . Still, I confess my immodest failing and will be careful to inhibit it in the future."

They went in to luncheon, where, when they had nearly finished, Phil found them. The introduction must have been trying to both men, but to Kay's surprise and pleasure the Westerner had a cool courteous poise that became him mightily. He was on his mettle, aware that in Brelsford he confronted all of Kay's alien and antagonistic world. Contrary to what might have been expected, Cameron's simplicity and the elder man's perspicuity and thoroughbred genuineness quickly brought the two into sympathy.

Kay grasped the opportune moment, and, pleading a little shopping to do, she left them together. But from the store she went directly to her cottage, and, changing to pajamas, she lay down on her bed to rest and think. The gambling dens would save money that afternoon, she reflected, with a smile. There was much to ponder upon, but Kay did not get very far with it, before she fell asleep.

Phil awakened her, coming in at five o'clock. He appeared excited and enthusiastic, and sat down beside her on the bed, something he had not done before.

156

"Say, Kay, this old flame of yours is some swell guy," declared Phil. "He's shore a regular fellow. I like him to beat the band. We've been all over town, playing faro, monte, roulette. I won a lot. It shore tickles me when I beat these Reno games."

Kay sat up to give him a little pull toward her and a searching look.

"You've been drinking champagne, Phil," she said severely. "I forbade that, you know."

"But, honey, only one bottle, and Brelsford ordered it."

"You should have confined yourself to one glass. We're to dine with Victor tonight, and that means more champagne."

"Aw, don't worry about me. I can hold my liquor . . . Dog-gone it, Kay, I feel great. Somehow, without saying so outright, your friend made me feel the bigness of my responsibility for you . . . the . . . the privilege I had . . . and that, since you had to pull such an awful stunt, I was the man to trust."

"You are, Phil. And Brelsford saw it and was man enough to convey it without flattering you. Oh, I'm glad he came . . . glad you like him . . . Right now he'll be giving Mother the unhappiest hour of her life."

"I'll say he will. I was there when they met, in the lobby, just now. Would you believe it, Brelsford had the nerve to introduce me to her? 'Kay's cowboy friend,' he said. And if looks could slay, I'd be daid now."

"Vic said that? Oh, delicious! Funny how life works out. Mother always hated cowboys because I loved to read about them . . . preferred Western heroes to dukes and fairy princes."

"Sounds like poetic justice to me . . . Kay Hempstead falling for a cowpuncher who's far from a hero."

"Oh! So she's fallen for you, has she?" rejoined Kay demurely. The boy was out of his head. "Don't tell it outside the family or it'll be front page news for our campaign."

"Kay, I gotta tell you the rest," he burst out joyously. "I met Mom, too, and she's licked. Aw, but I wanted to hug her. She said she'd go back to Dad and forgive him . . . forget it all . . . if I'd only give up that beautiful half-naked glory-eyed vampire I was traveling around with!"

"Oh, Phil! *No!*"

"Yes, by thunder! If it didn't hurt so, I could laugh till I cried."

"She called me all that? Phil, I just loved her, too. But she's justified . . . And what did you say?"

"I said I couldn't go back on you now . . . that you loved me . . . that I alone could keep you from the streets and dance halls. Oh, a lot of bunk like that. She wept. She said . . . 'I'll send for your dad. He'll fix this bad woman!' Aw, it's just too rich. If Dad comes and gets one look at you . . . the fire will be out."

"Phil, Mother, too, is collapsing. When Vic gets through with her, then the fire will be out there, too. Oh, Phil, to the victor belong the spoils!"

"I don't get you, lady," replied Phil dubiously. "Brelsford's name is Victor."

158

"Your head isn't clear, darling. You'd better sleep or rest a while. If you are very decorous and gentle about it, you may collect one . . . or more . . . of those kisses you raved about."

That night at dinner Phil was not proof against the portent of the hour, the glamour of Kay's star-like eyes and lovely person, of later assurance of his mother's poignant capitulation. He drank far too much champagne. He hugged Kay so shamelessly that she forgot her rôle, for once, and refused to dance again with him. It amused Brelsford, yet gave him a pang. For Kay divined that he thought there would be a tragic end to this farce. "Get that boy home," he advised while they were having their last dance. "He's true blue . . . too fine a lad for your sophisticated and decadent little comedy-drama. Cut the rest of your notoriety stunt. You can't undo the wrong you've done Cameron. But square it somehow. I'll go up to your mother. I predict unqualified retrenchment for her."

On the way out Phil bore himself well and appeared to be none the worse for his excess drinking. But the cold desert air, after the warm languorous atmosphere of the hotel, affected him so powerfully that he was drunk before they got back to their cottage. It was well that Kay had taken the wheel.

Phil stumbled indoors at her heels, breathing heavily, flushed of face. In the living room, where Kay let fall her furs, Phil made at her with a boyish ardor that yet had more heat and violence in it than he had ever exhibited. Kay let him take her in his arms, grief knocking at her heart.

"Phil, dear, you're drunk."

"Whosh drunk? Sweetie, I'm jus' gonna muss you all up."

"Not this gown, Phil. It won't stand pawing . . . Kiss me and go to your room."

"Shore, I'll kiss you . . . all right . . . but I ain't gonna go . . . Swell dress, Kay, but you jus's well might have nothun on. B'gosh, I'll take it off . . . Wash you pushin' me for? Say, lady, I'll show you how I used to break . . . wild filly."

There was good-natured humor about him that seemed to be succumbing to something raw and elemental. But he lost co-ordination between mind and muscle. He lost his violence, and his hands dragged at her, while he panted heavily and sleepily closed his eyes. Then he slumped down on the couch, nearly carrying Kay with him. To her intense relief his collapse obviated any further concern for herself, although in spite of his being drunk she did not believe she had anything to fear from him. She blamed herself for his condition. While she removed his coat, and collar and tie, and then his shoes, her mind worked swiftly. She recalled what Brelsford had advised. She must begin to undo the mischief, if that were humanly possible. How terrible it would have been for his mother to have seen him there! Then she put a pillow under his head. When he awakened, she thought, he would have some faint recollection of his condition. She would use that, exaggerate it, in order to make it a lesson. Then an

160

inspiration seized her that, outrageous as it seemed, irresistibly took hold of her.

Dead asleep as he was, she had no trouble in stripping him to his underclothes. Then she scattered her furs, her purse and handkerchief, her slippers, on the floor before the couch, quietly overturned the table with its several objects, disarranged the rug, and otherwise made that side of the room suggestive of a considerable struggle. That done, she stared at her work, at her insensible victim, conscious of an inward burning vibration. Then without turning off the light, she went into her bedroom and locked the door.

CHAPTER
SIX

At intervals during the night Kay awoke, and late in the morning her last restless nap was disrupted by heavy sounds in the kitchen.

Phil was knocking about out there. His footfalls had not their usual light quickness. She heard the splashing of water and blowing expulsions of breath. Presently Phil growled to himself and then went out, his steps crunching the gravel path.

Sunlight, bright and golden, streamed in Kay's window, throwing shadows of moving leaves upon her bed. A mockingbird, the second Kay had ever heard, sang from the hedge. Kay's oppression and the misgivings of the black night vanished like mist before the sun. A presentiment of what she knew not, vague and boding, did not hold in her consciousness.

Kay reached for her make-up box and mirror, which she had placed near at hand. Then propped up by pillows, she began a careful and elaborate preparation that must preserve her beauty and at the same time give her face and eyes the counterfeit of terrible havoc. "Not such a task at that," she mused ruefully. "I show my troubles." She pulled the blind down a little, to shade the sunlight somewhat, and composed herself to wait for Phil. And now that the hour was at hand — what would she say to Phil? Dare she go through with such a monstrous deceit? The injustice, the devilishness of her plan, the creed of *noblesse oblige* — all these shook her but did not change her. A stronger instinct, not wholly clear at the moment, held her tinglingly to her purpose.

Presently Phil's step, quick now, grated on the walk, and Kay sat up with her heart pounding in her breast.

He entered through the kitchen and came into the living room, where he halted with a sudden hard breath, like a gasp. What construction had he put upon the disarray of Kay's belongings, of the disorder of the room? Kay's courage almost failed her. But it was too late now. When Phil stamped to her bedroom door and knocked, she did not have the voice to answer. He tried the door, to find it locked. He knocked louder and called fearfully: "*Kay!*"

"Oh . . . who's . . . there?" she replied weakly.

"Who'n hell would it be?" he said impatiently. "Open this door."

"What for?"

"I want to see you."

"You think you do . . . but you don't, Phil Cameron."

This occasioned a long silence, during which, no doubt, poor Phil's fears were confounding him.

"Kay . . . damn it! I must see you."

"Promise not . . . to . . . to touch me."

"Yes, I promise," he replied harshly.

Kay slid out of bed and, unlocking her door, quickly ran back again.

163

Phil did not move for a moment. Then with violence he turned the knob and swept the door wide. As if the threshold had been an insurmountable wall, he halted there, stricken by his first sight of her.

"Aw . . . Kay!" he cried huskily, as if imagined fears had become realities.

Kay gazed back at him with all that was true in her feeling for him, mingled with all the reproach and anguish she could muster.

"I . . . I was drunk . . . last night," he went on brokenly.

She nodded her head in slow and sad affirmation.

"Did I . . . mistreat you?"

She turned her face away from his entreating look. "Phil, it was all my fault."

"My . . . God!" he gasped, and stumbled across the threshold to fall on his knees beside her bed, his head bowed, his hands clenching the coverlet. "I remember . . . something . . . I wanted to undress you . . . meant to . . . but I didn't think anything . . . lowdown . . . It was that champagne . . . made a beast of me . . . I didn't know . . . what I was about . . . Aw!" And he writhed in his shame.

"Phil, I am to blame," she said softly, checking her arms from folding around his neck.

"Shore you are. But that doesn't excuse me," he said, and, without any move to touch her, he slowly arose to his feet and stood staring down at her. "I'm sorry, Kay. That'll be about all for us. I cain't be trusted. I'm a . . . a . . . low-down dog! There's nothing for me to do but get out of here *pronto*."

164

"Phil . . . hush! You mustn't talk that way," she cried, swiftly realizing her mistake. He was a grim man now, despising himself, and capable of any rash deed. It was the West in him, the desert breed of him, that lacked materialism and loathed sensuality. In one instant more Kay realized how unselfishly and purely she was loved. It seemed to exalt her — to lift her above her morbid phantasms, her inexplicable exactions.

"This game we played was crazy," he declared, his eyes like pale flames. "You should have known better . . . unless you . . . aw, hell, I cain't think that . . . But I wasn't man enough to resist you. I gave in. We played the game. Look at you . . . and heah I am, sickened to death. All for what?"

"For our mothers, Phil."

"Aw, to hell with your mother! She wasn't worth it, nor mine either . . . the bull-haided old woman!"

"Come here, Phil!" cried Kay imperiously, and she held out her arms.

At that juncture there came a solid knock on the living room door, which was at the front of the cottage. The disruption brought Phil and Kay back to time and place, and the uncertainties of their position. Kay stared up at him, while Phil slowly turned toward the door. A second knock followed, heavier than the first, carrying an aggressive note.

Phil crossed the room. "Who's out there?" he called.

"Hello. Is this where Kay Hempstead stays?" called a resonant masculine voice.

Kay heard it, recognized it, and sprang up with a startled cry.

165

"Yes," replied Cameron.

"Is she in?"

"Yes, but not to reporters."

"Mister cowboy, I'm no reporter," came the militant retort. "You'll find that out quick."

"Hell you say," muttered Phil, his cold visage reddening, and he checked a sudden move to open the door. "Who are you? What do you want?"

"Tell Kay that Jack Morse from New York is here to see her."

Phil did not need to inform Kay what she had heard as well as he. She arose, donned a dressing gown, and hastened to the front door.

"Is it really you, Jack Morse?" she asked in surprise.

"Kay! Yes, it's Jack in the flesh. You'll see when you open this door."

"But Jack . . . please excuse me . . . I'll meet you at the Reno in half an hour."

"You'll see me right now, Kay Hempstead, if I have to smash open this door."

At that Kay's color receded to leave her white, and she stood undecided, her brow puckered, and with anger apparently overcoming her amazement. Phil laid a powerful hand on the doorknob.

"Well, I'll see who the hell this *hombre* is," he declared, and he flung open the door.

Kay had Morse vividly in mind before he brushed into the room, so that his virile presence, his great bulk, and dark visage added little. But his somber and questioning mien gave her a shock. Morse, in his champion athlete days, not long ago, had been Kay's hero, so far as football went. She had coquetted with him, then had kept up the friendship afterward. He, like Brelsford, was a friend of her family, and he had pressed his suit with all the rush and vim for which he had been famous in his university. But he had no claim whatever on Kay, and she resented this intrusion, the source of which she divined was her mother's frantic call for help.

Morse's contemptuous glance flashed over Phil to alight upon Kay, and there it changed markedly. Phil quietly shut the door behind him, and stood back, his eyes narrowed to piercing slits.

"Jack, now that you have forced yourself in here, kindly explain your uncalled for action," said Kay coldly, omitting any greeting.

"Your mother wired me. I came by plane," replied Morse.

"That could be your only excuse, of course. But you should have sent me a message and arranged to meet me at Mother's hotel."

"I just came from her. I couldn't wait. It was impossible to believe her. I had to see for myself."

"What?"

"If it is true that you are living openly with a cowboy?"

"Quite true," returned Kay, without a flicker of an eyelash.

"Are you . . . married?" went on Morse hoarsely.

"That is none of your business. But I'll tell you. No."

"It's true, then, what she told me? You've disgraced her . . . brought the name of Hempstead to disrepute

. . . become a gambler, an adventuress, lost to common decency, the companion of a cheap cowboy?"

Phil sprang forward, furious at Morse's insulting words, but Kay laid a restraining hand on his arm. "Wait, Phil," she commanded in no uncertain tone. Then, turning again to Morse, she said: "All true, Jack, except the cheap applied to my lover."

Those cool words, almost flippant, acted like a lash upon Morse.

"You do not introduce me?" he queried insolently.

"No. That isn't necessary or desirable, since you insult me."

"Insult you? For the love of . . . The more I see of women, the less I understand . . . and respect them."

"I am not interested in your opinions. And I must request of you, now that I have frankly clarified any doubts in your mind as to my status, to please take yourself back to my mother. Tell her that I said the honor of the Hempsteads was her concern before it was mine, and, as she chose to disregard it, I don't see why I shouldn't do as I please. She knows what kind of a man Leroyd is, and that she's making a fool of herself over him. He's after her money. He's gambling some of it away here in Reno."

"Well . . . who is decent these days? I shall dispense with any further interview."

"Jack, a graceful final gesture on your part would be to pan mother unmercifully."

"OK. If I have any stuff left after I get through with you . . . and this Western pup . . . Final gesture, you say? Well, it won't be graceful."

168

"Don't try to bully me, Mister Morse. You always tried it, and you never succeeded. Nor do I care to hear any of your bombast, for which you are famous."

"Kay, you're going to hear some of it straight," he said angrily.

"Oh, am I? Well, first let me tell you your motive. You're a jealous man, and you want to vent your jealousy on me, before Cameron, because I preferred him as a lover to you as a husband."

Kay's taunt found an immediate main, showing that she had gauged Morse with unerring and merciless precision.

"He's welcome to you, by God," rasped the Easterner stridently. "You, who were once Kay Hempstead, now a strumpet. Why, you look like a . . . like a streetwalker . . ."

Cameron leaped forward and whirled Morse so savagely that he staggered.

"Turn 'round, yuh!" he shouted, and his tawny hair stood up like the mane of a lion. "Western men don't talk that way to women. Out heah we'd call you a low-down dirty skunk!"

Then Phil lunged out, to strike Morse a terrific blow on his sneering mouth. The Easterner, staggering, took the table crashing down with him. His sudden fall shook the cottage.

Kay did not cry out, although she ran to the door of her bedroom, meaning to shut herself in. But she did not. Morse bounded up nimbly for so big a man. Blood gushed from his split lip, over his chin, and down his white collar. Passion had dominated him, but the smash

169

in the face eased and cooled him off. His training had been to fight. Physical violence was a stimulant, not a deterrent.

"Cowboy, I'll beat you half to death for that," he ground out, and made at Phil.

Kay could not take her fascinated gaze from the ensuing fight. At first, as the contestants began to swing and slug, she welcomed the rawness of these two animals fighting over her. The age-old combat. It liberated something hot and vicious in her, feelings she had never experienced. She was a barbarian and gloried in this lithe powerful stripling in unequal conflict with a giant. Phil was the nimbler on his feet. He landed oftener with his fists. But his blows did not tell upon his adversary as had the first one. He beat Morse about the face, but could not floor him again. On the contrary, Morse knocked Phil down repeatedly. The former began to whistle for his breath while the latter panted. Both began to sweat, which added to the flow of blood. They fought all over the living room, demolishing the furniture.

Kay's fierce sensorial perceptions yielded to the intelligence of a woman who had seen many contests of strength and endurance, some of which had been real prize fights. She grasped that the combatants were unequally matched. Phil was being terribly beaten. Yet he fought back with all his might and main.

"Oh, Jack!" she cried frantically, "that's enough. It's not fair. You're twice his size . . . You'll kill him!"

But Morse, deaf to her entreaty, if he heard it, rushed Phil, beat him back with right and left, then swung a

170

sodden blow that propelled him into a corner. Phil rolled over with a sucking intake of breath and rose, leaning on one hand. Between the hard breathing of the fighters, Kay heard the blood dripping from Phil's lowered face.

"Cowboy . . . you can . . . take . . . it . . . I'll tell the world," panted Morse, and he kicked his fallen rival. "But, by God . . . you're whipped too bad . . . to lie in your sweetie's arms . . . again very soon."

"I'm whipped plenty . . . your way," replied Phil thickly. "But wait a minute."

Morse righted a chair to sag into it. He mopped his lip that still bled. Kay stood in the door of her bedroom, staring at the prostrate Phil. She felt bursting to cry out, to run to him, yet she remained immovable and mute. She divined that this fight was not ended.

Phil got up, quickly it appeared, for one so battered, and staggered into the kitchen. Before Kay could unclamp her faculties, Phil came back with a gun in each hand. He confronted Morse to toss the left-hand gun into his lap.

"There, you slugger," he said, his voice like ice. "We'll take a fly at it Western fashion."

"What . . . at?" bellowed Morse, fumbling with the big blue gun. Except for bruises and bloodstains his face went deadly white. "You mean . . . shoot it out?"

"That's what I mean, Mister Morse."

"But Cameron . . . you . . . I . . . There's no call . . . for murder."

"No, if you've got any guts. But if you haven't, there'll be murder . . . For I'm going to kill you . . . you big loudmouthed bruiser . . . you filthy-minded Easterner! The West hasn't changed. You cain't get away with your vile insults . . . to her. Not out heah, Mister Morse . . . Throw that gun . . . you . . . before I bore you!"

It was then that Kay burst out of her paralyzed inaction, to find her senses and her spirit. She ran to Phil — almost brushing her breast with his leveled gun. "Phil! For God's sake . . . wait . . . listen!" she implored.

"Get out of my way, Kay. I don't want to kill you, too."

"Darling, you can't kill him. It'd be murder. *He* won't fight with a gun. He's afraid for his life."

"So it looks. But no matter. I don't care a damn." Bloody and magnificent he stood, not the boy Phil she had known, but a ruthless man in whom the heritage of the West called its fierce law. She sensed more than his succumbing to the creed of cowboy and pioneer. He welcomed this fight and the chance to force Morse to shoot him as a means to the end he believed he deserved.

"Listen to me or I'll fight for this gun," flashed Kay as she seized it with both hands.

"Let go. That's a hair-trigger. It might go off."

"Will you listen?" she besought him faintly.

"Yes, if you'll let go my gun."

She released her hold on it and swayed against his breast, which support she needed until she could rally. The unexpected contact of her disengaged his attention from Morse. Kay felt him shake. That moment was one of revelation. A strong and telling current of blood raced back from her heart to revive her. With her arms sliding up around him, her hands locking behind his neck, all doubt, all uncertainty ceased for her, and she knew that this moment of her surrender to her love would save him and herself.

"Phil, we have made mistakes," she began eloquently, "but do not crown them by a tragic deed, that would result in death for you and terrible misery for me. You are furious now. Not because Morse whipped you. What is that to you? He's twice your size and a slugger besides. Nor should you want to kill him because of what he called me. He thinks it's true. But you know it's false . . . Moreover, you are laboring under a delusion about what happened last night. It . . . didn't happen! I just helped you to believe so for a silly reason of my own. All this has faced me with the real truth. I love you, Phil. I am yours. I could not go back East without you, if I ever go . . . For the rest, what does that matter? My mother's trouble . . . your mother's . . . for which we disgraced ourselves to shame them, these matter little beside our own problem, which, darling, will be a problem no longer the moment you see the truth."

Kay felt Phil's arm over her shoulder, as evidently he made a move with the gun toward Morse.

"Get out and don't butt into me again," he ordered curtly.

Kay heard Morse thump the gun on the floor, then his dragging footfalls. He opened the door, shuffled out, and closed it.

"Kay, I hope he gets out of town before I recover from the talk you gave me. It was sure some talk. My God, what a woman can be and do! But that saved his life. I reckon mine, too."

She lay against him, exhausted. And whatever his doubt, his uncertainty, he found her warmth and sweetness and surrender beyond his power to withstand.

"Phil, it was true . . . all I said," she replied presently, in an unsteady voice.

"Aw . . . you've won, Kay. Don't rub it in. Lately I've reckoned you cared for me. But I couldn't believe it. You must now."

"Care for you? My dear boy, I love you . . . love you as I never loved anyone in my life."

"After last . . . night?" he whispered in her hair.

"Especially after last night."

"Oh, Lord! But I cain't be happy . . . I cain't ever."

"Phil, didn't I tell you that you were wrong about what you think happened when you were drunk?"

"Yes, I heahed you. It's a beautiful lie, my dearest. You're as noble and forgiving as you are lovely."

"I didn't lie. I swear to God."

"Kay, don't perjure your soul."

"Oh, you obstinate cow-headed cowboy!" cried Kay, beside herself. "If you love me, why won't you believe me?"

"I'm beginning to grasp the greatness of a woman."

"You drove me desperate. I'll give you one more chance. Do you . . . will you believe me?"

"No, sweetheart, I cain't."

174

"Very well, then," she retorted, and deliberately she raised her lips close to his with a low laugh.

"Don't play with me, Kay."

"I'm in dead earnest . . . Must I coax for kisses?"

"Kay . . . with this bloody nose?" he expostulated, half frantic.

"Darling, I didn't ask you to kiss me with your nose," she said, and, taking his handkerchief from his hand, she tenderly wiped the bleeding member.

"I must be a sight. My lip's cut. My face hurts all over."

She kissed his twitching mouth, which was suspiciously carmine in hue, and then the several bruises on his face. "There. That ought to soothe the pain . . . You don't look so very bad. Phil, I think by the dexterous use of my make-up, I can make you presentable . . . for our honeymoon."

"Mercy!" he gasped.

Then seriously she told him every little detail that had happened the night before upon their return to the cottage, and, as for her motive, she bared her soul to explain that strange and eternal feminine urge.

"Darling, you give me back something . . . 'most as much as the promise of your dear self," he returned solemnly.

"Come, let me wash the blood off you . . . and myself, too. Oh, that big bully . . . how I hate him. Yet, I ought to love him. He made me realize how I really love you!"

CHAPTER
SEVEN

On the eve of victory Kay and Phil forgot all about their mothers, forgot everything but the transport of their love, everything save their plan to be married and spend the honeymoon in Arizona before going on to California. To them divorce was a nightmare that had vanished in the sunlight of day. Marriage was the most beautiful dawning of a dream and glory, the consummation of all things, the hope and fulfillment of youth and life.

On the following day they were married by the famous minister of Reno, who joined together so many who, having failed once or twice, or even more, still followed the gleam.

"Phil, let's go inform our dear parents that as far as humanly possible we have made amends for our misconduct," said Kay radiantly. "And that we shall spend the rest of our lives proving the absurdity of such a place as the Reno divorce mill, and the joy and good of marriage."

They drove to the dealer from whom Kay had rented the car. She purchased it outright. Then they went to their cottage, and, while Phil loaded their baggage in the back seat, Kay lingered in the rooms that had unconsciously grown dear. How seldom things affected her like this.

Phil dropped Kay at the Hotel Reno. "I'll take the car to the garage, pay some bills, and be back *pronto*," he said. "I hope our glad news will finish your mother. It shore will Mom."

Kay went directly to her mother's apartment, striving for an indifferent mien, but eager to reveal the plot that had failed, and to confess her marriage. She found Mrs. Hempstead fully dressed and wholly devoid of some characteristic which Kay could not at once analyze.

"Oh, it's you, Kay. I thought you'd come flaunting in pretty soon."

"Good morning, Mother. I hope you are well," rejoined Kay brightly.

"I'm as well as could be expected under the circumstances. I needn't ask after *your* health. You're a picture of it. And your old beautiful self? God in heaven, how can you burn the candle at both ends, yet still retain your infernal youth and beauty?"

"Mother, my recipe is simple," replied Kay naïvely. "I eat and sleep properly, drink little wine and never cocktails, and keep my conscience clear."

"You have the impudence of your generation, my dear . . . Get it over with."

"What?"

"You evidently came to crow over me in my degradation."

"Not at all. I came to make up with you, if you will . . . and to say goodbye."

"Leaving, eh? I thought Morse would jar you out of your love nest, if Brelsford couldn't."

"Have you seen Jack since yesterday?"

"Yes, for a moment. He looked as if he'd been in an auto smash-up. And he acted queer, too. Said I was all wrong about you. Then he called me a decadent, silly, old dame, along with some more insulting things, and left to catch his plane."

"Morse hits harder, Mother, as Phil and I well know . . . Yes, you *are* all wrong about me. Listen to this." And Kay told her story, not sparing herself.

"Katherine Hempstead! You played that hoax on me . . . to save me? You disgraced yourself abominably to save me? All the time your atrocious conduct . . . your brazen immorality . . . was a sham . . . a trick to frighten me out of my rights?"

"All the time, Mother, darling. I'm sorry, and ashamed now. But when I got here, I couldn't move you."

"What's to become of the young man, Cameron? Brelsford got acquainted with him, said he was a fine fellow, a gentleman, evidently of good family. That you had been as conscienceless with him . . . wrecked his life, as you have so many men."

"Conscienceless, I confess. But I'm sure I haven't wrecked Phil. For this morning I married him."

Mrs. Hempstead uttered a faint shriek and fell back from her upright dignity into limp and abject prostration.

"You astounding . . . terrible young woman!" she ejaculated.

178

"Well, I'm settled, finally. I'm finished, Mother . . . except for love, home, husband, babies, happiness. You ought to be glad. Father will be and Polly."

"Thank God! This saves me. I want to know the cowboy who could work such magic in Kay Hempstead."

"You will like Phil. He's not a cowboy any more. That range life was his youth. He's a California planter now."

"Does he know you're worth millions?"

"I'm sure not. Of course, he saw that I had money. I spent it right and left. Funny thing, Mother, I couldn't lose. Whenever I gambled, I won. I'm away ahead of the game. Fact is, I bought my car with Reno winnings."

"Well, I lost," declared Mrs. Hempstead bitterly. "It was a lesson I needed. But you know, of course."

"I know nothing. What do you mean by lost?"

"The money I brought with me. Some thousands. My jewels . . . all gone."

"Mother! Did Leroyd . . . ?"

"You might not know he . . . appropriated my property. But you surely know he ran up a gambling debt of ten thousand dollars at Fillmore's private game."

"I don't surely know."

"But you must have seen this?" Mrs. Hempstead reached for a large purse on the table, from which she extracted a letter. This, with shaking hand, and shamed, averted eyes, she gave to Kay. The envelope contained some kind of a report on a single page. The printed heading denoted a detective agency. The details were in type. Kay's swift gaze ran over a full record of Leroyd's philandering and gambling while in Reno.

"Kay, you were right, I apologize," said her mother sadly. "Leroyd left day before yesterday, without a word to me."

"Well, of all things. I hardly guessed he was a gentleman crook . . . Oh, Mother, how cheaply you got rid of him. Just think."

"Yes, cheaply, from a material point of view . . . Kay, didn't you put a detective to watch Leroyd?"

"No, I never thought of such a thing. Honestly. Victor might have done it. But he never told me."

"He might have been just that clever. Fetch up your Westerner so that I can see what addition you have made to the Hempstead family. I sincerely hope *all* your sacrifices . . . your heedless wild actions have not been in vain."

Soberly Kay left her mother and went downstairs to meet Phil. But for her marriage she would have regarded the whole circumstance as an ironical joke on herself. Still there was Phil's mother to think of. And hoping that Phil's sacrifice of reputation would yet turn her back home, Kay crossed the lobby toward the drawing room to come face to face with Mrs. Cameron.

Mrs. Cameron hung on the arm of a tall, wide-shouldered, extremely handsome man about whom there appeared something familiar. He had a bronzed, clean-shaven face, wonderful eyes like gray daggers, and clustering chestnut hair whitened over the temples.

180

"Heah she is, Frank," announced Mrs. Cameron grimly.

"Air you Miss Hilda Wales?" queried this man perfunctorily, with marveling gaze sweeping her down and up.

"No," replied Kay, swiftly recovering her equilibrium, and she stood in smiling expectancy with all her natural poise.

"Then you must be Miss Katherine Hempstead?"

"No."

Phil's father wrenched his fascinated eyes from the gracious object of his interrogation, and turned to the little wife.

"Mom, you're off the trail," he said, troubled. "*This* girl shore cain't be that . . ."

"She is, Frank. I know her," declared Mrs. Cameron vehemently.

"But she doesn't look like one of those painted Hollywood actresses," protested the rancher.

"Oh, you men! She *is* an actress. That's her business. It was her angel face that led our son astray. She could fool God Almighty himself."

When Cameron turned to look again at Kay, he was plainly lost. In his eyes Kay read that, if all this were true about her, it did not matter, and he did not blame Phil.

"Mister Cameron, I have the honor to inform you that I am Phil's wife and your daughter-in-law," said Kay sweetly.

The horror and consternation that gripped Mrs. Cameron evidently did not extend to the steel-eyed

181

rancher. But he was sorely at a loss, between the devil and the deep sea.

"Missus Cameron, if you'll listen, I'll tell you why it's not so very bad for Phil," said Kay appealingly.

Just then Phil came running up opportunely, his face so happy that the sundry bruises and cuts detracted little from its comeliness.

"Dad!" he whooped, and made at his father, who certainly met him halfway. "Heah with Mom! Aw, you shore look good to my sore eyes."

"Howdy, Son. How'd you get bunged up?" replied the rancher coolly, as he let go of Phil.

"Had a little scrap, Dad. Gosh, I'm glad to see you and Mom together again . . . and heah with Kay. Has she introduced herself?"

"Wal, I'm not shore, but I reckon she's Hilda Wales, Kay Hempstead, and Mrs. Phil Cameron, all together. Am I correct?"

"Right, Dad . . . and am I happy," flashed Phil. "Mom, get that scared look off your face. Dad, it's all too wonderful to tell."

"So I savvy. But would you mind clearin' up all this bunk Mom has been feedin' me, since I got heah?"

"It's not bunk, but romance, Dad. I met Kay the night I got heah to Reno. We fell in love right then. At least *I* did. She had come out to stop her mother from divorcing her father. I had come to keep Mom from divorcing you. Well, we couldn't do a damn' thing with either of our mothers. So we planned to throw the wildest stunt we could think of. We played to the gallery . . . gambled, drank, drove, danced, lived together, just two young folk clean gone to hell. All to sicken and scare Missus Hempstead and Mom out of their haids . . . But, Dad, it was all a bluff. We played a swell game. Kay's friends came out and spilled the beans for us. They made us think of ourselves . . . that we couldn't go on. Besides, we had the game about won. So this mawning we were married."

"Wal, I'll be dog-goned," exclaimed the rancher with a hearty laugh. "Shore is some story. But couldn't you young folks have had all the romance *and* love without the shady stuff?"

Phil looked blank and somewhat crestfallen, while Kay began to see the light. If what she divined were true, then how cruelly had their agonies been wasted?

"Mom, you sent for Dad?" asked Phil eagerly.

"Indeed, I did not," returned his mother. "He came without being asked."

"Wal, Son, I reckon I'd've knuckled anyway, sooner or later," interposed the rancher in his cool slow drawl, and his keen eyes twinkled from Phil to Kay. "But the fact is Marcheta eloped with that Mexican, Lopez. Left me cold. And seein' the error of my ways, I hotfooted it to Reno to square myself with your mother."

"Marcheta? The black-eyed little hussy! And *I* was fond of her!" ejaculated Phil. Then awakening to the irony of his and Kay's past ventures, he turned to her: "What have we been up against? I just found out Leroyd ran off."

"Yes. Mother told me," returned Kay. "She let me read the record from the detective agency. I thought it was Brelsford. Phil, were you responsible for that?"

"Shore. I got wise to Leroyd and put the detectives on his trail. They were to mail reports about him to your mother at the end of a week. I forgot it . . . like I forgot everything else."

"Making your mother suffer all for nothing?" interposed Mrs. Cameron.

"No. I'll never believe that," declared Phil stoutly. "But Kay and I . . . look what *we* did . . . how *we* suffered . . . all for nothing!"

"Not at all, Phil," rejoined Kay softly. "We found love. And the West has won me . . . saved me, no doubt."

"Wal, all's wal that ends wal. I reckon there'll be a tightenin' of loose bridles, and a long ride down to sunset," added the rancher, his fine dark face alight.

Monty Price's Nightingale

Around campfires they cursed him in hearty cowboy fashion and laid upon him the bane of their ill will. They said that Monty Price had no friend — that no foreman or rancher ever trusted him — that he never spent a dollar — that he would not keep a job — that there must be something crooked about a fellow who bunked and worked alone, who quit every few months to ride away, no one knew where, and who returned to the ranges, haggard and thin and shaky, hunting for another place.

He had been drunk somewhere, and the wonder of it was that no one in the Tonto forest ranges had ever seen him drink a drop. Red Lake and Gallatin and Bellville knew him, but no more of him than the ranges. He went farther afield, they said, and hinted darker things than a fling at faro or a fondness for red liquor.

But there was no rancher, no cowboy from one end of the vast range country to another who did not admit Monty Price's pre-eminence in those peculiar attributes of his calling. He was a magnificent rider; he had an iron and cruel hand with a horse, yet he never killed or crippled his mount; he possessed the Indian's instinct for direction; he never failed on the trail of lost stock;

he could ride an outlaw and brand a wild steer and shoe a vicious mustang as bragging cowboys swore they could; and supreme test of all he would endure, without complaint, long toilsome hours in the piercing wind and freezing sleet and blistering sun.

"I'll tell you what," said old Abe Somers. "I've ranched from the Little Big Horn to the Pecos, an' I've seen a sight of cowpunchers in my day. But Monty Price's got 'em all skinned. It shore is too bad he's unreliable . . . packin' off the way he does, jest when he's the boy most needed. Some mystery about Monty."

The extra duty, the hard task, the problem with stock or tools or harness — these always fell to Monty. His most famous trick was to offer to take a comrade's night shift. So it often happened that while the cowboys lolled round their campfire, Monty Price, after a hard day's riding, would stand out the night guard, in rain and snow. But he always made a bargain. He sold his service. And the boys were wont to say that he put his services high.

Still they would never have grumbled at that if Monty had ever spent a dollar. He saved his money. He never bought any fancy boots or spurs or bridles or scarves or chaps; and his cheap jeans and saddles were the jest of his companions. Nevertheless, in spite of Monty's shortcomings, he rode in the Tonto on and off for five years before he made an enemy.

There was a cowboy named Bart Muncie who had risen to be a foreman and who eventually went to ranching on a small scale. He acquired a range up in the forest country where grassy valleys and parks lay between the wooden hills, and here in a wild spot among the pines he built a cabin for his wife and baby.

It came about that Monty went to work for Muncie and rode for him for six months. Then, in a dry season, with Muncie short of help and with long drives to make, Monty quit in his inexplicable way and left the rancher in dire need. Muncie lost a good deal of stock that fall, and he always blamed Monty for it. Some weeks later it chanced that Muncie was in Bellville the very day Monte returned from his latest mysterious absence. And the two met in a crowded store.

Monty appeared vastly different from the lean-jawed, keen-eyed, hard-riding cowboy of a month back. He was haggard and thin and shaky and spiritless and somber.

"See here, Monty Price," said Muncie with stinging scorn, "I reckon you'll spare me a minute of your precious time."

"I reckon so," replied Monty.

Muncie used up more than the allotted minute in calling Monte every bad name known to the range.

"An' the worst of all you are is that you're a liar!" concluded the rancher passionately. "I relied on you an' you failed me. You lost me a herd of stock. Put me back a year! An' for what? God only knows what! We ain't got you figgered here . . . not that way. But after this trick you turned me, we all know you're not square. An' I go on record callin' you as you deserve. You're no good. You've got a streak of yellow. An' you sneak off now an' then to indulge it. An' most of all you're a liar! Now, if it ain't all so . . . flash your gun!"

But Monty Price did not draw.

The scorn and abuse of the cowboys might never have been, for all the effect it had on Monty. He did not see or feel it. He found employment with a rancher named Wentworth and went at his work in the old, inimitable manner, that was at once the admiration and despair of his fellows. He rolled out of his blankets in the gray dawn, and he was the last to roll in at night.

In a week all traces of his weakened condition had vanished, and he grew strong and dark and hard, once more like iron. And then again he was up to his old tricks, more intense than ever, eager and gruff at bargaining his time, obsessed by the one idea — to make money.

To Monty the long, hot, dusty, blasting days of summer were as moments. Time flew for him. The odd jobs, the rough trails, the rides without water or food, the long stands in the cold rain, the electric storms when the lightning played around and cracked in his horse's mane, and the uneasy herd bawled and milled — all these things that were the everlasting torment of his comrades were as nothing to Monty Price.

And when the first payday came and Monty tucked away a little roll of greenbacks inside his vest and kept adding to it as one by one his comrades paid him for some bargained service — then in Monty Price's heart began the low and insistent and sweetly alluring call of the thing that had ruined him. Thereafter, sleeping or

190

waking, he lived in a dream with that music in his heart, and the hours were fleeting.

On the mountain trails, in the noonday heat of the dusty ranges, in the dark, sultry nights with their thunderous atmosphere, he was always listening to that song of his nightingale. To his comrades he seemed a silent, morose, greedy cowboy, a demon for work, with no desire for friendship, no thought of home or kin, no love of a woman or a horse or anything, except money. To Monty himself, his whole inner life grew rosier and mellower and richer as day by day his nightingale sang sweeter and louder.

And that song was a song of secret revel — far away — where he gave up to this wind of flame that burned within him — where a passionate and irresistible strain in his blood found its outlet — where wanton red lips whispered, and wanton eyes, wine dark and seductive, lured him, and wanton arms twined around him.

The rains failed to come that summer. The grama grass bleached on the open ranges and turned yellow up in the parks. But there was plenty of grass and water to last out the fall. It was fire the ranchers feared. And it came.

One morning above the low, gray-stoned, and black-fringed mountain range rose clouds of thick, creamy smoke. There was fire on the other side of the mountain. But unless the wind changed and drew fire in over the pass, there was no danger on that score. The wind was right; it seldom changed at that season, although sometimes it blew a gale. Still the ranchers grew more anxious. The smoke clouds rolled up and spread and hid the top of the mountain and then lifted slow, majestic columns of white and yellow toward the sky.

On the day that Wentworth, along with other alarmed ranchers, sent men up to fight the fire in the pass, Monty Price quit his job and rode away. He did not tell anybody. He just took his little pack and his horse, and in the confusion of the hour he rode away. For days he had felt that his call might come at any moment, and finally it had come. It did not occur to him that he was quitting Wentworth at a most critical time. It would not have made any difference to him if it had occurred to him.

He rode away with bells in his heart. He felt like a boy at the prospect of a wonderful adventure. He felt like a man who had toiled and slaved, whose ambition had been supreme, and who had reached the pinnacle where his longing would be gratified.

His road led to the right, away from the higher ground and the timber. To his left the other road wound down the ridge to the valley below and stretched on through straggling pines and clumps of cedar toward the slopes and the forests. Monty had ridden that road a thousand times. For it led to Muncie's range. And as Monty's keen eye swept on over the parks and the thin wedges of pine to the black mass of timber beyond, he saw something that made him draw up with a start. Clearly defined against the blue-black swelling slope was a white-and-yellow cloud of smoke. It was moving. At thirty miles' distance, that it could be seen to move at all, was proof of the great speed with which it was traveling.

"She's caught!" he ejaculated. "'Way down on this side. An' she'll burn over. Nothin' can save the range!" He watched, and those keen, practiced eyes made out the changing, swelling columns of smoke, the widening path, the creeping dim red. "Reckon that'll surprise Wentworth's outfit," soliloquized Monty thoughtfully. "It doesn't surprise me none. An' Muncie, too. His cabin's up there in the valley."

It struck Monty suddenly that the wind blew hard in his face. It was sweeping down the valley toward him. It was bringing that fire. Swiftly on the wind!

"One of them sudden changes of wind!" he said. "Veered right around! An' Muncie's range will go. An' his cabin!"

Straightway Monty grew darkly thoughtful. He had remembered seeing Muncie with Wentworth's men on the way to the pass. In fact, Muncie was the leader of this fire-fighting brigade.

"Sure he's fetched down his wife an' the baby," he muttered. "I didn't see them. But sure he must have."

Monty's sharp gaze sought the road for tracks. No fresh track showed! Muncie must have taken his family over the short-cut trail. Certainly he must have! Monty remembered Muncie's wife and child. The woman had hated him. But little Del with her dancing golden curls and her blue eyes — she had always had a ready smile for him.

It came to Monty then suddenly, strangely, that little Del would have loved him if he had let her. Where was

193

she now? Safe at Wentworth's, without a doubt. But then she might not be. Muncie had certainly no fears of fire in the direction of home, not with the wind in the north and no prospect of change. It was quite possible — it was probable that the rancher had left his family at home that morning.

Monty experienced a singular shock. It had occurred to him to ride down to Muncie's cabin and see if the woman and child had been left. And whether or not he found them there the matter of getting back was a long chance. That wind was strong — that fire was sweeping down. How murky, red, sinister the slow-moving cloud!

"I ain't got a lot of time to decide," he said. His face turned pale and beads of sweat came out upon his brow.

That sweet little golden-haired Del, with her blue eyes and her wistful smile! Monty saw her as if she had been there. Then like lightning flashed back the thought that he was on his way to his revel. And the fires of hell burst in his veins. And more deadly sweet than any siren music rang the song of his nightingale in his heart. Neither honor nor manliness had ever stood before him and his fatal passion.

He was in a swift, golden dream, with the thick fragrance of wine, and the dark, mocking, luring eyes on him. All this that was more than life to him — to give it up — to risk it — to put it off for an hour! He felt the wrenching pang of something deeply hidden in his soul, beating its way up, torturing him. But it was strange and mighty. In that terrible moment it decided

194

for him; and the smile of a child was stronger than the unquenchable and blasting fire of his heart.

Monty untied his saddle pack and threw it aside, and then, with tight-shut jaw, he rode down the steep descent to the level valley. His horse was big and strong and fast. He was fresh, too, and in superb condition.

Once down on the hard-packed road he broke into a run, and it took an iron arm to hold him from extending himself. Monty calculated on saving the horse for the run back. He had no doubt that would be a race with fire. And he had been in forest fires more than once . . .

Muncie's cabin was a structure of logs and clapboards, standing in a little clearing, with the great pines towering all around. Monty saw the child, little Del, playing in the yard with a dog. He called. The child heard and, being frightened, ran into the cabin. The dog came barking toward Monty. He was a big, savage animal, a trained watchdog. But he recognized Monty.

Hurrying forward, Monty went to the open door and called Mrs. Muncie. There was no response. He called again. And while he stood there waiting, listening, above the roar of the wind he heard a low, dull, thundering sound, like a waterfall in a flooded river. It sent the blood rushing back to his heart, leaving him cold. He had not a single instant to lose.

"Missus Muncie," he called louder. "Come out! Bring the child! It's Monty Price. There's forest fire! Hurry!"

He stepped into the cabin. There was no one in the big room — or the kitchen. He grew hurried now. The child was hiding. Finally he found her in the clothespress, and he pulled her out. She was frightened. She did not recognize him.

"Del, is your mother home?" he asked.

The child shook her head.

With that Monty picked her up along with a heavy shawl he saw, and, hurrying out, he ran down to the corral. Muncie's horses were badly frightened now. Monty set little Del down, threw the shawl into a watering trough, and then he let down the bars of the gate.

The horses pounded out in a cloud of dust. Monty's horse was frightened, too, and almost broke away. There was now a growing roar on the wind. It seemed right upon him. Yet he could not see any fire or smoke. The dog came to him, whining and sniffing.

With swift hands Monty soaked the shawl thoroughly in the water and then, wrapping it round little Del and holding her tightly, he mounted. The horse plunged and broke and plunged again — then leaped out straight and fast down the road. And Monty's ears seemed pierced and filled by a terrible, thundering roar.

He had to race with fire. He had to beat the wind of flame to the open parks. Ten miles of dry forest, like powder! Though he had never seen it, he knew fire backed by heavy wind could rage through dry pine faster than a horse could run. Yet something in Monty Price welcomed this race. He goaded the horse. Then he looked back.

Through the aisles of the forest he saw a strange, streaky, murky something, moving, alive, shifting up and down, never an instant the same. It must have been the wind, the heat before the fire. He seemed to see through it, but there was nothing beyond, only opaque, dim, mustering clouds.

Ahead of him, down the road, low under the spreading trees, floated swiftly some kind of a medium, like a transparent veil. It was neither smoke nor air. It carried pin points of light, sparks, that resembled atoms of dust floating in sunlight. It was a wave of heat propelled before the storm of fire. Monty did not feel pain, but he seemed to be drying up, parching. All was so strange and unreal — the swift flight between the pines, now growing ghostly in the dimming light — the sense of rushing, overpowering force — and yet absolute silence. But that light burden against his breast — the child — was not unreal.

He must have been insane, he thought, not to be overcome in spirit. But he was not. He felt loss of something, some kind of sensation he ought to have had. But he rode that race keener and better than any race he had ever before ridden. He had but to keep his saddle — to dodge the snags of the trees — to guide the maddened horse. No horse ever in the world had run so magnificent a race.

He was outracing wind and fire. But he was running in terror. For miles he held that long, swift, tremendous stride without a break. He was running to his death whether he distanced the fire or not. For nothing could

197

stop him now except a bursting heart. Already he was blind, Monty thought.

And then, it appeared to Monty, although his steed kept fleeting on faster and faster, that the wind of flame was gaining. The air was too thick to breathe. It seemed ponderous — not from above but from behind. It had irresistible weight. It pushed Monty and his horse onward in their flight — straws on the crest of a cyclone.

Ahead there was light through the forest. He made out a white, open space of grass. A park! And the horse, like a demon, hurtled onward, with his smoothness of action gone, beginning to break.

A wave of wind, blasting in its heat, like a blanket of fire, rolled over Monty. He saw the lashing tongues of flame above him in the pines. The storm had caught him. It forged ahead. He was riding under a canopy of fire. Burning pine cones, like torches, dropped all around him, upon him.

A terrible blank sense of weight, of agony, of suffocation — of the air turning to fire! He was drooping, withering, when he flashed from the pines out into the open park. The horse broke and plunged and went down, reeking, white, in convulsions, killed on his feet. There was fire in his mane. Monty fell with him and lay in the grass, the child in his arms.

Fire in the grass — fire at his legs roused him. He got up. The park was burning over. It was enveloped in a pall of smoke. But he could see. Drawing back a fold of the wet shawl, he looked at the child. She appeared unharmed. Then he set off, running away from the edge of the forest. It was a big park, miles wide. Near the middle there was bare ground. He recognized the place, got his bearings, and made for the point where a deep ravine headed out of the park.

Beyond the bare circle there was more fire, burning sage and grass. His feet were blistered through his boots, and then it seemed he walked on red-hot coals. His clothes caught fire, and he beat it out with bare hands.

Then he stumbled into the rocky ravine. Smoke and blaze above him — the rocks hot — the air suffocating — it was all unendurable. But he kept on. He knew that his strength failed as the conditions bettered. He plunged down, always saving the child when he fell. His sight grew red. Then it grew dark. All was black, or else night had come. He was losing all pain, all sense when he stumbled into water. That saved him. He stayed there. A long time passed till it was light again. His eyes had a thick film over them. Sometimes he could not see at all.

But when he could, he kept on walking, on and on. He knew when he got out of the ravine. He knew where he ought to be. But the smoky gloom obscured everything. He traveled the way he thought he ought to go and went on and on, endlessly. He did not suffer any more. The weight of the child bore him down. He rested, went on, rested again, went on again till all sense, except a dim sight, failed him. Through that, as in a dream, he saw moving figures, men looming up in the gray fog, hurrying to him.

199

★ ★ ★

Far south of the Tonto range, under the purple shadows of the Peloncillos, there lived a big-hearted rancher with whom Monty Price found a home. He did little odd jobs about the ranch that by courtesy might have been called work. He would never ride a horse again. Monty's legs were warped, his feet hobbled. He did not have free use of his hands. And seldom or never in the presence of anyone did he remove his sombrero. For there was not a hair on his head. His face was dark, almost black, with terrible scars.

A burned-out, hobble-footed wreck of a cowboy! But, strangely, there were those at the ranch who learned to love him. They knew his story.

On Location

The tracks of Wesley's strayed horse led up the cedar slope and over the windy ridge top into the pines. A roar of motor trucks heavily loaded came from the road down beyond the green slope. Wesley emerged presently at the edge of Bonito Park, where the forest thinned out and ended in the grassy oval shining like a silver lake under the black-belted, white-covered peaks.

A dark thread of road bisected the valley. Along it cars were moving, headed Wesley's way toward the desert. Riders appeared to be rounding up a big drove of horses. Wesley halted to light a cigarette, his eyes studying this scene, so unusual for lonely Bonito Park. A truck without sides rolled along. Sight of it, loaded with gleaming airplane propeller and engine, recalled to Wesley that Meteor Pictures had been on location there filming a Western.

Then Wesley espied his horse, Sarchedon, cantering around near the other horses, raising the dust like a colt.

"He would, the son-of-a-gun," soliloquized Wesley, as he rode on. "That darn' hoss is shore ruined. Ever since I lent him to Lee for that last movie!"

Trucks loaded with camping equipment and supplies passed Wesley into the forest. Evidently the company was going down into the Painted Desert. By the time Wesley rode up to the cabins that marked the site where the company had camped, the two score and more of horses had been bunched. Some were tossing nosebags high and others were kicking and snorting for grain. This bunch of Thoroughbreds belonged to a friend of Wesley's, Lee Hornell, an Arizonian who had made big money with the motion picture companies.

As Wesley approached the horses, he passed several parked automobiles, all occupied by actors, still with their make-up and costumes on. In the last car a striking beautiful blonde fixed flashing blue eyes upon him. Wesley stared back at her.

Then slim, hawk-nosed, red-faced Lee Hornell left a group at the roadside and called: "Howdy, Wes. Took you plumb long to find us here. We're leavin' for Red Lake."

"Howdy, Lee. Didn't know anything about it. What's that airplane propeller for?"

"Say, you backwoods cowpuncher, that's to throw up a dust storm."

"Dog-gone! These movie *hombres* are shore queer. I reckon you could use an elephant."

"You bet. Have you got one?"

"Shore have. A white elephant. That danged hoss of mine, Sarch."

"Sarch? Is he gone again? I should think you'd rather count his ribs than his tracks. We haven't seen him."

204

"You're a liar, Lee. Right there." And Wesley stretched out a gloved hand.

"Aw, hell! Wes, lend Sarch to me, won't you please, pard?"

"Not on your life. You damn' near spoiled him last time. Why, Sarch is nuts on sugar ever since that movie dame fed him a barrel."

A lanky cowboy in chaps approached Lee. "All grained, boss. Hadn't we better rustle after the trucks?"

Lee addressed a tall hatless individual who was nervously pacing to and fro with gaze on the road. "Mister Hinckley, shall I shoot the horses along?"

"No. Wait till Brubaker gets here. If Pelham's double doesn't come, we're sunk. You shouldn't have let the trucks go on."

"But, Mister Hinckley," protested Lee, "we're two days late on the Red Lake location. Rimmy Jim sent me word he had the Indians and a thousand mustangs waiting. Double or no double, Brubaker said we had to go."

The director threw up his hands and gave Lee a wild look. Then one of the group called that Brubaker was coming. A car like the head of a comet with a tail of yellow dust appeared, speeding across the park.

Wesley swung a knee over the pommel and casually glanced in the direction of the dazzling blonde. She met his eyes with a subtle smile that quickened his pulse.

"We've been held up two days waiting for Bryce Pelham's double," Lee was explaining. "Got a wild hoss stampede to film tomorrow. Workin' doubles for both stars. Hinckley is bughouse now."

205

"Wal, Lee, it's not skin off your nose," drawled Wesley. "Didn't you tell me once that these delays just lined your pockets?"

"Shore. But it's hell to work with these directors even when everything clicks."

In short order the dust-rolling car arrived with a roar and a clank. Out leaped a stout young man, his eyes popping, his collar open, waving a sheaf of telegrams.

"Where's Pelham's double?" yelled Hinckley.

"He's not coming."

Hinckley tore his hair and yelped and let loose a string of profanity. "Hell of a business manager you are," he ejaculated bitterly.

Brubaker did not even trouble to reply. He thrust the telegrams under the director's nose. It took a moment to force them upon Hinckley. "Ha!" he exclaimed, and ripped open a telegram to scan it contemptuously. Then with purpling visage he tore open another and another, all of them, suddenly to pitch them high and roar like a mad bull. "Retake . . . retake! Ha! Ha! Find double for Pelham. Ha! Ha! On no account let him risk life or limb! Ha! Ha! As if the conceited, sap-headed ass would! Hurry wild horse sequences! Budget overdrawn! Ha! Ha! . . . these squawking producers!"

Brubaker and several attendants surrounded Hinckley, and for a moment there was a discordant medley of voices. At length they quieted the distraught director, who emerged from the group, his face black as a thundercloud.

"Lee, line up your cowboys!" he ordered. "Bru, drag Pelham out here, so we can see if any of those ginks can match him."

206

Lee ran shouting to his men, while Brubaker hurried up to the last car in which Wesley had observed the beautiful blonde girl star. In a moment Hinckley's assistant appeared dragging a handsome young man. Booted and spurred, wearing blue jeans and a gun belt, this tall actor roused considerable interest in Wesley.

"What is it all about?" the actor protested, shaking himself free.

"Sorry, Bryce," replied the director, meeting him. "They didn't send Jerry or anyone. Not a double for you on the lot. I've got to pick one here."

"Here? Out of this lousy line of gawks?"

"No help for it. I'm on the spot, too. Don't rave now. All the shots are long shots, except the fight between you and the heavy. We'll shoot that somehow."

Whereupon Wesley had first-hand evidence of the blood pressure and high-strung temperament credited to actors. In fact, Mr. Pelham ranted like a tragedian, and Hinckley betrayed how rapturous murder would be for a director. He wheeled away from the gesticulating, emoting star to Lee's line of eager-faced cowboys.

"No ... No ... *No!* Hell no!" he wailed, as he strode down the line. By actual count there were twenty-six riders of the range, all typical, lean, bronzed, rough. A number of them could, no doubt, have doubled very creditably for Mr. Pelham in the dangerous parts of the rôle he was supposed to portray. Not improbably in the eyes of the director, their bowlegs alone elected them to a discard. The star and camera had to be satisfied.

207

"Lee, round up more . . . ," raved the director. Then his fierce gaze alighted upon Wesley. With three leaps and a lunge he reached Wesley to pull him out of the saddle, and with a shriek of relief and joy he attempted to line him up beside Pelham. But with a resounding thump on Hinckley's chest the surprised Arizonian frustrated that move.

"Look out!" shouted Lee, almost choking, as he sprang between the men. He put his hands back to get hold of Wesley. "Hinckley, you . . . he . . . this isn't Hollywood."

"Hell you say! I wish it was," retorted the director hotly. "What's eating you, Lee? This cowboy is the best double I ever saw for Pelham."

"That might well be. But you're not . . . approachin' it proper," panted Lee. "Mister Hinckley, this is Wesley Reigh, young rancher hereabouts . . . Wes, old pard, shake hands with Director Hinckley of Meteor Pictures."

"Lee, I reckon I ought to sock him," drawled Wesley coolly. "Jerking me off Brutus that way! Why the hoss might have busted a laig for me."

"Wes, if you sock anyone, it'll be me," yelped Lee, ready to weep. "Have a heart, old pard. Hinckley was beside himself. Big company on location. No double for the star. Enormous expense . . . Wes, you're the best sport in . . ."

"Pardon me, Mister Reigh. I am a bit upset," interposed Hinckley, whose brain had evidently begun to function. "Aren't you a . . . a range rider? You're togged out like a real cowboy."

"No offense, Mister Hinckley," replied Wesley easily. "I was just scared. Brutus might have piled me."

"Ah . . . I'm sorry. But you're a perfect double for Bryce Pelham. Same height. Only a little wider of shoulder. You're made for it . . . Help me out, Mister Reigh, and name your own wages."

"Aw, I wouldn't do that," declared Wesley. His confusion might have been partly due to the blue flame of the blonde star's eyes, which he happened to see bent upon him. She was close enough to have heard the conversation.

"Can't you ride?" exploded Hinckley.

"Reckon I don't fork a hoss so well any more."

"Lee, what's the dope? Will he do?" implored Hinckley.

"Say, Wes is stringing you," burst out Lee. "He's the best range rider in Arizona. Right up to date. His father is John Reigh, our biggest cattleman, running eighty thousand head. And Wes is foreman of six outfits. Ride! Say, he can ride any hoss, anywhere, any time. And that stunt you asked about. A cowboy ridin' full tilt . . . bendin' over to pick up a scarf or a dollar? Mister Hinckley, the Navajos won't let Wes ride any more at their chicken-pulls."

"Chicken-pulls. What are they?" inquired the director, seemingly greatly impressed.

"They bury a chicken in the ground up to its neck. They shave and grease that. The idee is for a rider to ride hell-bent-for-election and grab the chicken by the neck. Wes never fails."

209

Hinckley turned to Wesley with a relieved and appealing smile. "See here, Reigh. We've got you with the goods. It'd be easy for you to race your horse and pick up a running girl . . . who weighs only a hundred and five pounds. I'd like to introduce you to the actress whom you are to rescue. If you don't fall for a chance like that with Vera Van Dever, you'll be the first man."

Hinckley made for the last car, and engaged the blonde beauty in private conversation. Meanwhile, Wesley, feeling himself trapped in the interest of his friend Lee, and inexplicably weak, ventured to win some corroboration from the disgruntled actor.

"Mister Pelham, I'm shore you agree that I'd be a failure as your double?"

"You'd be a flop and a wash-out," returned the star resentfully.

Lee interposed eagerly: "Aw, Mister Pelham, you're daid wrong. If Wes looks the part, he'd fit it to a T. Why, he can act well. He's so good that the Normal College girls in town had him in their play."

"A hick actor, oh? That's worse," sneered Pelham, manifestly further alienated by this information. "I'm sick of insulting my public with doubles that a blind audience could see didn't resemble me. Moreover, I want a double who is an actor."

"But Mister Pelham," protested Lee, holding tightly to Wesley's arm when he started and reddened at these insulting remarks, "you movie stars won't risk gettin' crippled."

The star fumed under that, and his obviously sharp retort must have been checked by Hinckley's return.

This, however, in no wise inhibited Wesley's caustic remark: "Mister Pelham, if you're afraid of busting a laig or marring your beauty, why don't you insist on playing parts that don't call for a real man?"

Hinckley broke up this little by-play by drawing Wesley toward the car. "Listen, Reigh," he whispered tensely, "lucky break for you. Miss Van Dever likes your looks immensely. She's a big drawing card. Lent to us by Paragon. She hates Westerns. I hope to God you'll give her a kick in this one."

Next moment Wesley found himself tongue-tied before the loveliest girl he had ever seen. Her wonderful eyes and her soft hand drew him irresistibly, while her liquid voice lingered music all over his name and the words of pleasure she used in greeting him. Hinckley shoved him into the car and, slamming the door, yelled for the driver to step on it. Pelham let out a yell, too, but its content was indistinguishable. The car started with a crack and a whir. Wesley fell almost into the actress' arms which certainly opened to receive him.

"Rustled! Lee, the son-of-a-gun," cried Wesley aghast, sinking back helplessly.

Vera Van Dever clasped clinging hands round Wesley's arm and leaned to him. "Shanghaied, you splendid cowboy!" she cried gaily. "But don't blame me. Only I'm tickled pink. I saw and heard the whole show. I liked the way you took it all. It's refreshing to meet someone who isn't movie-struck!"

"Don't jolly me . . . please," rejoined Wesley, in an earnest effort to get his equilibrium. "It'll be bad enough without that. I'd like to help Lee out. I'll do my best, if only you . . . don't . . ."

"I won't, but believe me, Wesley, this is a tough break for Bryce Pelham. He's always scared to death some young extra or double will get his job. If you can act as well as a cigar-sign Indian, you'll give him a run . . . I'm fed up on Bryce. He's hard to work with. You'll inject some pep into these wild-horse sequences Hinckley puts such store in."

"I'm supposed to rescue you . . . pick you up . . . or something like?" ventured Wesley.

"You'll pick up my double, Betty Wyatt. Damn it, I'd do some of these stunts, if they'd let me."

"Can you ride a hoss?"

"Indeed, I can. To be sure I wasn't born on one, like Betty Wyatt, but I could pull these stunts well enough."

"Then why don't you?"

"Listen to you! Wesley, my bosses would faint at such a suggestion. I'm a dancer, you know. *That* is insured for one hundred thousand dollars." And lifting her skirt, she laid an exquisitely shaped silken-clad ankle over his knee.

"I . . . I reckon it's worth it," stammered Wesley, his gaze attracted as by a magnet. She left her little foot hanging over his leather-covered knee, and that, added to the soft warmth of her lissome body and the fragrance of her lovely head that had come imperceptibly on his shoulder, scattered his wits, as well as his reluctance to enter into this adventure.

The car sped on, up over the pine divide, down the grade into the cedars, and at last out upon the desert.

Miss Van Dever murmured at the colorful vista in the distance, but her enthusiasm did not extend to disengaging herself from Wesley's encircling arm. Still she asked many questions about the descent to the Little Colorado and the climb into the Painted Desert. After that she wanted to know all about Wesley — his ranch . . . his horses . . . his cattle . . . and his women.

"You mean my mother . . . sisters?"

"I meant your sweethearts. You must have some."

"Wrong again, Miss Van Dever."

"Call me Vera . . . But haven't you had sweethearts . . . been in love?"

"I reckon, after a fashion. But nothing ever came of it."

"Aren't you in love now?"

Wesley caught his breath at the subtle query, invested as it was with this alluring actress's beauty. He wanted to tell her that if he was not, he pretty soon would be.

"I mustn't know my stuff, Wesley," she said cryptically, and whatever that was, she proceeded to fill that lack, to his utter rout.

The car sped on. Wesley noted vaguely the bad lands below on Moencopie Wash. Beyond, at Tube, sight of silver-ornamented Navajos and bright blankets in front of the trading post intrigued Miss Van Dever to the point of stopping the car and dragging Wesley out. She clung to his arm and led him all over the post, evincing an interest in the Indians, especially the dusky little children, that enhanced, if possible, Wesley's already exalted opinion of her. They were still in the post when Lee's cars went roaring by.

At length, Miss Van Dever seemed inclined to resume the journey and her desire for conquest. She had just settled comfortably against Wesley when another automobile passed, and in this one he saw both Hinckley and Pelham peering at them. Miss Van Dever's silver laughter rang out.

"Are all cowboys as slow as you?" she murmured presently.

"I reckon not. Some of them are pretty swift," he returned boyishly.

"Wesley, in the movies, when the hero and heroine meet on the screen, some kid in the audience will yell . . . 'Now for the clinch!' "

"Yeah. I've heard that yell myself."

"Life is terribly short in this age," she said with a sigh.

Wesley was conscious that he was slow and stupid, but what he felt for this gorgeous creature went beyond flirtation. Her proud blue eyes and the poise of her head, notwithstanding the fact that it lay upon his shoulder, made it impossible for Wesley to react as he would have done to a saucy little minx of the range.

The afternoon was far spent. As the car climbed the long grade to the mesa, a sandstorm swooped down upon it. Penetrating dust and cold put an end to Miss Van Dever's sentiment, if that had been what it was. She drew on a veil, and, complaining bitterly of the cold and the horrid dust and rotten picture business, she had Wesley wrap her in a blanket, and she collapsed upon him. The driver had to proceed very cautiously through this yellow pall, so that they made but slow progress. When the dust cloud whistled by, Wesley could see a dull magenta ball low on the horizon. This was the setting sun.

They reached Red Lake at dusk. Miss Van Dever's maid, who had been in the front seat with the chauffeur, led her off into the darkness, directed by Brubaker. Lee met Wesley to grasp him as if he were a long lost brother.

"Wes, you bunk in my tent," said Lee. "Got a stove. It's colder'n hell. Snowed some . . . Say, those movie people are sure the real thing. Got any cowboy outfit I ever saw skinned to a frazzle. They work, I'll tell the world. My trucks got here at four o'clock. Tents all up. Baggage unpacked. Beds made. And the cooks will be yelling 'come an' get it' *pronto*. Wes, you got to hand it to these movie folks."

"Wal, I been handing it, all right," drawled Wesley dubiously. "How about your hosses, Lee? And more particularly Sarch and Brutus."

"Trucked them over with my best stock. They're eatin' their heads off right now."

"Which is what I'm needing. I had a biscuit and a cup of coffee at daylight this mawning."

"All same like good ol' ridin' days. Wes, I told Jerry and the boys not to push my hosses. They'll take a while gettin' here."

"Are you going to use them in that wild hoss stampede?"

"Yes. An' a thousand mustangs as wild as any broomtails you ever chased. Ha . . . here's the supper gong. Let's go rarin'."

215

Presently, under a huge tent, well-lighted, Wesley found himself straddling a bench to sit down at a white-clothed table, steaming with savory viands. And directly across from him a distractingly pretty girl with curly fair hair and stormy blue eyes that immediately appraised him thoroughly and impartially. There were several pretty girls, all good-looking.

"Wal, Lee, I reckon you had it correct," he drawled. "I'm in for a swell time." Lee, however, was too gastronomically active to talk. Whereupon Wesley endeavored to conjure up the enormous appetite he had hinted of. The supper was bountiful and as good as a Harvey dinner, which was the standard of cowboy excellence. Presently Wesley appeased his hunger to the extent of being able to look up from his plate. There were fully fifty persons at the long table, four of whom were young women. Neither Miss van Dever nor Pelham was present.

"Lee, who's the little peach across from me?" asked Wesley.

"That's Betty Wyatt. She doubles for the star. And you work with her. Tough break, huh, pard? She was shore lampin' you."

"Yeah. I'm sort of leery," grumbled Wesley, recalling in dubious dismay how easy he had been for Vera Van Dever.

"Hinckley gypped you, pard," returned Lee, speaking low. "He and Pelham had a row. You see these stars are married or engaged . . . or Gawd knows what. And Pelham was as sore as a wet hen because Hinckley threw you in with Van Dever. I've got a hunch they

216

framed you. Anyway, don't class Betty Wyatt with that proud golden-haired dame. Betty is Western, all over an' deep down. She's a Californian, hard boiled, sure, an' knows her stuff. The company calls her Nugget, an' it suits her, believe me."

"Yeah. So that crazy galoot framed me? Lee, wait till I go out and walk it off. Then you can introduce me to the little double."

Wesley stalked out into the night. The desert wind, sweeping along the ground, rustling the sage, stinging his face with tiny atoms of alkali dust, brought to mind the nature of this Red Lake. Striding away from the noise and glare of the camp, Wesley halted on the ridge below the great octagonal trading post, the one and only white man's habitation in the barren region. It looked like a black fort, dark and forbidding, silhouetted against the cold sky. Below spread the sand slopes, down to the wide valley where the pale gleam of water identified the small lake that gave the place its name.

He stood motionless a while, feeling as always the strange sense of kinship with this solitude and wasteland. Red Lake was a gateway to the sublime cañon country of the north. But for once Wesley did not wholly respond to this influence. He was still under the spell of Vera Van Dever, still smarting at Lee's hint that she had been set to use her charms in the interest of the director. Wesley repudiated this suspicion. Nevertheless, it galled him, and, finding that he could not shake it, he went back to camp in search of Lee.

Upon passing near a big white tent, Wesley heard his name spoken by someone inside. The silvery laughter of the actress pealed out like low bells. Then Hinckley's deeper voice cut in: "For Pete's sake, have a heart, Bryce. *I* told Vera to play up to the fellow. We had to land him for this double sequence."

"Oh, hell! Did you have to make me ride in an open car through that hideous sandstorm?" demanded Pelham hotly. "Did Vera have to ride sixty miles lying in his arms?"

"A little play like that in a good cause . . ."

"Bunk! She kissed him . . . and God only knows what else!"

Here Vera's mocking, sweet laugh sent a chill over Wesley.

"Registering jealousy, Bryce? I didn't think it was in you. No one but God ever will know what else I did. I'm a capable obedient star. I obey orders, which you never do. Hinck's order was to hold this big boy in the car if I had to sit on his lap and make love to him."

"Bah! I know you, Vera. You get a kick out of it!"

"I'll tell the world! There's one cowboy who is a sweet innocent kid. It was a dirty trick to vamp him."

"Well, I'll tell you both," ground out Pelham. "If you pull any more stuff like that again, I'll slug your sweet innocent kid and walk off the set."

Wesley thought it high time for him to walk off himself. In fact he ran, burning with shame, furious with himself, utterly amazed that so lovely a creature could be such a cheat, that she should be married or engaged to such a poor excuse for a man as the actor.

The nameless and beautiful emotion she had roused in Wesley died a violent death.

On the far side of the tents a bright campfire, surrounded by Indians and members of the company, brought Wesley to a walk. What a fool he was to run like that! Run from whom? He felt hurt, sick, disillusioned. He decided he would tell Lee that these double-crossing motion picture people could make their Western without him.

As he approached the fire, he espied the girl, Betty Wyatt, standing in the light, a vivid contrast to the dark cowboy figures and the lean picturesque Navajos. She wore a white coat, and her uncovered head blazed like gold. All feeling within Wesley seemed to rush to her. Here was something real, of his own world, not sham like all these moving picture people. This girl did the dangerous work, took the hard knocks that glorified the star.

In another moment Lee was introducing him to the heavy, to a girl who was to play the part of a Navajo maiden, to others of the company, and finally to Miss Wyatt. Out in the open, with the firelight playing on her face and the wind blowing her hair, she might have been recompense for a dozen stars, except that Wesley still felt like a burnt child.

"Lee has been building you up," she said gaily. "It'd never do to believe him."

"Don't. He's an awful liar. Like all cowboys, he loses his haid at sight of a pretty girl."

"And you're the cowboy exception to that rule?"

"Me? I'm no cowboy a-tall. I have to boss half a hundred of the lazy, loony buckaroos. But I wouldn't be corralled daid being a real one."

"You talk just like me. You look like one. I wonder?"

"Lady, if I've got to act like Pelham and save you, who're doubling for Miss Dever, wal, we're starting wrong."

"I hope you can't act like Pelham, any more than I can act like Miss Vera Van Dever," replied Betty, subtly changing. Wesley caught a trace of bitterness. The laughter and glow left her face. He had struck a wrong note. The intimation of antagonism, almost contempt, for the stars struck Wesley deeply and melted away his armor.

"That makes me shore we ought to get acquainted, outside of being doubles," he said simply.

"What you mean . . . acquainted?" He encountered a look that made him feel he would like to stand honest and square before this girl. Instinctively, she had put up the bars. It did not seem much of a compliment to cowboys in general and him in particular.

"Let's walk a bit. I cain't talk heah. I'll show you something worth seeing." And taking her arm, he led her away from the fire toward the ridge overlooking the valley.

"OK. But I'll freeze to death. I'm a California rose."

"You're limping," he said, surprised, and turned to look at her.

"Are you telling me? I got hurt the other day. My trick was to jump my horse off a cliff, down at Oak Creek. We went clear under. The water was so cold it damn near turned my blood to ice. I pulled the stunt OK. But riding out, I fell off too soon, and the horse hit me."

"Oak Creek! Why, it's high now, and icy, you bet. That was pretty risky, Miss Wyatt!"

"All in the day's work. That's my job," she replied flippantly. "I'm only a double."

"But do you have to . . . to take all these chances?" he queried earnestly.

"Of course, I do."

"Couldn't you go in for regular movie work . . . being an actress, you know, like Miss Dever?"

"Couldn't I? I tried to, for two long years, and almost starved to death. At that, I'd have made the grade if I'd . . . well, just skip it. One day I had a job riding with some extras. They found me out. I've been doubling ever since."

"And you hate it?"

"Oh, my God! But I stick on my horse somehow. Fifteen bucks a day! *She* pulls down two grand every week . . . Maybe I'll get a break some day."

"Shore you will," rejoined Wesley, and fell silent.

They passed Navajos, gliding by with moccasined tread, and came out of the shadow of the huge trading post, looming like a bluff, to the edge of the ridge. Wesley kept on to a jumble of big rocks, among which he threaded a careful way to a protected shelf.

"We'll be out of the wind heah," he explained. "Hell of a place for cold wind, blowing sand, and stinging alkali dust . . . this heah Red Lake. But it's great. See that white glow above the bluff across there? The moon

221

will slide up over the rim soon. And then you'll see why Arizona has it all over California."

But she did not look across. Instead she looked up at him. "All right, big boy. You've set the stage. Get going."

"Get going? I'm not going anywhere," he returned, puzzled.

"I've been led around like this by a hundred cowboys."

"Yeah?"

"And I'm always curious to see what kind of a line they hand out. They haven't much originality. Now you . . . what's yours?"

"Oh, I get you." Wesley laughed at her half-naïve, half-scornful explanation. Then he faced her to grasp that, as a matter of course, she expected him to take her in his arms. He wanted to. There was an allurement about her as strong as Miss Van Dever's, but entirely different. There was more . . . a hard simplicity and honesty far removed from the wiles of the actress.

"Lee said they called you Nugget. How come?"

"My hair, I guess. It's real color."

"And Miss Dever's?"

"Was red last picture."

"Nugget. I kind of like that. It means solid gold . . . Wal, Betty, if you expect me to talk and . . . and pet like a cowboy, you're in for disillusion."

"Good Lord! Am I hitting the pipe? But you *are* a cowboy."

"Shore. That was a bluff of mine. I'm an Arizona cowboy, dyed in the wool, like my dad was, and my

222

grandad. It makes no difference that I'm the luckiest dog ever . . . that I'm the boss of six outfits and eighty thousand head of cattle. Betty, I'm just a plain sap cowboy. That was shore proved today."

"Don't take it too hard. Vera's specialty is making saps out of men."

"Aw! How did you know? You saw us in the car?"

"Yes. And I wasn't the only one. Bryce Pelham tore his hair out by the roots. Did that tickle me? I'm telling you, big boy."

"Hinckley put up a job on me, Betty," explained Wesley shamefacedly. "He sicced that blonde onto me. To vamp me! Land me for this double job. I was easy. I fell for her."

"Oh, Wesley, you didn't fall in love with that . . . not really?" cried Betty heatedly.

"No. But just short of it. Only a little more of her would have . . . Wal, never mind, Nugget. Meeting you is a balance. I'm daid lucky."

"Meeting *me!*" she exclaimed incredulously, with her luminous eyes upon him, as if they had just seen him clearly.

"Yes. I can be my real self."

"But, big boy, I might be like lots of the movie girls . . . like *her.*"

"Yes, you might. But are you? Tell me straight."

"I'm every way but *that* way, I am."

"That is the only way I'm counting. Look, Betty. The moon. Heah's where you go back on California."

The environs of Red Lake, all in one instant, had been transformed as if by enchantment. A full moon had sailed up over the black rim to flood the valley with a transcendent glamour of silver light. Like a burnished shield the lake glistened and glimmered in the middle of the valley of sand. Except under the looming bluff opposite, all blackness, and weird shadow, and stark desolation had vanished in the magic of the moon. An ethereal softness fell upon the desert. Far across, through the opaque veil of light loomed up mesas and escarpments leading off to mystic obscurity.

There was life down below that had not been visible until the moon shone out. A bunch of cattle trooped around the lake, slaking the desert thirst of the day. A moving, round spot, gray in the moonlight, proved to be a flock of sheep coming in to water, shepherded by barking dogs. Off to the north straggled a line of mustangs driven by Navajo riders. Their mournful chant floated up on the cold air.

"How about it, Betty?" queried Wesley, after what seemed a long while.

"Ah! I forgot where I was," she murmured. "Arizona might win if . . . Let's go, Wesley. I'm frozen."

On the way back to camp it was she who held to his arm, not lightly, and she who was silent. There was something pregnant for Wesley in that silence and that contact, something that made him decide to accept the rôle of double if only because he might share the danger with this girl, and in some way possibly minimize it for her.

Five miles from Red Lake, on the vast slope of the upland desert, the motion picture company, with the cowboys and horses, and the Navajos with their hundreds of mustangs, had assembled to film the great stampede.

Hinckley had selected a sage ridge for the scene upon which he depended for the climax and punch of his picture. To Wesley's experienced eye no more magnificent setting could have been found in all Arizona. If it could be filmed! If the gusts of cold wind, blowing yellow veils of sand and dust, would hold off for the shooting! On the south side of a gentle rise of sage ridge, fairly well down, waited the immense drove of mustangs, corralled in the mounted circle of cowboys and Indians. This band was to be driven by shooting cowboys and yelling Indians up over the ridge top in a wild stampede. Four cameras had been set up to shoot the action, one on a high rock to the extreme left, two across the cañon upon which the ridge verged, and the last on the crest of the ridge, precariously close to where the mustang horses would run. The action faced the sage slope in the north and the ruined front of white bluff, and then the red rise of the mesa to the grand crowning wall of purple rock, that wound away into infinity.

All morning Hinckley labored with details, angles, light possibilities. At high-noon he was ready for action.

"Now Lee, trot out this buckaroo you wished on me," he shouted stridently. "Oh, man, he's got to be good!"

On the moment Wesley was trying to assure Betty that his horse, Sarchedon, would not run her down.

225

"He's grand. But, oh, so wild!" she exclaimed, as she ventured to caress the noble arch of neck. "See how he flinches. Wesley, I'll have to ride him or die."

"Betty, you won't have to *die* to own him," flashed Wesley.

"Cowboy! What will I have to do?"

Lee dashed up to disrupt that colloquy. His hawk eyes glinted. Dust sifted off his sombrero. In charge of the cowboys and Indians, with the great drive at hand, he looked cool and hard, equal to the responsibility invested in him.

"Come, pard. Do your stuff."

Wesley rode out upon the ridge with him, where they were met by Hinckley, Brubaker, Pelham, and the cameramen. The director had eyes only for Sarchedon.

"What a horse! Does he know what's coming off?"

"I'll say he does."

"All right, Reigh. See that red scarf there. Ride back to your stand. When I wave my arms, put that roan devil in high, and pick up the scarf at top speed."

Wheeling Sarch back, Wesley trotted to the spot designated and turned to await the signal. When it came, he spurred Sarch into a run across the ridge. In a few jumps the roan was going like the wind. Then, with Sarch at the top of his stride, Wesley swung down in perfect timing, to snatch scarf and tuft of sage off the ground. He had not tried that trick for a long time, but it was easy. Not easy, however, was it to pull Sarch out of that gait. He wanted to run. Wesley slowed him presently and turned to ride back to the group, which Wesley observed had been joined by Betty. At a

226

distance he noted her strong resemblance to Miss Van Dever in stature and coloring. Moreover, she was dressed in smallest detail as the star had been the day before.

"Good," said Hinckley, rubbing his hands. "You'll do, cowboy. But don't ride down so thundering hard. I know I told you to. Never mind . . ."

"The faster, the better," interrupted Pelham somberly excited. "And let him cut in quicker, so his back will be to the cameras."

"Bryce, I'm directing this sequence," retorted Hinckley irritably. "Hell of a lot you'd care, if he ran Nugget down. It's a tough spot for her."

"She's doubling for Vera, isn't she? This is our big scene. It's got to be fast, hard."

"Rehearse," snapped the director, turning from the tense actor. "Reigh, listen. Vera comes riding up the slope in front of the stampede. When the mustangs show over the ridge, we trip her horse. Vera is thrown over his head. See! It'll be some fall. If she's unhurt, she'll be on her feet when you ride down to snatch her from under the hoofs of death. See! She'll catch your hand and spring to help you. *But,* if she broke her leg or got knocked senseless, which can happen to doubles, she'll be flat on the ground, and you'll have to pick her up to save her life. However, it's more than likely Vera will roll free and come up on her feet. See?"

"No. You say Vera?"

"Oh, you dumb cluck! Vera is Nugget."

"All right, I see now. As far as I'm concerned, you needn't rehearse this part. I'll get her, up or down."

227

"She weighs one hundred and five," retorted Hinckley in terse voice. "Show me how you can snatch her flat off the ground."

"Wait, Wesley," interposed Betty earnestly. "Under my blouse I'm wearing a belt of strong cloth. It's laced, but it's loose. Be sure you grab that."

Wesley smiled reassuringly at the girl. She was pale and fully aware of her danger, but gave no sign of flinching. As he rode back to his stand, he cursed this business that risked the life and limb of an unknown and courageous girl to swell the fame of a public idol. When he turned to face the gradual descent of the ridge, he saw Hinckley with hand uplifted and down on the sage Betty on her knees, waving at him. Then she slid over, face downward, in her protecting arms. The director yelled at the same time that he swept up his arm.

Wesley did not allow the roan to get his head this time. Nevertheless, Sarch hit from a lope into a run. Wesley glued his eye upon the little patch of blue that was Betty lying on the sage. Never, even in his rodeo days, had he felt this stern and set co-ordination between his faculties and his muscles. He forced himself to imagine he heard the thunder of thousands of hoofs close behind him. Then he ran down upon Betty, swooped like a desert hawk, and buried his clutch in her blouse. Braced for the expected drag, he felt the jerk of her weight, but he swept her clean off the ground as if she were an empty sack. Up he swung her into his arms.

"Ouch! You got my skin!" shrieked Betty. Then as he released that rigid grip she sagged to gaze up at him with telltale eyes. "Oh, Wes, you're one grand cowboy! I was scared to death. But now I'd double on the edge of hell, if you and Sarch were on the job."

"Wal, I reckon I'd go to hell for you at that," replied Wesley grimly, and, holding her at ease, he rode back to let her slide to the ground before the director and his group. They appeared to be in an exceedingly hot argument. Wesley gathered presently that some of them, particularly Pelham, were keen for the shot to be taken exactly as the action had been rehearsed that time. Hinckley, backed by the heavy, balked at the risk to Betty.

"Hold out! Give me air! Let me talk!" roared the director, his hair hanging wet over his flaming eyes. "It was great stuff, Bryce. Great for you! But it'll be good enough with Vera on her feet, if she's able to get on them."

"Alive or dead, *that* is the way she'll do it . . . or I'm through," rang out the star.

Hinckley appeared on the verge of apoplexy. His face turned purple. His neck bulged. "All right! All right!" he ejaculated hoarsely. "Have it your way, Pelham. But this is my swan-song with you. I'd starve to death before I'd go on location with you again."

"You'll starve, old dear, if I give you the works at the studio," returned the star viciously.

"All set. Let's go," rasped the director.

"Hinckley, wait," called Wesley. "Make this clear to me. You want this stunt repeated exactly as I did it?"

229

"Exactly. And you're a marvel, if you pull it. Just you watch me. When Vera . . ."

"You mean Betty Wyatt," interrupted Wesley. "I'm not saving Miss Van Dever's life."

"Yes . . . yes . . . When Betty comes in sight, you watch me for your cue. This red scarf."

"How far will she be in front of the stampede when you trip her hoss?"

"Damn' close, believe me. Vera . . . I mean Nugget . . . shows first . . . her horse plunging . . . rearing. The mustangs show pell-mell. Right there we'll trip her horse. At the same instant you'll get my signal. The rest depends on you, and it's a hell of a lot, cowboy!"

"It'll be OK, Hinckley, only I cain't wait for your signal."

"You cain't what?" yelled the director, imitating Wesley's pronunciation in his excitement. His eyes popped wide.

"Mister Hinckley, I see it this way," returned Wesley forcibly. "You don't know Indian mustangs. I do. They're wild. Once the cowboys open up with guns that bunch of broomtails will bust into high. I've got to use my own judgment about distance. You're subjecting Betty Wyatt to grave peril. It oughtn't be done. But if you let me ride in there, not too soon to crab your picture, nor too late to allow for unforeseen chances, I'll guarantee to pull the stunt."

"You wait for my signal," bellowed Hinckley.

"Mister, I won't even look at you. I'll watch Betty and the mustangs. Get that?" returned Wesley forcibly, and, turning Sarch, he rode off to his post. A clamor burst upon his ears, so trenchant, so raucous that Wesley nearly succumbed to the humor of it. For a moment it looked like Hornell leaned from his horse for a last word with the director, then erect with his inimitable seat in the saddle, he loped away toward the black uneasy blot of mustangs and their guards. His red scarf streamed over his shoulder. Betty Wyatt appeared on a spirited white horse, riding to her stand. One glance sufficed for the Arizonian — she could ride. Vera Van Dever sat upon a high rock. Her mocking laugh jarred Wesley's strung nerves. Other members of the company were grouped nearby. Pelham appeared to be bullyragging the director, who swung his megaphone on high as if to brain him. The star retreated with sullen stride.

Then, suddenly, the director spread high his arms, as if to embrace the perfect location. It was the homage of the artist. He appeared instinct with a rapt passion.

Wesley awoke to the reality of his surroundings. The desert scene had gathered an appalling beauty. A strong wind came rippling the bright sage. It was dry and bitter with a hint of invisible alkali. The lone cedar behind Wesley began to swish its violet-tipped foliage and moan a presage of desert storm. The sun, banked all around by huge columnar clouds, like purple ships with sails of silver, poured a dazzling light down upon the location about to be photographed. It brought out the caves and caverns of the ragged cañon, black in contrast to the pitiless white of the terraced cliffs. Dark cloud-shadows sailed swiftly up the vast sage-slope.

231

And the grand purple wall, catching the full effulgence of the sunlight, blazed in incredible glory.

In the west the sandstorm had gathered, and it was swooping its advance puffs of yellow dust and sheets of gray alkali along the colored desert floor toward the ridge. Farther back a low dense pall approached with an irresistible sweep, like an unearthly army hidden behind its sky-high banners.

Wesley suddenly understood. He had been late to grasp what had stricken the director motionless, his arms uplifted. The elements had combined to glorify his picture. This scene, with its counterfeit of drama and stampede, would be truer than any actual race of frightened wild horses the West had ever seen. The rescue of Betty Wyatt would typify the innumerable and unrecorded feats of heroism that the pioneers, the gold seekers, the hunters and scouts, the range riders of the plains had performed with never a thought of their greatness.

"*Cam-e-ra!*" Hinckley's megaphoned voice rolled stentoriously over the ridge, to bellow back in echo from the cañon. Lee's gun, held aloft, belched fire and smoke. Its sharp crack loosed a terrific din of shots and yells.

Like a tidal wave, ragged with bobbing crest, the horde of trapped mustangs rolled into thundering action. The roar of ten thousand hoofbeats drowned the boom of guns and bawl of throats. Wesley felt the solid earth shake under his horse. The splendid spectacle drew a piercing yell from him, which seemed soundless in his ears. Across the chosen gateway of the ridge raced a flood of lean wild horses, twinkling hoofs, and flying manes — a terrifying stampede, rolling on like a juggernaut, smoking and streaking dust, straight at the frightened white horse and its apparently bewildered rider. Betty's cue in the sequence was to appear trapped. Hinckley had not needed subterfuge or acting. Lee had seen the peril. So had Wesley. The girl was trapped. The speed of those wild mustangs, maddened by the guns and yells, had been the unknown quantity of the director. But the cowboys had foreseen it. Wesley was ready for it. In that crucial instant, Betty ceased to play double for Vera Van Dever. She wheeled the white horse to goad him for her life.

Savagely spurred, Sarchedon shot like an arrow from a bow. As Wesley cut in after Betty, the storm of wild mustangs zoomed over the ridge top. Fury of roar enveloped him. Fifty strides ahead, Betty's racing horse hit the invisible tripping wire. He plunged to a terrific fall, hurtling Betty far over his head. Like a catapulted diver she winged that graceful flight. But when she struck, the force was so great that she plowed through the sage, twisted sideways, rolled over and over, to lie prone, crumpled on her face.

Wesley hauled mightily on his rope-strengthened bridle. Sarch, with that rumbling avalanche at his heels, was almost impossible to check. It took two iron arms. He bore down on the blue form inert in the sage. Deadly grim and sure, Wesley bent far over in the saddle, suddenly to stiffen his legs and sweep with lowered arm. His clutching hand caught Betty — closed with steel fingers on blouse, belt, flesh. He held while Sarchedon's momentum swung the girl off the ground. Wesley felt his bones and muscles wrench. But she seemed light as a feather. Up on the pommel — safe! He reeled. A haze of red blinded him. He felt the mighty stride, the smooth action of the great horse under him. He heard the devastating thunder of hell at his heels. Sarchedon, carrying double, could not outrun the mustangs.

With clearing sight and brain, Wesley swerved Sarch to the left. His plan had been to gain the cedars. A red demon-like head, smoking, with eyes of fire and mane of flame, forged past Wesley. Lean wild ponies, specters in the flying dust, came abreast of Sarch. The engulfing stampede rolled like a maëlstrom upon him.

Wesley saw cedars close at hand, dim through the whipping streaks of dust. Sarch would gain this shelter. His shoulder collided with a racing mustang. It went down to roll with four hoofs beating the air. Sarch lunged up a rise of ground, behind the cedars.

The muddy cataract of mustangs poured down the slope. All sound ceased for Wesley. As the yellow pall raced on with the stampede, Wesley covered Betty's bloody face with her silken scarf and bent his head to endure.

Like Sarchedon he was inured to the hardships of the desert. This was a dust-laden storm, not one of the sandstorms that buried horses and men, and changed landscapes. It would pass quickly. Again his deafened ears admitted the rumbling roar of hoofs. They were rolling on, receding, lessening in volume. And soon the whistling wind obliterated all sounds of the stampede.

234

ON LOCATION

That, too, swooped by with a parting shriek. Wesley lifted his head to wipe his wet and stinging eyes.

Sunlight again, pale, steely. The air was cold and acrid. It clogged Wesley's nostrils. Indian yells whooped from the slope. Sarchedon stood champing his bit and snorting. For him the incident was closed.

Wesley removed the scarf from Betty's face. Her eyes were wide open, dark with retreating pain or terror, beautiful in the realization of deliverance. Her mouth was redder than lipstick had made it. Bits of sage adhered to the raw flesh where points of blood began to show. Dust failed to hide a cut over her temple. Gently Wesley wiped the stains away.

"Wes," she whispered. "We . . . pulled it?"

"Right-o. And I reckon we're all heah. But let's make shore." He felt her arms, her collar bones, her ribs, her legs, fearful that pressure would extract a groan from her. But all bones appeared intact. Not till he shifted her to his left arm, thus pressing her back, did she cry out.

"Ooooo! Have a heart . . . big boy!"

"Where did I hurt you, Betty?"

"My back. Holy cats! You tore my skin off."

"I reckon. But you're OK. We pulled it, and I'll bet, by God, no movie ever before equaled that stunt. Oh, how the sun and storm acted for us! What a setting, Betty! The desert gave us all the glory."

"I'm awfully glad . . . But scared? Oh, my . . . that mob of beasts! I almost fainted off my horse."

"You did a grand stunt."

235

"Yeah? All the same, till I saw Sarch . . . Oh, but he's wonderful. Wes, will you let me ride him . . . take my picture on him?"

"I shore will. He's yours."

"Mine?"

"Yes, darling."

"Darling! Oh, you cowboy!"

"I mean it, Betty. I've lived a long time in two days. These last few minutes . . . The hellinest ride I ever made . . . to save the girl I love."

"Don't . . . don't kid me," she said weakly.

"I'm terrible in love with you, Betty."

"Oh, Wes! I fell for you on sight. Was I jealous of that hateful, lovely movie star? I'm telling you . . . But now . . . oh, Wes, is it a break for little Betty?"

"If you want to put it that way. Only I reckon the break is mine . . . Betty, would you give up your career . . . as double, and sometime star yourself . . . to be the wife of a young rancher? I can give you all a Western girl could desire . . . But that glittering career . . ."

"Hush! Beside what you offer, darling, that career is a bursted bubble." She put her arms around his neck and lifted trembling, stained lips to meet his kiss.

Yells disrupted that ecstatic moment for Wesley. "Honey, they're yelling," he said, lifting his head. "I reckon they figure us daid."

"But we're alive, Wesley, alive, alive!" she flashed rapturously.

He rode out of the cedars with her and across the trampled sage-slope to the ridge top. Hinckley with his company awaited them in strained expectancy. Wesley's keen eye caught the cameraman shooting his ride across the sage, with Betty in his arms.

"Cowboy! Don't tell me she's badly hurt," cried Hinckley. "It'd spoil the greatest finale I ever shot."

"I reckon she's OK. But it shore was a bad spill," replied Wesley, and he swung out of the saddle to set Betty on her feet.

"Betty Wyatt, you're disfigured for life!" exclaimed Miss Van Dever in a tone that betrayed more than compassion.

"Yeah? To make you more famous, Vera," flashed Betty.

Hinckley embraced Wesley, then wrung his hand in exceeding gratefulness. "Oh, boy! You were great, Reigh! It was a wow . . . a knockout! The cameramen shot it all, every single detail to where the stampede and storm swallowed you. I never saw your beat for a rider and an actor."

"Wal, I was in dead earnest," drawled Wesley.

"You'll be famous. I'll offer you a contract."

Before Wesley could reply, Pelham interposed with his handsome visage distorted by jealousy and passion.

"Not with Meteor, you won't, Mister Hinckley. And you'll have to retake that sequence."

"Retake?" gasped the director. "For Pete's sake . . . why?"

"Because I won't stand for it. I warned you. This lousy conceited cowboy turned his face to the cameras."

"Ah-h! Can you beat that? I ask you!" shrieked Hinckley. "Ha! Ha! He's handsomer than you, Bryce.

Sure, I get it. But look here. That shot is in the little black boxes. And when the studio sees it, your contract will fade out for this real guy."

Wesley strode forward to confront the frenzied actor. "Mister Pelham, this heah doubling stunt is done," drawled Wesley in cool contempt. "I reckon you'll take back your dirty crack."

"Aha! All swelled up, eh?" retorted the actor wickedly. "Spooning with the star one day and stealing my thunder the next . . . too much for the glorified cowboy, eh? Here's another crack!"

As swiftly as he ended, he struck Wesley a resounding blow. But for Hinckley, who blocked his fall, Wesley would have gone down hard. In an instant he recovered to rush at the actor.

The move appeared to liberate something dynamic in Hinckley. "Back! Back! Give them room!" he yelled, fiendishly inspired. "On your job, Jimmy. Don't miss this! *Cam-e-ra!*"

Wesley heard, but his enforced entrance to an unforeseen contretemps, only increased his wrath and his purpose to give this crazy actor the beating he deserved. If it came to a rough and tumble, gloves and chaps and spurs would enhance his advantage. Wesley made at Pelham vigorously, meaning to give and take until he got his opponent's measure. During this period of the fight Wesley had the worst of it. Pelham showed a smattering of science. He could box. But no other of his blows upset Wesley. They lacked what a Westerner called beef. Moreover, they had not been at it for more than a few moments, when the actor began to sweat and pant. Compared with the range rider, he was soft.

This dawned on Wesley with an exceeding satisfaction which mitigated in some degree his surrender to rage. Pelham, manifestly realizing that he would not last long, redoubled his efforts to beat Wesley down.

The fight then became fast and furious. For every blow Wesley dealt, he received two. But his were sodden. Those to Pelham's midriff had decided effect. Once, in the whirl of battle, Wesley caught a glimpse of Betty Wyatt's face. It was decidedly no longer pale nor distressed. If the fight had been going against Wesley, Betty would not have betrayed such sheer primitive joy. Wesley heard her shrieks high above the shouts of the other spectators. Hinckley yelled through his director's megaphone a booming proof that his ruling passion had gone into eclipse. "Kill the ham actor, cowboy! Kill him!"

To Pelham's credit, he took a grueling punishment without a yelp. But he was obviously so possessed by fury that he would have to be knocked out. Wesley recognized that, and the moment. The actor's blows no longer harried him, kept him back. Regaining his breath, Wesley bored in. As the fight had progressed, his feeling had augmented with expended physical force. Blood on his face, on his hands, his own blood mixed with his antagonist's, maddened him, and he felt the lust to kill.

Plunging on the actor, then, Wesley beat down his guard, banged him with right and left. A sharp uppercut to the nose upset Pelham, who sat down absurdly. Scarlet poured from his mashed nose. Whipped, tragic, he bounded up gamely, only to meet the same rain of swift blows. Back he staggered. Then Wesley swung with all he had left — and turned abruptly away.

Betty came running to him as he untied his scarf. "Oh, Wes! Wes! Are you hurt?"

"Wipe me off . . . Betty . . . I cain't see," panted Wesley.

Lee joined them, his hawk-eyes matching the fight in his convulsed face. "Aw, pard! Every time he hit you, he hit me!"

"Yeah? I'll bet you don't feel what I feel. How's the handsome star?"

"Senseless yet. Mebbe daid. But he shore took it. Wes, we gotta hand bouquets to these motion picture folks. I heahed Van Dever say . . . 'Served him just right, the big stiff. Always throwing a monkey wrench into the works. But this picture with me in that stampede . . . riding to that fall . . . oh, what a climax! And oh, you cowboy, you can have me!'"

"Wal, I'll be dog-goned!" ejaculated Wesley.

"Lee, she can't have that cowboy," interposed Betty with flashing eyes.

Hinckley waved to the cowboys and Indians, driving the tired mustangs back up the slope. Then he bellowed through his megaphone: "All in the little black box! Let's call it a day and a picture. Scram!"

Death Valley

Of the five hundred and fifty-seven thousand square miles of desert land in the Southwest, Death Valley is the lowest below sea level, the most arid and desolate. It derives its felicitous name from the earliest days of the gold strike in California, when a caravan of Mormons, numbering about seventy, struck out from Salt Lake, to cross the Mojave Desert and make a short cut to the gold fields. All but two of these prospectors perished in the deep, iron-walled, ghastly sinkholes, which from that time became known as Death Valley.

The survivors of this fatal expedition brought news to the world that the somber Valley of Death was a treasure mine of minerals, and since then hundreds of prospectors and wanderers have lost their lives there. To seek gold and to live in the lonely waste places of the earth have been and ever will be driving passions of men.

My companion on this trip was a Norwegian named Nielsen. On most of my trips to lonely and wild places I have been fortunate as to comrades or guides. The circumstances of my meeting Nielsen were so singular that I think they will serve as an interesting introduction. Some years ago I received a letter, brief, clear, and well-written, in which the writer stated that he had been a wanderer over the world, a sailor before the mast, and was now a prospector for gold. He had taken four trips alone down into the desert of Sonora, and in many other places of the Southwest, and knew the prospecting game. Somewhere he had run across my story "Desert Gold" in which I told about a lost gold mine. And the point of his letter was that, if I could give him some idea as to where the lost mine was located, he would go find it and give me half. His name was Sievert Nielsen. I wrote him that to my regret the lost gold mine existed only in my imagination, but, if he would come to Avalon to see me, perhaps we might both profit by such a meeting. To my surprise, he came. He was a man of about thirty-five, of magnificent physique, weighing about one hundred and ninety, and he was so enormously broad across the shoulders that he did not look his five feet ten. He had a wonderful head, huge, round, solid, like a cannonball. And his bronzed face, his regular features, square, firm jaw, and clear gray eyes, fearless and direct, were singularly attractive to me. Well-educated, with a strange calm poise and a cool courtesy, not common in Americans, he evidently was a man of good family, by his own choice a rolling stone and adventurer.

Nielsen accompanied me on two trips into the wilderness of Arizona, on one of which he saved my life, and on the other he rescued all our party from a most uncomfortable and possibly hazardous situation — but these are tales I may tell elsewhere. In January 1919, Nielsen and I traveled around the desert of

244

southern California from Palm Springs to Picacho, and in March we went to Death Valley.

Nowadays a little railroad, the Tonapah and Tidewater Railroad, runs northward, from the Santa Fé over the barren Mojave, and it passes within fifty miles of Death Valley.

It was sunset when we arrived at Death Valley Junction — a weird, strange sunset in drooping curtains of transparent cloud lighting up dark mountain ranges, some peaks of which were clear-cut and black against the sky, and others veiled in trailing storms, and still others white with snow. That night in the dingy little store I heard prospectors talk about float, which meant gold on the surface, and about high grade ores, zinc, copper, silver, lead, manganese, and about how borax was mined thirty years ago, and hauled out of Death Valley by teams of twenty mules. Next morning, while Nielsen packed the outfit, I visited the borax mill. It was the property of an English firm, and the work of hauling, grinding, roasting borax ore went on day and night. Inside, it was as dusty and full of powdery atmosphere as an old-fashioned flour mill. The ore was hauled by train from some twenty miles over toward the valley, and was dumped from a high trestle into shutes that fed the grinders. For an hour I watched this constant stream of borax as it slid down into the hungry crushers, and I listened to the chalk-faced operator who yelled in my ear. Once he picked a piece of gypsum out of the borax. He said the mill was getting out twenty-five hundred sacks a day. The most significant thing he said was that men did not last long

245

at such labor, and in the mines six months appeared to be the limit of human endurance. How soon I had enough of that choking air in the room where the borax was ground! And the place where the borax was roasted in huge round revolving furnaces — I found that intolerable. When I got out into the cool clean desert air, I felt an immeasurable relief. And that relief made me thoughtful of the lives of men who labored, who were chained by necessity, by duty or habit, or by love, to the hard tasks of the world. It did not seem fair. These laborers of the borax mines and mills, like the stokers of ships, and coal-diggers, and blast-furnace hands — like thousands and millions of men, killed themselves outright or impaired their strength, and, when they were gone or rendered useless, others were found to take their places. Whenever I come in contact with some phase of this problem of life, I take the meaning or the lesson of it to myself. And as the years go by my respect and reverence and wonder increase for these men of elemental lives, these horny-handed toilers with physical things, these uncomplaining users of brawn and bone, these giants who breast the elements, who till the earth and handle iron, who fight the natural forces with their bodies.

That day about noon I looked back down the long gravel and greasewood slope that we had ascended, and I saw the borax mill now only a smoky blot on the desert floor. When we reached the pass between the Black Mountains and the Funeral Mountains, we left the road, and were soon lost to the works of man. How strange a gladness, a relief! Something dropped away from me. I felt the same subtle change in Nielsen. For one thing, he stopped talking, except an occasional word to the mules.

The blunt end of the Funeral Range was as remarkable as its name. It sheered up very high, a saw-toothed range with colored strata tilted at an angle of forty-five degrees. Zigzag veins of black and red and yellow, rather dull, ran through the great drab-gray mass. This end of the range, an iron mountain, frowned down upon us with hard and formidable aspect. The peak was draped in streaky veils of rain from low-dropping clouds that appeared to have lodged there. All below lay clear and cold in the sunlight.

Our direction lay to the westward, and at that altitude, about three thousand feet, how pleasant to face the sun! For the wind was cold. The narrow shallow wash leading down from the pass deepened, widened, almost imperceptibly at first, and then gradually until its proportions were striking. It was a gully where the gravel washed down during rains, and where a scant vegetation, greasewood, and few low cacti and scrubby sage struggled for existence. Not a bird or lizard or living creature in sight! The trail was getting lonely. From time to time I looked back, because as we could not see far ahead all the superb scene spread and towered behind us. By and by our wash grew to be a wide cañon, winding away from under the massive, impondering wall of the Funeral Range. The high side of this magnificent and impressive line of mountains faced west — a succession of unscalable slopes of bare ragged rock, jagged and jutted, dark drab, rusty iron, with gray and oblique strata running through them far as eye could see. Clouds soared around the peaks. Shadows sailed along the slopes.

Walking in loose gravel was as hard as trudging along in sand. After about fifteen miles I began to have leaden feet. I did not mind hard work, but I wanted to avoid over-exertion. When I am extremely wearied, my feelings are liable to be colored somewhat by depression or melancholy. Then it always bothered me to get tired while Nielsen kept on with his wonderful stride.

"Say, Nielsen, do you take me for a Yaqui?" I complained. "Slow up a little."

Then he obliged me, and to cheer me up he told me about a little tramping experience he had in Baja, California. Somewhere on the east slope of Sierra Madre his burros strayed or were killed by mountain lions, and he found it imperative to strike at once for the nearest ranch below the border, a distance of one hundred and fifty miles. He could carry only so much of his outfit, and, as some of it was valuable to him he discarded all his food except a few biscuits, and a canteen of water. Resting only a few hours, without sleep at all, he walked the hundred and fifty miles in three days and nights. I believed that Nielsen, by telling me such incidents of his own wild experience, inspired me to more endurance than I knew I possessed.

As we traveled on down the cañon, its dimensions continued to grow. It finally turned to the left, and opened out wide into a valley running west. A low range of hills faced us, rising in a long sweeping slant of earth, like the incline of a glacier, to rounded spurs. Halfway up this slope, where the brown earth lightened, there showed an outcropping of clay — amber and cream and cinnamon and green, all exquisitely vivid and clear. This bright spot appeared to be isolated. Far above it rose other clay slopes of variegated hues, red and russet and mauve and gray, and colors indescribably merged, all running in veins through this range of hills. We faced the west again and, descending this valley, were soon greeted by a region of clay hills, bare, cone-shaped, fantastic in shade, slope, and ridge, with a high sharp peak dominating all. The colors were mauve, taupe, pearl-gray, all stained by a descending band of crimson, as if a higher slope had been stabbed to let its life blood flow down. The softness, the richness, and beauty of this texture of earth amazed and delighted my eyes.

Quite unprepared, at time approaching sunset, we reached and rounded a sharp curve, to see down and far away, and to be held mute in our tracks. Between a white-mantled mountain range on the left and the dark-striped lofty range on the right I could see far down into a gulf, a hazy void, a vast stark valley that seemed streaked and ridged and cañoned, an abyss into which veils of rain were dropping and over which broken clouds hung, pierced by red and gold rays.

Death Valley! Far down and far away still, yet confounding at first sight! I gazed spellbound. It oppressed my heart. Nielsen stood like a statue, silent, absorbed for a moment, then he strode on. I followed, and every second saw more and different aspects, that could not, however, change the first stunning impression. Immense, unreal, weird! I went on down the widening cañon, looking into that changing void. How full of color! It smoked. The traceries of streams or shining white washes brightened the floor of the long dark pit. Patches and plains of white, borax flats or alkali, showed up, like snow. A red haze, sinister and somber, hung over the eastern ramparts of this valley, and over the western drooped gray veils of rain, like thinnest lacy clouds, through which gleams of the sun shone.

Nielsen plodded on, mindful of our mules. But I lingered, and at last checked my reluctant steps at an open high point with commanding and magnificent view. As I did not attempt the impossible — to write down thoughts and sensations — afterward I could remember only a few. How desolate and grand! The faraway, lonely, and terrible places of the earth are the most beautiful and elevating. Life's little day seemed so easy to understand, so pitiful. As the sun began to set and the storm clouds moved across it, this wondrous scene darkened, changed every moment, brightened, grew full of luminous red light and then streaked by golden gleams. The tips of the Panamint Mountains came out silver above the purple clouds. At sunset the moment was glorious — dark, forbidding, dim, weird, dismal, yet still tinged with gold. Not like any other scene! Dante's Inferno! Valley of Shadows! Cañon of Purple Veils!

When the sun had set and all that upheaved and furrowed world of rock had received a mantle of gray, and a slumberous, sulphurous, ruddy haze slowly darkened to purple and black, then I realized more fully that I was looking down into Death Valley.

Twilight was stealing down when I caught up with Nielsen. He had selected for our camp a protected nook near where the cañon floor bore some patches of sage, the stalks and roots of which would serve for firewood. We unpacked, fed the mules some grain, pitched our little tent, and made our bed all in short order. During the meal we talked a little, but afterward, when the chores were done and the mules had become quiet and the strange thick silence had settled down upon us, we did not talk at all.

The night was black, with sky mostly obscured by clouds. A pale haze marked the west where the afterglow had faded; in the south one radiant star crowned a mountain peak. I strolled away in the darkness and sat down upon a stone. How intense the silence! Dead, vast, sepulcher-like, dreaming, waiting, a silence of ages, burdened with the history of the past, awful! I strained my ears for sound of insect or rustle of sage or drop of weathered rock. The soft, cool desert wind was soundless. This silence had something terrifying in it, making me a man alone on the earth. The great spaces, the wild places as they had been millions of years before! I seemed to divine how through them man might develop from savage to a god, and how alas! he might go back again.

When I returned to camp, Nielsen had gone to bed and the fire had burned low. I threw on some branches of sage. The fire blazed up. But it seemed different from other campfires. No cheer, no glow, no sparkle. Perhaps it was owing to scant and poor wood. Still I thought it was owing as much to the place. The sadness, the loneliness, the desolateness of this place weighed upon the campfire the same as it did upon my heart.

We got up at five-thirty. At dawn the sky was a cold leaden gray, with a dull gold and rose in the east. A hard wind, eager and nipping, blew up the cañon. At six o'clock the sky brightened somewhat, and the day did not promise so threatening.

An hour later we broke camp. Traveling in the early morning was pleasant, and we made good time down the winding cañon, arriving at Furnace Creek about noon, where we halted to rest. This stream of warm water flowed down from a gully that headed up in the Funeral Mountains. It had a disagreeable taste, somewhat acrid and soapy. A green thicket of brush was, indeed, welcome to the eye. It consisted of a rank, coarse kind of grass, and arrowweed, mesquite, and tamarack. The last-named bore a pink, fuzzy blossom, not unlike pussy willow, which was quite fragrant. Here the deadness of the region seemed further enlivened by several small birds, speckled and gray, two ravens, and a hawk. They all appeared to be hunting food. On a ridge above Furnace Creek, we came upon a spring of poison water. It was clear, sparkling, with a greenish cast, and it deposited a white crust on the margins. Nielsen, kicking around in the sand, unearthed a skull, bleached and yellow, yet evidently not so very old. Some thirsty wanderer had taken his last drink at that deceiving spring. The gruesome and the beautiful, the tragic and the sublime, go hand in hand down the naked shingle of this desolate desert.

While tramping around in the neighborhood of Furnace Creek, I happened upon an old, almost obliterated trail. It led toward the ridges of clay, and, when I had climbed it a little way, I began to get an impression that the slopes on the other side must run down into a basin or cañon. So I climbed to the top.

The magnificent scenes of desert and mountain, like the splendid things of life, must be climbed for. In this instance I was suddenly and stunningly confronted by a yellow gulf of cone-shaped and fan-shaped ridges, all bare, crinkly clay, of gold, of amber, of pink, of bronze, of cream, all tapering down to round-knobbed lower ridges, bleak and barren, yet wonderfully beautiful in their stark purity of denudation; until at last far down between two widely separated hills shone, dim and blue and ghastly with shining white streaks like silver streams — the Valley of Death. Then beyond it climbed the league-long red slope, merging into the iron-buttressed base of the Panamint Range, and here line on line, and bulge on bulge, rose the bold benches, and on up the unscalable outcroppings of rock, like colossal ribs of the earth, on and up the steep slopes to where their density of blue-black color began to thin out with streaks of white, and thence upward to the last noble height, where the cold pure snow gleamed against the sky.

I descended into this yellow maze, this world of gullies and ridges where I found it difficult to keep from getting lost. I did lose my bearings, but, as my boots made deep imprints in the soft clay, I knew it would be easy to back track my trail. After a while this labyrinthine series of channels and dunes opened into a wide space enclosed on three sides by denuded slopes, mostly yellow. These slopes were smooth, graceful, symmetrical, with tiny tracery of erosion, and each appeared to retain its own color, yellow or cinnamon or mauve. But they were always dominated by a higher one of a different color. And this mystic region sloped and slanted to a great amphitheater that was walled on the opposite side by a mountain of bare earth of every hue, and of a thousand ribbed and scalloped surfaces. At its base the golds and russets and yellows were strongest, but ascending its slopes were changing colors — a dark beautiful mouse color on one side and a strange pearly cream on the other. Between these great corners of the curve climbed ridges of gray and heliotrope and amber, to meet wonderful veins of green — green as the sea in sunlight — and tracery of white — and on the bold face of this amphitheater, high up, stood out a zigzag belt of dull red, the stain of which had run down to tinge the other hues. Above all this wondrous coloration upheaved the bare breast of the mountain, growing darker with earthy browns, up to the gray old rock ramparts.

This place affected me so strangely, so irresistibly that I remained there a long time. Something terrible had happened there to men. I felt that. Something tragic was going on right then — the wearing down, the devastation of the old earth. How plainly that could be seen! Geologically it was more remarkable to me than the absolutely indescribable beauty that overcame me. I thought of those who had been inspiration to me in my work, and I suffered a pang that they could not be there to see and feel with me.

On my way out of this amphitheater a hard wind swooped down over the slopes, tearing up the colored dust in sheets and clouds. It seemed to me each gully had its mystic pall of color. I lost no time climbing out. What a hot, choking ordeal! But I never would have missed it even had I known I would get lost. Looking down again, the scene was vastly changed. A smoky, weird, murky hell with the dull sun gleaming magenta-hued through the shifting pall of dust!

In the afternoon we proceeded leisurely, through an atmosphere growing warmer and denser, down to the valley, reaching it at dusk. We followed the course of Furnace Creek and made camp under some cottonwood trees, on the west slope of the valley.

The wind blew a warm gale all night. I lay awake a while and slept with very little covering. Toward dawn the gale died away. I was up at five-thirty. The morning broke fine, clear, balmy. A flare of pale, gleaming light over the Funeral Range heralded the sunrise. The tips of the higher snow-capped Panamints were rose-colored, and below them the slopes were red. The bulk of the range showed dark. All these features gradually brightened until the sun came up. How blazing and intense! The wind began to blow again. Under the cottonwoods with their rustling leaves and green so soothing to the eye, it was very pleasant.

Beyond our camp stood green and pink thickets of tamarack, and some dark velvety-green alfalfa fields, made possible by the spreading of Furnace Creek over the valley slope. A man lived there, and raised this alfalfa for the mules of the borax miners. He lived there alone, and his was, indeed, a lonely, wonderful, and terrible life. At this season a few Shoshone Indians were camped near, helping him in his labors. This lone rancher's name was Denton, and he turned out to be a brother of a Denton, hunter and guide, whom I had met in Lower California.

Like all desert men used to silence, Denton talked with difficulty, but the content of his speech made up for its brevity. He told us about the wanderers and prospectors he had rescued from death by starvation and thirst; he told us about the incredible and horrible midnight furnace gales that swept down the valley. With the mercury at one hundred and twenty-five degrees at midnight, below the level of the sea, when these furnace blasts bore down upon him, it was just all he could do to live. No man could spend many summers there. As for white women — Death Valley was fatal to them. The Indians spent the summers up on the mountain. Denton said heat affected men differently. Those who were meat eaters or alcohol drinkers could not survive. Perfect heart and lungs were necessary to stand the heat and density of atmosphere below sea level. He told of a man who had visited his cabin, and had left early in the day, vigorous and strong. A few hours later he was found near the oasis unable to walk, crawling on his hands and knees, dragging a full canteen of water. He never knew what ailed him. It might have been heat, for the thermometer registered one hundred and thirty-five, and it might have been poison gas. Another man, young, of heavy and powerful build, lost seventy pounds weight in less than two days, and was nearly dead when found. The heat of Death Valley quickly dried up blood, tissue, bone. Denton told of a prospector who started out at dawn strong and rational, to return at sunset so crazy that he had to be tied to keep him out of the water. To have drunk his fill then would have killed him! He had to be fed water by spoonful. Another wanderer came staggering into the oasis, blind, with horrible face, and black swollen tongue protruding. He could not make a sound. He also had to be roped, as if he were a mad steer.

I met only one prospector during my stay in Death Valley. He camped with us. A rather undersize man he was, yet muscular, with brown wrinkled face and narrow dim eyes. He seemed to be smiling to himself most of the time. He liked to talk to his burros. He was exceedingly interesting. Once he nearly died of thirst, having gone from noon one day till next morning without water. He said he fell down often during this ordeal, but did not lose his senses. Finally the burros saved his life. This old fellow had been across Death Valley every month in the year. July was the worst. In that month, crossing should not be attempted during the middle of the day.

I made the acquaintance of the Shoshone Indians, or rather through Nielsen I met them. Nielsen had a kindly, friendly way with Indians. There were half a dozen families, living in squalid tents. The braves worked in the fields for Denton, and the squaws kept to the shade with their numerous children. They appeared to be poor. Certainly they were a ragged, unpicturesque group. Nielsen and I visited them, taking an armload of canned fruit and boxes of sweet crackers, which they received with evident joy. Through this overture I got a peep into one of the tents. The simplicity and frugality of the desert Piute or Navajo were here wanting. These children of the open wore white men's apparel and ate white men's food, and they even had a cook stove and a sewing machine in their tent. With all that they were trying to live like Indians. For me the spectacle was melancholy. Another manifestation added to my long list of degeneration of the Indians by the whites. The tent was a buzzing beehive of flies. I never before saw so many. In a corner I saw a naked Indian baby asleep on a goat skin, all his brown warm-tinted skin spotted black with flies.

Later in the day one of the Indian men called upon us at our camp. I was surprised to hear him use good English. He said he had been educated in a government school in California. From him I learned considerable about Death Valley. As he was about to depart, on the way to his labor in the fields, he put his hand in his ragged pocket and drew forth an old beaded hatband, and with calm dignity, worthy of any gift, he made me a present of it. I had been kind. The Indian was not to be outdone. How that reminded me of the many instances of pride in Indians! Who yet has ever told the story of the Indian — the truth, the spirit, the soul of his tragedy?

Nielsen and I climbed high up the west slope to the top of a gravel ridge swept clean and packed hard by the winds. Here I sat down while my companion tramped curiously around. At my feet I found a tiny flower, so tiny as to almost defy detection. The color resembled sage gray, and it had the fragrance of sage. Hard to find and wonderful to see — was its tiny blossom! The small leaves were perfectly formed, very soft, veined and scalloped, with a fine fuzz and a glistening sparkle. That desert flower of a day, in its isolation and fragility, yet its unquenchable spirit to live, was as great to me as the tremendous reddening bulk of the Funeral Mountains looming so sinisterly over me.

Then I saw some large bats with white heads flitting around in zigzag flights — assuredly new and strange creatures to me.

I had come up here to this high ridge to take advantage of the bleak, lonely spot commanding a view of valley and mountains. Before I could compose myself to watch the valley, I made the discovery that near me were six low gravelly mounds. Graves! One had two stones at head and foot. Another had no mark at all. The one nearest me had for the head a flat piece of board, with lettering so effaced by weather that I could not decipher the inscription. The bones of a horse lay littered about between the graves. What a lonely place for graves! Death Valley seemed to be one vast sepulcher. What had been the lives and deaths of these people buried here? Lonely, melancholy, nameless graves upon the windy desert slope.

By this time the long shadows had begun to fall. Sunset over Death Valley! A golden flare burned over the Panamints — long, tapering, notched mountains with all their rugged conformation showing. Above floated gold and gray and silver-edged clouds — below shone a whorl of dusky, ruddy bronze haze, gradually thickening. Dim veils of heat still rose from the pale desert valley. As I watched, all before me seemed to change and be shrouded in purple. How bold and desolate a scene! What vast scale and tremendous dimension! The clouds paled, turned rosy for a moment with the afterglow, then deepened into purple gloom. A somber smoky sunset, as if this Death Valley was the gateway of hell, and its sinister shades were upflung from fire.

The desert day was done, and now the desert twilight descended. Twilight of hazy purple fell over the valley of shadows. The black bold lines of mountains ran across the sky and down into the valley and up on the other side. A buzzard sailed low in the foreground — fitting emblem of life in all that wilderness of suggested death. This fleeting hour was tranquil and sad. What little had it to do with the destiny of man! Death Valley was only a ragged rent of the old earth, from which men in their folly and passion had sought to dig forth golden treasure. The air had a solemn stillness. Peace! How it rested my troubled soul! I felt that I was myself here, far different from my habitual self. Why had I longed to see Death Valley? What did I

260

want of the desert that was naked, red, sinister, somber, forbidding, ghastly, stark, dim and dark and dismal, the abode of silence and loneliness, the proof of death, decay, devastation, and destruction, the majestic sublimity of desolation? The answer was that I sought the awful, the appalling and terrible because they harked me back to a primitive day where my blood and bones were bequeathed their heritage of the elements. That was the secret of the eternal fascination the desert exerted upon all men. It carried them back. It inhibited thought. It brought up the age-old sensations, so that I could feel, although I did not know it then, once again the all-satisfying state of the savage in nature.

When I returned to camp, night had fallen. The evening star stood high in the pale sky, all alone and difficult to see, yet the more beautiful for that. The night appeared to be warmer or perhaps it was because no wind blew. Nielsen got supper, and ate most of it, for I was not hungry. As I sat by the campfire, a flock of little bats, the smallest I had ever seen, darted from the woodpile nearby and flew right in my face. They had no fear of man or fire. Their wings made a soft swishing sound. Later I heard the trill of frogs, which was the last sound I might have expected to hear in Death Valley. A sweet high-pitched melodious trill, it reminded me of the music made by frogs in the Tamaulipa Jungle of Mexico. Every time I awakened that night, and it was often, I heard this trill. Once, too, sometime late, my listening ear caught faint mournful notes of a killdeer. How strange, and still sweeter than the trill! What a touch to the infinite silence and loneliness. A killdeer — bird of the swamps and marshes — what could he be doing in arid and barren Death Valley? Nature is mysterious and inscrutable.

Next morning the marvel of nature was exemplified even more strikingly. Out on the hard gravel-strewn slope I found some more tiny flowers of a day. One was a white daisy, very frail and delicate on long thin stem with scarcely any leaves. Another was a yellow flower, with four petals, a pale miniature California poppy. Still another was a purple-red flower, almost as large as a buttercup, with dark green leaves. Last and tiniest of all were infinitely fragile pink-and-white blossoms, on very flat plants, smiling wanly up from the desolate earth.

Nielsen and I made known to Denton our purpose to walk across the valley. He advised against it. Not that the heat was intense at this season, he explained, but there were other dangers, particularly the brittle salty crust of the sinkhole. Nevertheless, we were not deterred from our purpose.

So with plenty of water in canteens and a few biscuits in our pockets we set out. I saw the heat veils rising from the valley floor at that point one hundred and seventy-eight feet below sea level. The heat lifted in veils, like thin smoke. Denton had told us that in summer the heat came in currents, in waves. It blasted leaves, burned trees to death as well as men. Prospectors watched for the leaden haze that thickened over the mountains, knowing then no man could dare the terrible sun. That day would be a hazed and glaring hell, leaden, copper, with sun blazing a sky of molten iron.

A long sandy slope of mesquite extended down to the bare crinkly floor of the valley, and here the descent to a lower level was scarcely perceptible. The walking was bad. Little mounds in the salty crust made it hard to place a foot on the level. This crust appeared fairly strong. But when it rang hollow under our boots, then I stepped very cautiously. The color was a dirty gray and yellow. Far ahead I could see a dazzling white plain that looked like frost or a frozen river. The atmosphere was deceptive, making this plain seem far away and then close at hand.

The excessively difficult walking and the thickness of the air tired me, so I plumped myself down to rest, and used my notebook as a means to conceal from the tireless Nielsen that I was fatigued. Always I found this a very efficient excuse, and for that matter it was profitable for me. I have forgotten more than I have ever written.

Rather overpowering, indeed, was it to sit on the floor of Death Valley, miles from the slopes that appeared so far away. It was flat, salty, alkali, or borax ground, crusted and cracked. The glare hurt my eyes. I felt moist, hot, oppressed in spite of a rather stiff wind. A dry odor pervaded the air, slightly like salty dust. Thin dust devils whirled on the bare flats. A valley-wide mirage shone clear as a mirror along the desert floor to the west, strange, deceiving, a thing both unreal and beautiful. The Panamints towered a wrinkled red grisly mass, broken by rough cañons, with long declines of talus like brown glaciers. Seamed and scarred! Indestructible by past ages, yet surely wearing to ruin!

From this point I could not see the snow on the peaks. The whole mountain range seemed an immense red barrier of beetling rock. The Funeral Range was farther away and, therefore, more impressive. Leagues of brown chocolate slopes, scarred by splashes of yellow and cream, and shadowed black by sailing clouds, led up to the magnificently peaked and jutted summits.

Splendid as this was and reluctant as I felt to leave, I soon joined Nielsen, and we proceeded onward. At last we reached the white, winding plain that had resembled a frozen river, and which from afar had looked so ghastly and stark. We found it to be a perfectly smooth stratum of salt glistening as if powdered. It was not solid, not stable. At pressure of a boot it shook like jelly. Under the white crust lay a yellow substance that was wet. Here appeared an obstacle we had not calculated upon. Nielsen ventured out on it, and his feet sank in several inches. I did not like the wave of the crust. It resembled thin ice under a weight. Presently I ventured to take a few steps, and did not sink in so deeply or make such depression in the crust as Nielsen. We returned to the solid edge and deliberated. Nielsen said that by stepping quickly we could cross without any great risk, although it appeared reasonable that, by standing still, a person would sink into the substance.

"Well, Nielsen, you go ahead," I said, with an attempt at lightness. "You weigh one hundred and ninety. If you go through, I'll turn back!"

Nielsen started with a laugh. The man courted peril. The bright face of danger must have been beautiful and alluring to him. I started after him — caught up with him — and stayed beside him. I could not have walked behind him over that strip of treacherous sinkhole. If I could have done so, the whole adventure would have been meaningless to me. Nevertheless, I was frightened. I felt the prickle of my skin, the stiffening of my hair, as well as the cold tingling thrills along my veins.

This place was the lowest point of the valley, in that particular location, and must have been upwards of two hundred feet below sea level. The lowest spot, called the Sink Hole, lay some miles distant, and was the terminus of this river of salty white.

We crossed it in safety. On the other side extended a long flat of upheaved crusts of salt and mud, full of holes and pitfalls, an exceedingly toilsome and painful place to travel, and, for all we could tell, dangerous, too. I had all I could do to watch my feet and find surfaces to hold my steps. Eventually we crossed this broken field, reaching the edge of the gravel slope, where we were very glad, indeed, to rest.

Denton had informed us that the distance was seven miles across the valley at the mouth of Furnace Creek. I had thought it seemed much less than that. But after I had toiled across it, I was convinced that it was much more. It had taken us hours. How the time had sped! For this reason we did not tarry long on that side.

Facing the sun, we found the return trip more formidable. Hot, indeed, it was — hot enough for me to imagine how terrible Death Valley would be in July or August. On all sides the mountains stood up dim and obscure and distant in haze. The heat veils lifted in ripples, and any object not near at hand seemed

265

illusive. Nielsen set a pace for me on this return trip. I was quicker and surer of foot than he, but he had more endurance. I lost strength, while he kept his unimpaired. So often he had to wait for me. Once, when I broke through the crust, he happened to be close at hand and quickly hauled me out. I got one foot wet with some acid fluid. We peered down into the murky hole. Nielsen quoted a prospector's saying: "Forty feet from hell!" That broken, sharp crust of salt afforded the meanest traveling I had ever experienced. Slopes of weathered rock that slip and slide are bad; cacti, and especially cholla cacti, are worse; the jagged and corrugated surfaces of lava are still more hazardous and painful. But this cracked floor of Death Valley, with its salt crusts standing on end, like pickets of a fence, beat any place for hard going that either Nielsen or I ever had encountered. I ruined my boots, skinned my shins, cut my hands. How those salt cuts stung! We crossed the upheaved plain, then the strip of white, and reached the crinkly floor of yellow salt. The last hour taxed my endurance almost to the limit. When we reached the edge of the sand and the beginning of the slope, I was hotter and thirstier than I had ever been in my life. It pleased me to see Nielsen wringing wet and panting. He drank a quart of water apparently in one gulp. And it was significant that I took the longest and deepest drink of water that I had ever had.

We reached camp at the end of this still hot summer day. Never had camp seemed so welcome! What a wonderful thing it was to earn and appreciate and realize rest! The cottonwood leaves were rustling; bees were humming in the tamarack blossoms. I lay in the shade, resting my burning feet and aching bones, and I watched Nielsen as he whistled over the camp chores. Then I heard the sweet song of a swamp blackbird. These birds evidently were traveling north and had tarried at the oasis.

Lying there, I realized that I had come to love the silence, the loneliness, the serenity, even the tragedy of this valley of shadows. Death Valley was one place that could never be popular with men. It had been set apart for the hardy diggers for earthen treasure, and for the wanderers of the wastelands — men who go forth to seek and to find and to face their souls. Perhaps most of them found death. But there was a death in life. Desert travelers learned the secret that men lived too much in the world — that in silence and loneliness and desolation there was something infinite, something hidden from the crowd.

Strange Partners at Two-Fold Bay

These are really two separate accounts of the same events relating what must constitute one of the most astonishing alliances between man and animals ever known. The first story, my father's rousing tale, came from what he had learned in newspapers and magazines about some amazing events in Australia. These accounts were later corroborated by Dr. David Stead, then of the Sydney Museum in Australia. This story was not published until 1955, more than sixteen years after my father's death. At my persuasion, it then appeared in *American Weekly Magazine*.

The second account is my version of the same incidents, which resulted from my visit to Eden, Australia, the little town where this all took place, and after reading a carefully researched book by Thomas Mead, published in 1961 by Angus and Robertson in Sydney. Although Dad's story was by far the more thrilling, what I learned was even more exciting and meaningful to me because of the curious, almost poignant, relationship that existed among three generations of the Davidson family and Old Tom, the acknowledged leader of the band of killer whales that visited Eden regularly each fall for a span of close to eighty years.

However, my father's story does contain a few inaccuracies, the most notable being that Two-Fold Bay was not geographically as he described it; in fact, it is two huge, open, semicircular bays — almost like extinct volcanic craters with a small, crooked tongue jutting out in the middle toward the east that furnishes a small harbor for the vessels of the little fishing port of Eden.

Another inaccuracy is his relating that when the whales breached on being attacked, they would make a roaring sound like a bull. As we know now, almost all sea mammals communicate with high-pitched squeaks because water is a much better conductor of sound than air.

Otherwise, the events of this story, as I discovered, are amazingly accurate, and what I did was merely to document what he had related in his version. Nevertheless, perhaps the two most important facts I learned beyond what he had written were about the extraordinary intelligence of these animals (that has since been documented by many research studies performed recently with killer whales in captivity), and the fact that, in general, their longevity period seems to be as long, if not longer, than our own.

But enough of this. I'm sure that what you are about to read will capture your imagination as have few stories ever written, and it will verify the old dictum that sometimes truth is, indeed, stranger than fiction.

"Look!" cried whaler John Davidson, "there he breaches again." The three other men in the tiny whaleboat scanned the water in the direction of their leader's outstretched arm. Almost as Davidson spoke, the huge humpback whale appeared on the calm surface of Two-Fold Bay, some six hundred yards distant, engaged in a furious battle with a school of deadly orca, known more commonly as killer whales. At this juncture, the first of the accompanying boats from the little Australian fishing village of Eden came within hailing distance of their leader. "Hey Dad," yelled Davidson's son, George, from the first boat. "What happened? Did he break off?"

"No, Son," replied the elder, "the whale was attacked by a school of orca. We had to cut the line."

"Aw," groaned young George. "Why didn't you hang on a little longer?"

Young Davidson's boat came up and passed his father's and went on; all eyes were intent on the fury ahead. The elder Davidson had to call twice to make them stop. The other boats came along then, and the rowers rested on their oars.

Suddenly young George shouted: "They're bearing down on us!"

"So they are," responded Barkley excitedly. "If they come up under us, it will be all over."

"Back away, men," ordered Davidson.

Meanwhile, the orca and the whale had sounded again, and there was only an oily slick on the water where they had gone down. Then the sea opened suddenly again directly in front of the boat. The great blunt nose of the whale emerged beyond a white ripple, and there was a loud puff of expelled breath and then a whistling intake. Not an orca was in sight. Young

273

Davidson suddenly straightened and raised the great harpoon high over his head. In magnificent action, he cast the iron. It sped true to the mark and sank half its length in the shiny hump. The young men in the boat with Davidson screamed their elation. The whale lunged and, crashing the water, disappeared. In another instant the boat stood almost on end, its stern sunk deeply and the bow rising to an angle of forty-five degrees. George Davidson clung to the thwarts while his comrades hung onto the seats to keep from being spilled out. The whale line stretched out stiff and straight, and in that precarious position the boat sped over the surface, leaving two enormous white furrows behind.

"By God," cried Barkley, "that boy has fastened onto the whale again. What an arm. He's a born harpooner."

"He's a born fool," rasped out the father, and, standing up, he cupped his hands to his mouth and thundered: "Cut that line!"

But young Davidson gave no heed, even if he did hear, which was improbable. The boat raced on and increased its speed. The leader ordered the other boats to row hard in pursuit. It was evident that John Davidson was deeply concerned over the fate of his son and the others, in view of the tales related by whalers of orca capsizing small boats and attacking men in the water. While his companions worked furiously at the oars, he scanned the bay ahead. They rowed a mile or more before he spoke. Finally he said to the others, with great relief: "Thank God, they're still afloat. There. The whale is on the surface again, and the orca are tearing into him. George's boat is up with them. The bloody fools are still fast to the whale." In the succeeding moments while the three boats were gaining, the whale was driven down seven times, but he was prevented from making any long runs. At last the leader's boat came within hailing distance.

"Cut that line, I tell you," roared the father.

This time young Davidson turned and waved his hand. "Looks good, Dad!" he shouted. "These orca are doing us a good turn."

"You young fool," bellowed Davidson, "they'll turn your boat over in a second."

"Dad, we were scared stiff. Two of the orca came up to us, and one went right under the boat, the other bit at the line, but he only pulled. Seems to me that if these orca were going to harm us, they would have done it."

"That beats me," said Barkley, laying hold of Davidson's arm. "He may be talking sense. Don't make him cut the line."

It was evident that young George could not be forced from his object. The whale and his enemies sank once more, and the skiff began to sail over the water again.

In several moments the humpback rose again to try for a short blow before he was attacked and literally smothered by the pack of killers. There were at least a dozen of them. A big white spotted orca leaped high out of the water and landed squarely upon the whale's nose in what appeared to be a most singular and incredible action. Boats and quarry were soon in the lee of the headland on the south shore and well in the smooth waters of the bay. The whale showed five times

275

at shortening intervals. Then, some miles up the bay, he began to swim in circles. The attack of the orca had frustrated his escape and exhausted him. The orca continued to harry the whale whenever he rose, and the huge black and white fellows doggedly kept leaping upon his nose. These beasts must have weighed five or six tons, and, every time, they managed to submerge the nose of the whale before it could draw a good full breath.

The fray worked into shoal water, increasing the furious activity of the orca. The whale now floundered in three fathoms not far from the shore where friends and families of the whalers had come down to see the battle. From whaler Davidson's boat there rang a sharp command: "Pull close, George! Spear him the next time he comes up!" The boatmen pulled the slack line in and laid it in the bow while young Davidson stood with his ten-foot lance waiting for the critical moment.

The whale heaved up again, slowly rolling and gasping, this time the orca paying little attention to the boat in their furious attack. However, as the rowers pulled their boat closer to the whale, the orca left off their attack, but could be seen cruising around in front. As the first skiff came right upon the rolling quarry, young Davidson elevated the huge spear and plunged it into the great beast. A geyser of blood shot high in the air. The whale let out a gasping, gurgling roar and began to beat the water with his tail in great white splashes. Quickly the boatmen backed water to a safe distance.

276

All eyes were turned upon the death throes of the great humpback. He slapped the water with thunderous crashes. He rolled in a sea of blood. His great head came out, jaws gaping, with the huge juicy tongue hanging out. Immediately the orca were upon him, tearing the tongue out of his mouth, and then, as the whale slowly sank, they could be seen biting out great mouthfuls of blubber. The whale sank slowly to the bottom in less than three fathoms of water. Presently the orca disappeared, and the great humpback lay dying in convulsions in a great cloud of murky water. As soon as the blood had drifted away on the current, the second boat put down a huge hook and anchored it in the whale. Then all boats rowed ashore where the whalers climbed out to the wild acclaim of their friends and families. As far as the whale was concerned, it would be necessary to wait a day or so until internal gases built up to bring the beast to the surface. Then he could be rowed ashore and cut up.

Excitement ran high in Eden that night. The capture of the whale presaged the beginning of an industry after a discouraging time of many years during which great numbers of huge tiger sharks had continually torn up the fishermen's nets, destroying the normal fishing industry along this part of the Australian coast.

Orca, the giant ancient enemy of whales, had been known along the coast of New South Wales and Two-Fold Bay for over seventy years. That is about as long as the memory of the oldest inhabitant. Of course, the killer whales must have ranged up and down this coast for thousands of years, as long, indeed, as whales have inhabited these waters.

There had to be a whale industry before any notice was taken of the orca and their predatory habit of chasing whales. A peculiar kind of whaling had been developed by Davidson and his men at Two-Fold Bay, probably as primitive as was ever devised by man. The whalers used what were little more than large rowboats, harpoons with long ropes, and long-poled lances with which to put the finishing stroke to the whales. Their method had been largely unsuccessful in that they had been afraid to go out into the open sea after their quarry. They patrolled the mouth of the bay until a whale came in. Then they would attack it and take a chance on being able to hold the whale within the confines of the bay. Most of the whales they sighted had been too wary, and the few monsters they actually harpooned soon departed with most of their inadequate gear. However, because of the persistence of some of the younger men under Barkley, who had been a whaler in New Zealand, and the fact that the normal fishing industry of Eden was dying, the whalers had kept up their dogged efforts.

The capture of the first whale depended a great deal upon the formation of Two-Fold Bay. It is a body of water difficult to describe. The mouth of the bay is comparatively narrow, and the inlet soon runs shallow towards the upper end, folding back upon itself, to account for its picturesque name. The background is about the same as everywhere along the New South Wales coast, very rugged and wild with white sandy beaches, green benches, and forests of eucalyptus running up to the mountain ranges that grow purple in the distance. The little town of Eden is not only picturesquely situated, but felicitously named.

This particular morning the whalers had been unusually lucky, and had sighted whales only a couple of miles out and well within the calm water of the bay. The elder Davidson's boat was first to come within throwing distance of one of the giant humpbacks. Barkley, heaving the heavy iron harpoon, had made fast to a whale and the fight was on, to the grim concern of the older men and the yelling chorus of the younger. The whale made off with three or four hundred yards of rope and then slowed down. The three other boats followed, rowing as swiftly as they could, but losing ground. But, as usually happened, Davidson's craft was towed to the mouth of the bay. Presently the whale came to the surface and began to thrash around in a commotion of white water. Barkley, standing in the bow, holding the rope, suddenly let out a yell — "Orca, by Lord!" — and pointed ahead. "Look, look. See those big black fins standing up? They belong to bull orcas. Bad luck. It's as much as our lives are worth to go near that bunch."

Davidson and the other two men in the boat saw the big black fins swirling around the whale, forcing him down, and Davidson cried: "Bad luck, indeed! We'll have to cut him loose," and he made a move with a naked blade.

Barkley motioned him to stop. "Let's wait. There's five hundred yards of good rope out there, and we can't

279

afford to lose it." The whale sounded, and the orca disappeared. The strain on the whaling line slackened. Presently, as the men waited in tense excitement, the big humpback came to the surface surrounded by the thumping, splashing school of orca. The boat was close enough for the fishermen to hear the bellowing roar of the whale and the vicious splashing of the killer whales.

Barkley had heard a whale roar before in its terror, but the other men had not. It was a strange, strangling sound. Then one of the orca leaped into the air, a huge black glistening body with white spots, and landed squarely on top of the whale. Sounding with a tremendous splash of his tail, the big humpback went out of sight as did his tormentors. Again the whale line went whistling off the bow. As the boat gathered momentum and rose on its stern, fairly flying through the water, Davidson leaped forward and cut the line. The boat settled down, slid ahead a few yards, and finally came to a stop. The whalers, gray-faced and sweating, eyed each other in silence. Finally Barkley, wiping his face, spoke: "I guess there wasn't anything else to do, but it's hard to swallow the loss of all that fine rope and the whale, too."

"We're lucky to get rid of him," spoke up one of the other men.

This would have been the end of it had not the younger men rashly made fast to the whale again and, with what seemed the almost incredible aid of the orca, succeeded in capturing him.

That night the men of Eden speculated excitedly on their good luck.

"Men" said Barkley, "I've got to believe my own eyes. These orca are as keen and bold as any hounds that ever chased a stag. Nearly every whale killed in deep water sinks to the bottom. The orca know this. If they kill a whale in the open sea, it sinks before they can satisfy their hunger. This bay is a trap. The orca often hang out here and patrol the mouth until a school of whales comes along. Then they deliberately separate one from the others and drive him ashore. That accounts for the skeletons of whales we occasionally find here in shallow water. But, of course, every battle with a whale doesn't end successfully for the orca. They're intelligent enough to see that we're a help. They intercepted this whale and sent him back."

Young George answered: "As the chase kept on, they showed less fear of us."

"Well," spoke up his father, "I wonder . . . it remains to be seen whether they'll do it again."

On the second day, about noon, while the whalers were at work, cutting up their humpback, a scout came running down to the wharf to shout the exciting news that there was white water in the offing. Whaler Davidson took his glass and went to an elevated place to take a look. A school of whales was passing the mouth of the bay, and one of them had already been cut adrift from his fellows and was being hemmed in and driven into the bay by the whale killers. Davidson went back to his men with the exciting information, and two boats made ready to go out.

When they were about a mile off, it was evident that there was a big school of orca, and that they were proceeding with remarkable energy to prevent the whale from getting back down the bay. According to Davidson, who had the glass: "There's a small bunch right at him and a larger number back a ways in a half circle and then a line of others stretched across the bay where the water is deep."

The whale, finding himself in shoaling water, made determined and persistent efforts to break the line of his tormentors, but, whenever he charged back, a half dozen bulldogs of the sea charged him and tore at his head, compelling him to sound and turn. From the shore, watchers could see the long green shadow moving up the bay and also the flashing black and white orca at his head. The pursuit in a straight line soon ended, and a ring of orca encircled the whale. They were on top of him every moment, and, as his efforts to rise to breathe were frustrated, he grew bewildered, frantic, and nearly helpless, although the pursuing orca still kept a safe distance from his tremendous tail. There came a time when the humpback slid up on his side with a crooked-fin orca the whalers had dubbed Humpy, hanging onto his lip like a bulldog. What a strange blubbering roar the whale made. It was a loud noise and could be heard far beyond the village. Presently the whale shook free of Humpy and went plunging again, around and around. He was so big and powerful that the orca could not stop him, and Old Tom, as the whalers had named the orca with the white spots, could not wholly shut up the whistling blowhole. This humpback might have escaped his relentless enemies if he had had deep water. But between him and the dark blue water of the bay were stretched two lines of menacing orca that charged him in a body when he headed toward the opening.

It became apparent then that the orca would require the help of the whalers to finish the humpback. Davidson sent out his son and a crew of four, also a second boat with four more men. The men were still afraid of the orca, but there did not seem to be any reason for this. The orca, with the exception of Old Tom and Humpy, kept away from the boats. And it was astonishing and incredible to see their renewed ferocity when the whalers came upon the scene. Young Davidson soon harpooned the whale, which lunged out and then tried to burrow in the mud at the bottom in its mad endeavor to sound. But the whale was prevented from going any distance in a straight line. He was driven around to where a harpooner in the second boat soon made fast to him. They had him from two sides now. When the second harpoon went home, it struck a vital place, for it energized the whale to a tremendous rolling and heaving and a mighty buffeting of the water with his great tail. Out the long black head came again with the white smoke from the blowhole accompanied by a strangling whistle. Three of the orca were now hanging onto his lips, wiggling their shiny bodies with fierce and tenacious energy. Old Tom cut the water in a grand leap to alight fairly on the side of the whale's head and slip off, raising a great splash. That appeared to be a signal for the remaining orca to charge in close. In a maëlstrom of white and bloody water, the whale and his attackers fought a few moments in a most ferocious manner. At the end of this attack, the whale heaved up with his great jaws spread, and, as he sank back, the orca in a solid mass tore at the enormous tongue.

Not long after the carnage had settled, several huge triangular-shaped fins were seen headed out to sea. So far as the orca were concerned, the engagement was ended. They swam away, leaving the whalers with a seventy-foot humpback, and establishing the fact for all who had seen the incident that they had leagued themselves with the whalers.

Then began a strenuous season for the whalers and all who were concerned in the disposition of the great carcasses. The inhabitants of Eden labored early and late. Seldom did they have a whale cut up and his carcass towed away to the other side of the bay before the orca would drive in another victim.

All through June the partnership between the whalers and the orca grew more successful. The news had long since traveled all over Australia, and many visitors made the long journey to the little hamlet to verify the strange and romantic tale. During July the whalers processed seven whales, which was about all they could handle with their limited equipment. Then toward the close of that month, the whales passed by in fewer numbers until only a stray was seen, here and there. When at last they were gone, the orca were seen no more. The whalers speculated upon what had become of them and concluded that they had followed the whales. They were all sorry to see the orca go, hardly hoping that they would ever turn up again. But on the first of June the next year, on the very first day the whalers went out, they were amazed and delighted to see the orca patrolling the mouth of the bay. Old Barkley expressed the opinion that he thought they were as glad to see the whalers as the whalers were to see the orca. He proved his point when Old Tom, Humpy, and another orca they had dubbed Hooker, deliberately swam close to the boat to look them over — as if to identify them.

The orca were back, and it was certain that the well-known leader of the pack and others that had been named the summer before had returned to Two-Fold Bay. Barkley identified Big Ben and Typee, while the elder Davidson recognized Big Jack and Little Jack and an enormous lean orca without any white marks they called Blacky. In less than two hours from the time the orca showed themselves to the whalers, they had a humpback headed into the bay. In due course they drove it into shallow water where the combined energies of whalers and orca soon added another humpback to their list.

There were more whales that summer and more orca to help in the pursuit of them. When that season ended, it was an established fact that a crew of whalers had enlisted a school of whale killers to help them in their work.

Even more remarkable, on at least two occasions the orca had driven in a whale and helped to kill it, but made absolutely no attempt to tear at the tongue, the juicy morsel that attracted them so powerfully. After the kill had been executed and the whale had sunk to the bottom, the orca had left without further mole-station.

Davidson had done a good deal of thinking about this and had talked to his comrade Barkley about it. They decided that if the whale killers did not tear out the tongue of a crippled whale and otherwise chew him up, it meant that they were not hungry. The deduction to be made, then, was that this intelligent school of orca, or at least the leaders, Old Tom, Humpy, Hooker, and one or two others, cut a whale adrift from its herd, chased him inland, and deliberately helped kill him for no other reason than to maintain their partnership with the whalers.

One night Davidson saw his conclusion borne out in a startling manner. Shortly after he had gone to bed, he was awakened by a succession of loud rapid reports almost like pistol shots. He listened wonderingly. His house was some distance from the bay, but he had often heard the splashing of great sharks or the blowing of porpoises and other marine sounds that went on in the dead of night. When it occurred again, somewhat more clearly, he decided it was a fish of some kind.

Davidson called to his son, who slept in the next room: "George, slip on some clothes and grab a lantern and go down to the wharf and see what's making that noise."

"What noise?" asked George sleepily.

"Don't you hear it? Listen."

Again the sound rang out — short, sharp, powerful smacks on the water. George let out a whoop, and his bare feet thudded on the floor. "Sure, I hear that," he answered. "Something's up for sure." He dressed, lighted a lantern, and rushed out.

He was gone so long that the elder Davidson nearly fell asleep waiting for him. But at last a light gleamed through the murky darkness, accompanied by the rapid tread of bare feet. George entered, letting the cool misty air in with him.

"Dad, what do you think?" he burst out. "Our band of orca have brought in a big whale, and some of them are lobtailing while the others are fighting the whale. Struck me funny. What would they be doing that for?"

"No reason in the world, Son, except to wake us up and tell us to come down and do our part. Go wake up the men and hurry down to the wharf," he ordered, as he got out of bed. Davidson dressed hurriedly, putting on his great raincoat, and, lighting the lantern, he sallied forth into the black night. Several times before he reached the wharf, he heard loud buffetings on the water. As he drew closer, he also caught the sharp splashes and quick blows that he recognized were made by orca. Then he heard the strangled obstructed puff of a whale trying to breathe. A second later came the unmistakable and fearsome sound of the whale roaring like a wounded bull.

"By Halifax," Davidson uttered. "I thought I had seen and heard everything before, but this beats me all hollow." He halted on the wharf and cast the beam of his lantern out upon the dark waters. He could see fifty feet or more from where he stood, and, as he watched, there came a surge of water, a short deep whistle and intake of air, and a huge orca, blacker than the night, with his white spots showing like phosphorescence, plunged in the track of the lantern to show the gleaming eye and the tremendous seven-foot fin of Old Tom. Davidson yelled with all his might. It was as if he were talking to the orca. The orca made a plunging sound and vanished. Then out of the darkness came rapid cracking slaps of the giant tail on the water, loud and sharp as the shots from a rapid-fire gun.

Davidson stood there marveling. The lobtailing ceased. Out there in the bay, a hundred or two hundred yards, resounded the rush and slap and roar of battle between a cornered whale and his enemies. Then lights appeared from all directions, and soon Davidson was joined by a dozen men. They were excited, eager, and curious to know what it was all about.

"Our pet hounds have chased in a whale, and they're fighting him out there," replied the chief.

"What can we do?" asked Barkley. "It's dangerous enough in the daytime, let alone at night."

"There's no danger for us, if we keep out of the way of the whale."

"But we ought to wait until more light," objected Hazelton.

"It's a long while till dawn. Our orca have brought in a whale, and they have signaled us to come and help. We couldn't let them down now. We'll take four boats. I'll call for volunteers."

Twelve of the score or more men signified their willingness to take the risk. This was enough to man the boats. When all was in readiness, leader Davidson shouted for them to follow him and headed out over

288

the black waters of the bay. While two of the crew rowed the lead boat, another held the lantern high, and Davidson stood in the bow of his boat with his harpoon in readiness.

"Back water!" he called presently. "Steady. Rest your oars. Now everybody listen. We got to tell by the sound." From the thrashing and swishing of the water, it appeared that the whale and his attackers were approaching the boats. After an interval of quiet, when undoubtedly the whale and the orca were underwater, there came a break just ahead, and, as the long black snout of the whale appeared, it emitted a resounding blast as loud as a steam whistle. Davidson poised the harpoon aloft. He was a big man, and he easily held the heavy iron. As the whale came sliding by, he cast the harpoon with unerring and tremendous force. In the light of the lantern, it appeared to sink half its length in the side of the whale.

"Get away! Get away!" boomed Davidson as he sank to his knees with the line in his hands.

With a thunderous surge the whale answered the inthrust of the steel. He leaped half out of the water. As he came down, big waves rocked the boat, nearly capsizing it. Then the whole pack of orca were upon their victim. The sounds of watery combat and the frenzied plunging of the whale united in a deafening din. Orca and whale passed out of the lantern's illumination. Davidson yelled at the top of his lungs, but his words were indistinct. The lights of the other boats came close. The whale sounded with his demons hanging onto him, and in the sudden quiet yells became distinguishable.

"I'm fast, men, good and hard," called the leader. "The line is going out. He's circling. Better hang close to me so that, when he comes 'round, you can get another iron in him ... Mike, lend a hand here. They're blocking him ... turning him ... We can risk a tow ... Hey, you all back there, hang close to us, it's getting hot."

Davidson's boat was now being hauled through the water at a considerable rate. The line showed the whale to be circling, but the lantern, that had been set down, cast very little light ahead. However, the lanterns of the crew behind Davidson helped. Suddenly the line slacked, the boat slowed down, the turmoil of orca and whale ceased again. "He's sounded!" yelled Davidson. "Now look out!" His warning cry was echoed by the men in the nearest boat. They had seen a gleam in the water ahead in time for them to row aside, just missing the blunt nose of the whale as it heaved out. Again that whistling strangled intake of breath, a hollow rumbling roar, then the surge of a tremendous body in friction against the water, and after that the swift cutting splashes of the orca and the dull thuds of their contact with the whale. The second boat did not escape an upset. It capsized, and all the men were thrown into the water. The third boat sped to the rescue, and, just as quickly, young Davidson, in the bow of the fourth boat, with a magnificent throw, made fast to the sliding black flanks of the whale. The two boats towed by the whale passed the others and sped into the night. Soon the orca stopped the crippled whale and killed it. When

290

gray dawn broke soon after, the orca had left the scene of carnage, and the whale had sunk.

The successful summer passed, and another followed. The fame of the whale killers continued to spread abroad, bringing many people to the bay, and the little hamlet of Eden grew apace. The whaling business flourished, and there was some talk of installing more modern methods of hunting the leviathans. But nothing ever came of it. The whalers preferred their own method and the help that was given them by the orca. So the years passed, bringing few changes. The older whalers passed on or moved away or gave up their work to sit in the sun and tell tales about their great experiences with the orca. Davidson's son George became the leader of the whalers, and other young men took the place of the old. For thirty years there was little alteration in the number and actions of the orca. Led by Old Tom and Humpy and Hooker, this pack of sea wolves patrolled the mouth of Two-Fold Bay and hunted within reach of the harpoons. And as they grew more proficient in their attacks, they also grew friendly with their human allies.

It was related of Old Tom that he grew mischievous and liked to play pranks, some of which gave the whalers a great deal of concern. Several times he made off with the anchor of a small boat, dragging the boat behind him. This was play, and after a while the whalers seemed to enjoy the experience as much as the orca. But the first time that Old Tom took the line fastened to a harpooned whale and ran off with it, the whalers were frightened and concerned, and had a difficult time

291

recovering it. There didn't seem to be any reason for this behavior except playfulness on the part of the big fellow. The remarkable thing was that this trick of Old Tom's never lost them a whale.

He and old Humpy often swam alongside the small boats with every appearance of friendly interest. The whalers never entirely gave up their fear of falling overboard when orca were around. A heritage of confidence had come down to them from the older whalers, but it applied only to Old Tom and Humpy and Hooker and possibly one or two others. The young whalers were still afraid of the less tame and friendly orca.

Most notable of all stories told by the old whalers, and handed down to their sons, was the time the orca, either by mistake or design, drove a sperm whale into the bay. Sperm and blue whales were rare along the coast, and the whaling men had given the sperms a wide berth. Owing to the superior bulk and speed of this species, and the fact that they have great teeth in the lower jaw, and habitually charge boats when attacked, sperm whales are considered most formidable and dangerous foes.

That day, two boats were out ahead, the crews composed of younger men. Then two other boats, with some experienced whalers among the crews, followed the first two and found them fast to a whale they didn't know was a sperm. The older men, reluctant to show a shy spirit by cutting this whale loose, came to the assistance of the bold young whalers. They fought the big beast all the way up the bay to the shoal water.

292

Here again the whalers were treated to an exhibition of the amazing intelligence of the orca. When the sperm headed toward one of the skiffs, Old Tom and his partners would lay hold of the whale, carefully avoiding the great jaw, and fight him and nag him until he changed his course. This was one whale Old Tom did not try to stop breathing, for a major reason, the blowhole of the sperm was clear out at the end of his nose and much nearer the formidable jaws and huge teeth than in other species of whale. As a consequence, this fight was a longer one, fiercer and harder than any the whalers had ever seen. It was owing, of course, to the superior strength and stamina of the sperm, and the impossibility of the orca's interfering with his breathing. But when the whale reached the shallow water, the whole pack attacked him, and they made up in ruthless fury what they had lost in the way of technique. The men now pressed in and tried to get another harpoon in the sperm.

The whalers had noticed a number of huge tiger sharks following in the wake of the bloody mess, and this fact did not lend any pleasure to the thought of a capsized boat. George Davidson's skiff finally drew in close to the sperm, and George, by a very long throw, got his harpoon into the side of the whale — but it did not hold. Suddenly the sperm turned as on a pivot. The slap of his great tail staggered the boat and threw George into the water. Cries of alarm rose from the other whalers. The boat from which George had fallen passed him with its momentum, and, before the crew could back water, two of the great orca deliberately

293

swam up to Davidson. The sperm whale was still close, rolling and thrashing around, and everywhere were other orca and a number of the big gray tiger sharks. One of the men, standing in the bow of the skiff with a rope, yelled at the top of his lungs: "It's Old Tom and Humpy! They're not going to hurt George!"

And marvelous to relate, that is the way it was. Old Tom and Humpy, who had been friends with the whalers for fifty years, swam on each side of young Davidson and guarded him until his own swimming and a rope tossed from the first boat made his rescue possible. The orca actually followed until George was safely in the boat.

The fight with the sperm was then renewed, and in time, when the whale's weakening enabled the whalers to get in two more harpoons, the fight eventually ended up with victory for the men from Eden. Orca and sharks chewed up the whale pretty badly, but they could not injure the great head which formed at least a third of this species' body and which contained the valuable sperm oil. However, several of the orca seemed to have been injured in this fray. One was seen to swim away after the others as if he were crippled.

No yarn handed down from the old whalers to the young compared to this one. And the young whalers made the most of it. From that day, Old Tom and Humpy became heroes. But when Old Tom's body washed ashore in Two-Fold Bay shortly afterward, the villagers were stunned. Some were in favor of sending the skin to Sydney to be mounted, but the whalers would have none of this. They built a memorial for Old Tom right there in Eden.

Humpy and the other orca well-known to the whalers were often seen in the ensuing years. But whales finally became so scarce that the whalers did not go out, and the orca took to other hunting grounds. Finally the whaling business waned and died, but never the romance and wonderful doings of the orca whale killers. It was said by many that the friendly orca had all died, but others thought they'd roamed on to better hunting waters.

There are men now living in Eden who will take pleasure in verifying the story I have here told. Some will tell it conservatively; others will embellish it with the most remarkable fishing yarns that were ever invented. And they say an occasional fight between orca and whales can be seen to this day off the mouth of Two-Fold Bay.

Of Whales and Men
by Loren Grey

Eden is a quiet little town of perhaps forty-five hundred people, whose major industry is mostly fishing, some sporadic logging nearby, and a huge chip mill, located on the bay some ten miles across from the town. Two-Fold Bay itself is a magnificent open harbor with eleven beaches, most of them relatively deserted, many in view of the town. There are several better-class motels in Eden, but tourists are still relatively scarce. The only contact is by road from Sydney — a distance of some three hundred miles — or Canberra, the Australian capital city, which is one hundred and fifty miles away. But I soon learned that Eden's history does not revolve solely around its departed whaling or logging industries. In fact, a shipping magnate, a visionary entrepreneur named Benjamin Boyd, arrived in Eden in 1842, and dreamed of Two-Fold Bay as a third deep-water harbor, equidistant between Melbourne and Sydney, and with a center of commerce rivaling both. One of his first promotions, in 1845, was to build a magnificent hotel on the southeast shore of the bay, the remnants of which still stand today. Boyd also started a shipping run between Sydney and Melbourne with stops at Fort Jackson, Fort Phillip, and Two-Fold

299

Bay. Furthermore, he bought thousands of acres of property on which to raise cattle and sheep, and established the first permanent whaling station in Eden, although this was before the time of the Davidsons and their orca allies. But Boyd's administrative abilities apparently did not match his vision. In 1849, the whole venture sank into bankruptcy. An administrator was appointed from Sydney, and Boyd was relieved of his position and holdings in Eden. He then turned his attention to gold prospecting, and sailed his yacht, *The Wanderer*, to try his hand at mining in California, but after a year of fruitless effort he started back. On the 15th of October, 1851, he stopped at the Ponape on the Caroline Islands. Here, accompanied by a native, he went ashore to attempt some duck shooting. Sounds of gunfire were heard from aboard his yacht, but no trace of Boyd was ever found when a search was made ashore. There were rumors that the islanders had killed, cooked, and eaten Boyd, but no facts ever came to light.

Later efforts were made to turn Two-Fold Bay into a shipping center, particularly with the discovery of gold at Kiandra in 1859. But the gold rush subsided as quickly as it came, and the adroit business promoters in Sydney, who did not want a rival, blocked all efforts by the local residents to build a railroad connecting Sydney, Eden, and Melbourne.

And perhaps it is just as well. Most of the townspeople with whom I talked appeared to be content to let Eden remain as it was and is today. They seem almost bemused by the stunning tales of Eden's

past and particularly of the legendary whale killers —
as if it were almost a lost and forgotten fable.

I visited Billy Grieg who, at age ninety, is the last
surviving member of the whalers that went out in
George Davidson's little boats when Old Tom and
Humpy were still about. But he was shy and ill at ease,
so I did not press him for details of the past. However,
it was Bert Eagen, the garrulous old caretaker of the
tiny Eden Museum, located in the center of town, who
gave me more than my fill of fascinating tales about the
great days of the past. The skeleton of Old Tom is
preserved there in its full splendor, along with many
other artifacts, paintings, and replicas covering more
than a hundred years of Eden's history. Of course, Bert
Eagen could hold forth endlessly on any number of
other subjects relating to Eden and its history.
However, much of his talk about the whale killers
concerned Old Tom and his uncanny intelligence and
obvious affinity with the Davidson family rather than
with the competing whalers and their boats. Much of
what he said is also documented by Tom Mead in his
carefully researched book, *Killers of Eden*, in the form
of interviews with George Davidson, his wife, Sarah,
and surviving children, and other members of the
whalers' crews still living at the time — as well as
numerous old newspaper clippings and photos of the
killer whales that are still available in a booklet
published by the museum.

By the time young George Davidson was twenty-five
years old and taking over for his father, who was
nearing retirement, he was already aware that Tom

was different from the other killer whales. On one occasion George fell overboard while their boat was fastened to a whale, at a time when there were hordes of huge sharks in the vicinity. Tom immediately left his pursuit of the whale, came down, and swam by George Davidson to keep the sharks at a safe distance till he could climb back in the boat. Tom also had a habit which, in the beginning, was very frightening to the whalers. Often when a whale was fastened, he could grab the harpoon rope with his teeth and pull the boat toward the whale with great speed. But the apprehension among the boat crews subsided when they realized that he was only being playful. At no time did he ever act in a manner that endangered their safety.

On another occasion, a harpooned whale had escaped into deeper water and sounded. The men had to cut the last of their ropes, or the craft would have been pulled under by the whale. The whalers were disconsolate because they had lost their quarry as well as many hundreds of feet of valuable rope. But, suddenly, the whale reappeared about half a mile away with the killers still harassing it. When the boats caught up, they found that Tom was hanging onto the rope they had abandoned for lost.

Some time after the turn of the century, some of the other whalers began using a gun with an explosive charge in it, which had been developed to kill the whales after they had been harpooned. George Davidson had warned the opposition boats against this practice because he felt that this would upset the killer whales, and perhaps frighten them away. But the other whalers went ahead and used it anyway. The next day two whales had come into the bay, and, after the first charge was used, the killers were only willing to stay with a whale that Davidson's boats had harpooned. His boats were always painted green, easily identified by the orca, and after that they left opposition boats strictly alone. As a result, in all his years of whaling, George Davidson never used a gun in his attempts to subdue a whale in Two-Fold Bay.

The Davidsons also found out that, when the killers would find a whale at night and chase it into the bay, they would signal to the whalers by slapping their tails loudly on the water — which in whaling parlance is called lobtailing.

As a result of this kinship with these strange creatures of the deep, George Davidson, his family, and his crew prospered. George's son, Jack, grew up and was working alongside his father on the whaling boats, and the alliance kept up till the 1920s. But by this time, George and his men had become aware that things were not the same. Some of their old friends were missing, although the pack was still led by Old Tom, with Humpy, Hooker, and the Kincher, Charlie, and young Ben as his lieutenants. Humpy and Hooker were showing signs of age, although Old Tom strangely enough seemed to retain his perpetual youth.

Then tragedy struck the Davidsons. Jack and his wife, Ann, had taken their dinghy with their five children out over the surf at the mouth of the Kiah River, where they had established the whaling station, to go to Eden for supplies. It was a perfect November Sunday, with a cloudless sky and a mild breeze just barely ruffling the calm waters of the bay. Norman Severs, a member of George's crew, and his wife, Elsie, had come over to the Davidsons' for Sunday dinner.

But George was uneasy that afternoon — Jack seemed to be taking longer to return than usual. "Looks like a storm brewing," he said to Norman. "We've had good weather too long."

"Barometer's OK, but there was a fair sea building up when we came across," Norman replied.

"Well, I'll go down and take a look for Jack," George said.

It was only a few minutes later that they heard George's frantic voice calling: "Come quick, Norman, and you, too, Elsie. Jack's boat has capsized on the bar . . . hurry for God's sake!"

George, Norman, and Elsie rushed down to the shore and managed to get a whale boat out onto the now thunderous surf. They reached the overturned dinghy and were barely able to drag Ann and Tommy aboard just as she and the little girl clinging around her neck lost consciousness. In another minute she would have slid from her desperate hold and gone under the waves. But there was no sign of Jack, Roy, or little Patricia.

All the boats that were available from Eden turned out to search for the bodies. The next day they found the children, but there was still no evidence of Jack. Incredibly enough, Old Tom was there, swimming back and forth where the dinghy had capsized, as if he were trying to guide them to where the body was — and he did not leave there for days on end. Only once did he abandon his lonely patrol outside the bar, when other killer whales had driven a huge humpback into the harbor. The fight was long and frenzied, but eventually the injured whale managed to reach the open water and escape. Old Tom immediately returned to his vigil at the bar. After five days, they began to believe that the sharks had, indeed, gotten Jack. But Old Tom was still out there patrolling, so perhaps there was hope.

On the sixth day, Bill Grieg and Archer Davidson, two of George's men, discovered Jack's body very close to where Tom had been circling. The next day the Davidsons took Jack's body in their launch out over the bar to Eden for the funeral. Incredibly, Old Tom was still there, and followed the launch all the way over to Eden. When the body, in its simple wooden casket, was finally lifted onto the dock, Tom made a circle as if to salute them, then turned out and headed toward the open sea. That was the last they saw of him until the following May at the start of another winter whaling season. George often thought about this episode in later years, particularly after Old Tom's death, with a mixture of sadness and near reverence. Tom had then become a member of the family as much as Sarah, his other surviving children, and his grandchildren.

But somehow, after Jack's death, things were no longer the same. While George Davidson whaled several more years with casual crews, he had lost his enthusiasm since the death of his son. Furthermore, the whaling they had known was just about over. For one thing, the killers seemed to be dying off one by one. The pack had dwindled down to Old Tom, Humpy, and a few of the younger orca. Then Humpy disappeared. Alex and Bill Grieg saw him for the last time when fishing one day near South Head, and they knew Humpy would not come back for another fishing season. He was like a feeble old man taking his last journey to the Antarctic, which was the only home he knew.

The next winter, Old Tom came back alone. Even though many whales passed the bay, and there were younger orcas to lead, he refused to go out and round them up. He was no longer interested in how many of them there were. He would go down to the river mouth and flop about as he had done in his more active days, when summoning up the whalers to come for their quarry. Suddenly — although it seemed hard to believe — Old Tom was dead. It was a lonely, cold, early spring day — September 17, 1930 — when Tom's body was spotted and towed ashore by George and his crew. There were many ideas brought forth as to what to do with the body. Some thought it would be best to have it mounted. But George himself decided to preserve the skeleton, in the hope that eventually a museum would be built to house it — as was finally done in 1938.

In retrospect, one can only wonder what kind of intelligence these great mammals really possessed. The killer whale had been venerated by primitive tribes all over the seas long before civilization as we know it began. Even in Eden, there is a legend about a fierce Polynesian tribe that lived and disappeared long before the aboriginals, who literally worshipped the orca and believed that, if they lived heroic lives, they would be reincarnated as killer whales. Indians in British Columbia have woven eyes and fins of the orca into their ceremonial blankets, but only the greatest chiefs could wear such a covering with the full whale woven into its design. There seems to be no comparable reverence known for any other sea creature. Although we are only beginning to find out how the dolphin and the orca think, some of the facts presented in this story should be of help to scientists in their investigations, as well as of interest to any lover of the wild. For one thing, the orca appears to possess a life span similar to, if not greater, than our own. Their method of communication is similar in its complexity and organization to that of the dolphins, which have only recently begun to be studied. That killer whales, as have the dolphins, can develop a strong sentimental attachment to human beings seems to have been verified here as well.

There are, of course, the skeptics who would attribute all these events to a form of conditioning rather than independent thinking. Killer whales, dolphins, dogs, and apes have been trained by humans to develop superior organizational abilities as a result of conditioning. But in this case, the whales trained themselves. And what kind of conditioning could explain Old Tom's behavior after Jack Davidson's tragic accident, particularly when he followed the launch with Jack's body all the way to Eden, almost as if to pay his respects before the funeral. Was it instinct that kept him patrolling at the mouth of the Kiah River for days until

Jack's body was found? And what brought him back to Two-Fold Bay when he knew his own death was near? Was it because he knew the waters were safer there from the sharks who were the inevitable enemy of old and crippled killers? Or was it because he had lost all his old friends, that he came back to the one place where he knew other friends were waiting? Who can tell?

Whatever speculations one can make about the motivations or intelligence of the orca, I think few can deny that this tale — along with the legends about the dolphin, Pelorus Jack, who for more than forty years is reputed to have guided literally hundreds of sailing vessels through the treacherous reefs which separate New Zealand's North Island from the South Island — ranks well up among the greatest sea stories of all time.